The Flower of Grass

D1264529

James E. Robinson is a professional songwriter, singer, author, therapist and speaker. *Midwest Book Review* called Robinson's first book, *Prodigal Song: A Memoir*, "...a moving and life-affirming portrayal, spiritually rewarding and reader inspiring". *The Flower of Grass* is his first novel. He lives in Tennessee with his wife and two children.

To learn more about Jim and his work, please visit www.ProdigalSong.com and www.jameserobinson.com

The Flower of Grass

A novel by

JAMES E. ROBINSON

MONARCH
BOOKS

Oxford, UK & Grand Rapids, Michigan, USA

Copyright © 2008 by James E. Robinson.

The right of James E. Robinson to be identified as author of
this work has been asserted by him in accordance with the
Copyright, Designs and Patents Act 1988.

All rights reserved. No part of this publication may be repro-
duced or transmitted in any form or by any means, electronic
or mechanical, including photocopy, recording or any informa-
tion storage and retrieval system, without permission in writing
from the publisher.

Published in association with The Literati Agency, Franklin,
TN. www.TheLiterati.net

First published in the UK in 2008 by Monarch Books
(a publishing imprint of Lion Hudson plc),
Wilkinson House, Jordan Hill Road, Oxford OX2 8DR
Tel: +44 (0) 1865 302750   Fax: +44 (0) 1865 302757
Email: monarch@lionhudson.com
www.lionhudson.com

ISBN: 978-1-85424-879-4 (UK)
ISBN: 978-0-8254-6286-3 (USA)

Distributed by:
UK: Marston Book Services Ltd, PO Box 269, Abingdon, Oxon OX14 4YN;
USA: Kregel Publications, PO Box 2607, Grand Rapids, Michigan 49501.

Unless otherwise stated, Scripture quotations are taken from
the Holy Bible, New International Version, © 1973, 1978, 1984
by the International Bible Society. Used by permission of
Hodder and Stoughton Ltd. All rights reserved.

This book has been printed on paper and board independently
certified as having come from sustainable forests.

British Library Cataloguing Data A catalogue record for this
book is available from the British Library.

Printed and bound in Malta by Gutenberg Press.

For Teresa, Mary Ruth and James Bryan.
And for Bryan Haislip.
And in memory of Billy Fry.

The grace of grass growing she has;
Of leaves blowing, of daisies bowed
Before the rain. Clouds at morning
  Have such a sweet simplicity.
  Her feet go laughing everywhere.
There are not birds so blithely free,
So singing quick, so apt as she.
  I love her April ways. I pray
She may not change. As now she is
  I have asked heaven to keep her.
                        —Z. Bryan Haislip

Prologue

The man drove across the bridge.

From high above the wide, reaching waters he found himself hovering between light and dark. To his left the sprawling Tennessee River extended its antler-shaped tributary waters into the last remnants of the night, blue and barely hanging on, until both water and sky merged into the gray mist and became one. To his right, at the east edge of the earth, the horizon and river met and barely glowed there together. Dawn appeared veiled, uncertain whether to begin or end, to be born or buried.

At the crest of the great arched bridge John Allen found himself suspended somewhere between past and present. The years had passed, and yet the dense and primal woods seemed unchanged. Beneath the rolling canopy of trees he knew the forest floor would be etched with tracks of possum and rabbit and raccoon, the soft sand sloping to the river's edge dappled by prints where deer had come to drink the twilight-tinted water. Even isolated within the sterile confines of his rental car, from atop the tall bridge he could see where most could not, underneath the quilted wood and into a shrouded past.

From the thick bordering tree line a blue heron lifted into the reluctant morning on wide, heaving wings, then vanished into the cobalt haze hanging like smoke along the banks, giving a soaring impression of arrested time, peaceful and prehistoric. John's throat tightened; he realized the place had not aged since he had last seen it, and with this came the feeling that he had been the only lonely and deluded thing moving in another direction all these years. Floating there above his two estranged selves, the young and the old, caused an expectant kind of fear to course through his chest, like the pulsating heart of a man about to fall from some great height.

His foot lifted—he suddenly felt that he and the car and the speed were all wrong, an irreverent intrusion into a sacred place, and that unless he slowed to the same speed as the rest of this world, the whole scene might vanish like a wonderful dream upon waking. He wished he could stop his mind, memory, movement. He was afraid to reach the other side of the river, and afraid to turn back. But down he came, and once across the bridge he knew he was close; another hour or so and he'd be there.

He ached with a longing he did not fully understand.

Once off the main highway, the car pointed towards town like an old horse heading home; John felt he could get there without even steering, if need be. He had come too far now, and so resigned himself to the role of detached observer, pulled along a path from which there was no easy escape.

He knew before seeing them when and where certain things would appear: the Stockard place, surrounded by the same undulating meadows dotted with brown and black cows...then the hills flattening into broad fields littered with the rotting stalks of harvested sorghum and corn... then back to sloping grazing land. Here and there skeletons of old barns leered from somber shadows, occasionally flanked by towering silos looming above the gloom like abandoned lighthouses.

As he came closer toward town, houses appeared— small, insignificant structures occasionally peeking out from mile after mile of rolling, heavily forested hillsides. As the flecks of flickering light and soft-smoking chimneys were each quickly consumed by secluding woods, the man felt uprooted, as if a hard rain might wash him away.

Ahead through the fog the forest finally began a gradual retreat along both sides of the road, crowding back to make room for the town. The old sign was showing some rust:

WELCOME TO TRANQUILITY
A Place for Family

John flexed his grip on the steering wheel. He felt surprisingly alert, considering all the red-eye hours flown; he had wanted to get there early, before the town had shaken itself fully awake. His sister knew he was coming, but not exactly when. It would feel safer to drive around in his anonymity and just look at things for a while, before stepping out onto the alien surface of what had once been his home.

Home. He had a sense that time had been standing still, waiting for his return. Something young within him stirred. He felt both connected and afraid.

John Allen had come back to say goodbye. But he was too late; there would be no atonement. Any last hope for a bridge across the abyss separating father and son was now gone. And though he knew his father had been buried two days earlier, his mind and heart were haunted by many things not yet laid to rest. Now the land and air remembered who he had once been, and undying voices whispered his name. His father's voice was one. But not the only one.

She was here.

For much of his life he had not gone a single a day without a sense of her presence. Now, all these years later, he could again feel the reality of her nearness.

As he crossed back over into the world of his past, a new truth entered him, one that until that moment he had not allowed himself to consider.

She would not be the same, any more than he was the same.

John Allen had come home. But he would no longer know the place, nor would it know him. No matter how familiar this world looked, he would be nothing more than a stranger in it now.

1

The woman stood at the kitchen window and looked out across the frozen fields.

The short brown grass of the yard stretched from the back of the old house for about fifty yards before gradually losing itself in the long, leaning weeds of the unkempt pasture. A few motionless cows could be seen huddled together against the wind near the south fence. The faded fog lay low over everything, in the half light of not-quite morning.

Jessie had looked out this window onto this scene all her life. She had been born in the house. When she was a little girl her mother had put a step-stool in front of the sink so that the two of them could wash dishes together, and she had watched moon and sun and rain and wind pass through and over the fields, a hundred seasons rolling through their cycles—the new life of spring, then sultry summers that exhausted the earth and everyone on it, until fall finally laid its calming colors over the hills like a quilt, readying the woods for the deep sleep of winter.

Now it seemed as if the world had stopped turning, and that winter would remain forever. Her reflection in the glass hung superimposed over the sleeping soil like the face of a ghost. On most days she could look out into the bright day with the eyes of a little girl, but today the translucent image held in its tired eyes the oppressive proof of passing time. She stared straight through the unfamiliar face in the window, far out into the hanging mists.

Another phantom face floated in from behind her own. Jessie felt a light touch on her shoulder.

"You look lost, little girl."

"I *feel* lost," she said, almost a whisper. She reached across her chest to lay her hand on her mother's. Then she blinked and took in a breath. "I'm fine," she said, forcing some life back into her voice. "Just tired. I've been up half the night." Her dark brows narrowed, the way they did when she set her strength against a challenge, but she did not quite break her gaze away from the window. "I'll never, ever get used to him working the midnight shift, even if he has to do it another ten years. It ruins everything, I swear it does. Tuck and I are becoming like strangers. Neither one of us can figure out day from night anymore..."

"He does what he has to, Jessie."

"I know." Jessie allowed herself one more look into the reflection and saw her mother wearily close her eyes. *At least she feels good enough to be out of bed,* she thought. *Maybe today will be a good one...*

Jessie squared her shoulders against the foolishness she had again let sneak into reality. *Daydreaming,* she chastised herself, *like some silly schoolgirl. This won't do...*

"I'll get us some coffee," she said, turning her back on the reticent dawn. "Come sit down, Momma." She took hold of her mother's arm and guided her toward the kitchen table. "It's a mystery to me why that God-forsaken plant starts a shift in the middle of the night," she said, careful to sound more defiant than depressed. "And now with him taking on twelve-hour shifts, and overtime when he can get it. It's ridiculous, especially in the winter. By the time he gets home the day's half gone..."

"Lord knows he works hard, hard as your father used to," Belle said, then, "Goodness, child, you don't have to hold me up. I can walk just fine." But she let her daughter help her sit. "All those hours in that place, driving back and forth over that river all the time."

"You settled?"

"Yes, Jessie. Don't dote on me so. I'm not helpless. Not yet, anyway."

Jessie's mouth tightened. "Momma," she said. She didn't feel the strength for an argument. She turned and went to the stove.

"Well. I do worry about him, though." Belle paused to catch her breath. "Your daddy scratched a living out of this land, so at least he was close by. But times are different." She looked toward the window. "If it wasn't for Tuck, we'd never have been able to keep this place. For as long as we have, anyway."

Jessie felt a familiar slow sadness come up in her. Her mother had always been the untiring voice of hope in the house, remaining strong even when Jessie would sometimes falter during the interminable season of her father's illness. But in the past year, as Belle's pain had steadily worsened, the resignation would slip out sometimes—"There's nothing much left to sell, I'm afraid. Two old pickup trucks, Tuck's and that rickety old thing your daddy left you..."

"Don't you talk bad about my truck," Jessie half-teased, trying to lighten her voice. "I *love* my daddy's truck."

"*Any*way. That old tractor and rusted-out bush-hog, this house and what's in it...and now the fields growing nothing but broomstraw..."

"Momma."

"Of course, it's not like I'm going to be here much longer..."

"*Mom*ma."

"There's no need pretending, little girl. I'm not sure I can outlive winter this time around."

"Don't *say* that," Jessie said, unable to rein in the tone. She knew her mother well, understood that her words reflected more a spirit of acceptance than complaint. But even so she could feel her own frustrations rising. *Stay calm,* she told herself sternly, but it had always been a struggle. She had emerged from the womb red-faced, her mother often said, and from her first breath demonstrating a famous temper; even the well-seasoned Nurse White had long afterward remembered the screams as "rancorous".

Keeping her back to her mother, Jessie crossed her arms and hugged her worn terrycloth robe tighter against the cold. "Momma, you know good and well that you and I will be kneeling down together in your flower garden come spring."

Her mother was quiet. Then, "Hmm. Well, I'm not afraid of coming face to face with my Jesus, little girl. But I'd be lying if I said I wouldn't love to see one more spring..."

Jessie felt almost too tired to hold back the sorrow. She shut her eyes tight against the tears and tried to calm her breathing. Finally she said, "Donna told me yesterday that, come spring, she's pretty sure she can put me back on at the dress shop. Part time, anyway. It's just that business slows down so during the winter..."

"Well, goodness, it's not like she ever paid you anything to speak of."

"It was *some*thing, Momma. But it's best I'm here to take care of you, anyway."

"I don't need taking care of. Look at me. I'm strong as a mule this morning."

"Momma."

"You stay too cooped up in this house all the time, Jessie, that's for certain. You work yourself to death around here trying to take care of me, taking care of everything day in and day out for so long now..." Belle sighed. "It's like you've never had a whole life of your own..."

Jessie turned and lifted her chin. "I have the life I want. I do what needs doing. I've never been afraid of work, Momma, you taught me that. There's not one thing about my life that's been forced on me. I've *chosen* my life. Please don't *lec*ture me."

"And please don't *sass* me, little girl."

Both women could be formidable. They looked at each other hard. And then both seemed to see it at the same time—the long winter and even longer illnesses had hung over the house for too long; it was good to again recognize some of the old fire flaring up in each other's eyes.

Belle broke first, tried to hide the smile but couldn't, and Jessie's followed.

"Good Lord, little girl. Just look at us. Seems like you and me are about the only friends either of us has these days, and listen to us squawkin'." She reached out her hand; Jessie came and took it between both of her own, lifted it up gently under her chin.

"I'm sorry, Momma. I'm flighty as a sparrow, I guess."

"Well. That's my good girl. I know you're...tired. We both are. But we'll stick together, won't we? We'll make it." She lightly brushed the back of her fingers against her daughter's cheek. "Anyway, thank God for Tuck. And never once has he complained, never once."

"Tuck loves you, Momma."

"I know. But still...a man wants his own home."

"This *is* home. Yours. Mine. Tuck's. We've both told you that a hundred times." Her voice was gentler now. "It's just the way things worked out. He knows how much this place means to you, and to me." Jessie saw Tuck in her mind and felt the strange mix of admiration and regret that for the past week had struggled for ownership of her heart. Today remorse lay heavy as the clouds, and a vague guilt alongside. She gave her mother's hand a squeeze and moved back to the sink at the window. "He's a good man," she said finally. She filled the coffee pot with water, then wiped a soapy sponge over a section of countertop she'd already scrubbed only an hour before.

"He sure loves you, Jessie. That boy has loved you since you were both little things. It's not every woman can claim being loved like that, with a whole heart. But then, that's how you've always loved, too. Ever since you were little. Dogs, horses, it didn't matter." Belle chuckled. "Never less than your whole heart..."

But Jessie's thoughts had drifted through the glass again, all the way to the trees, and this time kept going, to the hidden place she sometimes went, far out in the deep waters of her secret soul. This place belonged to her alone, and even the briefest of journeys there had sometimes saved her life. She could hear the sound of her mother's voice, and then, faintly, another sound, drawing her back...

The old clock soft-chimed from its place on the living room mantel. Jessie moved silently to the chair beside her mother. The women stilled to a kind of reverence, silently counting...four, five, six. When the last chime had faded away, the hollow ticking from the central room patiently reestablished itself throughout their home; they heard it now, softly, from their table in the kitchen, and both knew that when they next lay in their beds at the opposite end of the house its rhythm would steady them to sleep as it had countless nights before. Before Dub's death the sound had inhabited their world as an unconscious thing, essential yet unnoticed, like breathing in and out. Listening now, both women felt comforted by its kind constancy.

Jessie knew the words her mother would say, more or less, before she spoke them.

"Every day, for as long as I was married to him, your father would faithfully wind that clock." Belle's voice was very small in the quiet. "Far as I can remember, he never let it run down, not once, except when he'd have it all taken apart sometimes, tinkering with it. Goodness, how the man loved that clock. It was the only thing of much value that his own daddy left him. And now that sweet, sweet Tuck." Her eyes misted. "Just took it over, from the first day Dub was too sick to stand. Just took that little brass winding key and put it in his pocket without asking me, or waiting for me to ask him. I reckon he'd just made up his mind that keeping that old clock running would be his natural responsibility from then on, as head of this house..."

"I know." Jessie sounded somewhat lifeless. "He's never been anything but good to me, or to you, Momma, no matter what."

"Well. Anyway, you're half mean to him sometimes."

"Momma, please. Let me fix you some eggs."

"Not this morning, Jessie."

"You need to eat, Momma."

"I'm not hungry. You're the one who needs to eat. You're too skinny. Tuck says so, too."

Jessie was already up and at the stove, heating the skillet. "I'll fry some sausage," she said. "A nice breakfast will do you good."

After the dishes had been cleared away the two sat at the kitchen table in dim, amber lamplight, warming their hands against the sides of their cups. Jessie held her face above the steam and let it rise moist onto her skin, eyes closed, praying a silent prayer of thanks for their time together. She knew her mother was too sick to be up, but she also knew better than to refuse her efforts. Any day her mother could get out of bed and function for very long was a blessing.

Opening her eyes, Jessie noticed how thin and small her mother's arms looked, sticking out from the sleeves of her housecoat. Over time her body had been so ravaged that the once vibrant woman now appeared shadowy and colorless, like a poorly drawn sketch on old paper. Jessie felt pangs of sadness again rising up in her at seeing this systematic, dehumanizing cutting away of her beautiful mother, but then turned instead to the more familiar feeling

17

of resentment. She had learned over time that anger, however unbecoming, was still less debilitating than grief. Her mother was a fighter, too; the hair grown back since the last round of chemo had come in white and wispy, but Belle wore it uncovered without embarrassment.

The old woman broke the quiet.

"Do you want to talk about it?"

"No, I don't." The words came out harder than Jessie wanted, and she closed her eyes.

"Do you know if he's here yet?" Belle's voice was gentle.

"No. It's been a week since I saw Maggie at the grocery. She told me he wasn't going to make it in time for the funeral...that was all she knew. I could tell she wasn't even sure if she should tell me that much..." Jessie consciously straightened in her chair, rebuking any appearance of weakness. "It's not such a big deal, Momma. He can do as he pleases, it's no concern of mine."

"Hmm," Belle sighed. "Well. God rest Big John's soul."

"John Allen was mean as a snake, Momma. Meaner. All he ever did was hurt people. Good riddance, I say."

"Jessie. It's not our place to judge. It's hard to know a man's true heart."

"No it isn't," Jessie said. "It's easy. A man proves his heart by his actions."

"God forgives," Belle said.

"Well, good for Him," Jessie said. "Sometimes I can't." As soon as she'd spoken she knew her words had betrayed a deeper meaning, and that her mother would know, too. She massaged fingertips against both temples. "I'm sorry. I'm just tired."

"I know," Belle said.

"Not tired, really," Jessie admitted, the weariness wearing away at her resolve. "Trapped. I feel *trapped*, Momma. Surely you've felt like that."

"Yes. I have."

"There must have been times when you wondered, at least *wondered* about whatever kind of life is out there, other places and people..."

"Everybody dreams, little girl," Belle said gently. "But life isn't all dreaming. Life's about living out what's in front of you, and trying to accept whatever life brings us, one day at a time, as a gift. Sometimes it looks like something we want, and other times it looks like something we'd just as soon avoid." The old woman paused. "But life's coming, one way or the other. It's offered up to us, and we can reach out our hands for it or turn our backs on it. Wanting can be a good thing, Jessie. But *having* is better, because having is *real*."

"The world outside of these woods is real, too, Momma. Just as real as this one."

"Maybe. Some of it, anyway. But lots of folks go chasing after things they think are important, when in fact none of it really amounts to a hill of beans. Sometimes people reach for things they want, and grab on as tight as they can. But when they open up their hands, there's nothing...nothing but air." Belle held out her empty palm. "I don't mean to preach at you, little girl. But what we think means the most to us isn't worth a hoot sometimes, that's all. The dream becomes more important than the gift we're already holding."

"But sometimes the dream is real."

The old woman looked at her daughter. "*Love* is real, Jessie. And love is never, *never* selfish."

Jessie shook her head, slowly. "How can we know, Momma? How can we ever *know* what's real and what's not?"

"You're the only one who can figure that out, Jessie. You're the only one." Belle knew the words were insufficient. *But she's held on to me for too long as it is,* she thought.

Stillness settled.

Jessie took a deep breath and pulled her long, brown curls back with both hands into a bunched knot on top of her head. Her eyebrows arched and lifted like dark wings readying for flight.

"I've got to start sleeping better. This won't *do*."

Belle smiled. "You still don't like to cry, do you, little girl?"

"No."

"Ever since you were a child. So strong-headed! My gracious, those big brown eyes of yours would fire up and even your daddy would back down..."

Jessie came out of herself and looked. Nearly four years had passed since her father's death, but her mother's face still sometimes showed the same grief she'd worn at the funeral. She hadn't been whole since.

"I had Daddy wrapped around my little finger," Jessie said.

"Oh mercy, yes, you did. You sure did."

They sat quietly, the way old friends do, unafraid of the silence.

Belle bent suddenly forward.

"Momma?" Jessie's heart leaped. She reached and touched her mother's slumping shoulder.

"I'm fine," the old woman said. "It was just...a little one. Whew!" She leaned back, forcing a smile.

"Do you need to lie down?"

"No, I'm all right. Just had to catch my breath." Belle blinked back tears, and reached to touch her daughter's face.

"Oh, my sweet Jessie," she said. "How time fleets away. Time, and love. We can't harness either one of them. We go through the days thinking we've got all the time and the love we need..."

Both women dabbed at their eyes with paper napkins. The old woman smiled at something only she could see...then moaned and again bent over the table.

"Oh, God, Momma..."

"No, no, I'm all right." Belle lowered her face so Jessie couldn't clearly see, clenched her teeth against the pain, forcing it back by strength of will. She inhaled as deeply as she could and pulled herself up.

Their eyes met.

Jessie couldn't hide her fear.

Belle spoke clearly and quickly.

"Like I always say, little girl, time fleets away. One day me and your daddy looked up and there you were nearly grown, the prettiest young woman in the county, by far. Mercy, I couldn't believe it. I can barely believe it now."

Please, Lord, Jessie silently prayed, *keep her pain away. Let her keep talking with me a while, the way it used to be...*

"Go back some, Momma," she said, her voice almost childlike. "Tell me again, about when you and Daddy met."

The woman perked up. "Lands, child, don't you ever get tired of this tale?"

"No."

Something changed in Belle's face as she spoke, like light moving across shadow. "Well, he was just about the most handsome man in the world, is all. I was nothing more than a girl, really, a young and silly girl..."

From the next room, chimes.

One, two...

Sad, intractable.

...three, four...

The sound of time passing.

...five, six, seven.

And then the old woman heard another sound tugging her towards the past, a thing both faint and familiar, a middle-of-the-night crying that long ago would have had her up like a flash and down the dark hallway.

"Come here, little girl," Belle said.

Jessie came to her mother and knelt into her frail frame. And she couldn't stop her shoulders from shaking, all

21

the hard, hindered tears pouring out, finally finding their way. Jessie felt the iced-up streams inside her thaw, join, and flow like a river from her heart. She covered her face with her hands.

"Oh, Momma..."

"It's okay, baby."

And the old woman wished she had more strength to share. The thoughts and feelings came fast into her as she held tightly to all that was left of her life. She knew, deep down, that Jessie and Tuck were meant to be together. But in this brief moment she also allowed herself to feel her daughter's long suffering, intimately, and to wish against reason that things hadn't happened as they did, that her only child hadn't decided to stay and help her tend to Dub for so long, watching him wither with such slow cruelty, and now the same thing with her dying, too. She regretted that she hadn't told Jessie to run, just *run* while there was still a chance, to follow what she knew to be the real truth and not look back, knowing that life might break her and love might kill her but at least she would have tried, at least she would have known.

And now the empty land lay out hard and barren all around, and holding Jessie was all Belle knew to do, all she had ever known. She stroked the back of her daughter's soft neck and closed her eyes and let her own grief flow out, the two of them locked together in lonely loss, just held her tight against her fading frailty, loving her with whatever life was left, saying the only words she knew to say...

"I wish he wasn't coming back, little girl," the old woman whispered. "I wish he wasn't coming back."

2

John drove through the mist toward town.

Passing the cemetery on his right, he felt a chill, and involuntarily pressed down harder on the gas. Daring a glance, he saw the gravestones poking their rounded heads up out of the fog like ghosts.

Driving toward the court square, he began experiencing a feeling that fell somewhere between nostalgia and claustrophobia. A person could drive from one city limit marker on the south border to the marker on the north in less than ten minutes; for the first eighteen years of his life, these had been the borders defining his whole world. He found himself alarmed at what felt like a forced familiarity—The Dairy Dip, the old Winston Diner, the little Presbyterian church, all the same. The squat brown brick building that had once been an auto parts store was now an insurance office. The fix-it shop at one time owned by the King boys had become an empty cinderblock shell with the windows broken out, and the old salvage barn had a new coat of coffee-colored paint on the metal roof, with big white letters that read: ELI'S GUNS, AMMO, & SPORTING GOODS. But little else had changed.

Maybe it was the wearying weather. But the place seemed to have a weaker pulse, somehow, a little less life in it. Not a dying place, exactly, but one with less glow in its cheeks than he'd remembered. The tired town moving past the windshield wasn't unlike his own image in the rear-view mirror—a face not old but no longer young, a blurred reflection back to a time before the sky had drained of color.

He came to the four-way stop, then slowly cruised the town court square. The place was not yet awake; tired little shops stood huddled around the aged courthouse in the frozen morning. A couple of storefronts had new names painted on the windows, but several spaces well remembered from his childhood were now abandoned, with peeling paint and faded For Rent signs. A few childhood images remained stubbornly ensconced: J.B.'s Grocery, Tranquility Cleaners, Hadley's Hardware. The bank still sat alongside the post office, but the ancient Five & Dime, against whose cool plate glass window John had pressed his young and hopeful face each Saturday morning, had not survived. The old brick building sat empty, foil insulation covering its windows like silver dollars on a dead man's eyes.

John drove past the three-chair barbershop he had known as Tater's, now called Bob's. And then he saw the place he remembered best, Swain's Drug Store. A knot of fear twisted in his stomach; he felt a strong, irrational desire to escape. Not knowing what else to do, he drove past the store and started around the square again.

On his third pass the fluorescent lights inside the drugstore flickered on behind large plate glass windows, and like a drawn moth the car pulled almost against his will into the front parking space. Through the glass wall he saw the counters and shelves, then Swain's squat figure coming from the rear, readying things for business.

John sat with the motor running like someone considering robbing the place, keeping the getaway car at ready. He could feel the muted thud of his heart against his chest. Finally he turned off the engine, walked to the glass door, and knocked.

Swain turned and for a moment froze. His face went from blank to bewildered. And then, smiling and shaking his head, he shuffled with a familiar limp to unlock and open the door.

"Good Lord in heaven!" he said. "Johnny Allen!"

"Hi, Swain."

"Good Lord," Swain said, softer this time. He came out onto the sidewalk, letting the door shut behind him, and put his hands on John's shoulders. "Good Lord in *heaven*."

"You look old, Swain."

"I *am* old," he said. "But not much older than *you*." Little white frost-clouds came from both their mouths. "How long has it been? Fifteen years?"

"A little more than that."

"Hmm...graduating class of '73. Am I right?"

"Right." John smiled. "Still got that amazing memory, huh Swain?"

"Yeah, the body's wearing out, but the mind's sharp as steel. So, hard as it is to believe, here we are just crankin' up a new year, 1989, so that means...sixteen years. *Sixteen*. Just don't seem possible. 'Course I saw you once since you first left, some years back, from a distance anyway, at your mama's funeral..."

"Well, I was in and out of town faster than I wanted to be. My schedule..."

"Oh, sure, sure. Everybody understood that, Johnny. It was a time...for family, for being with your family and all..."

"Yeah."

"Well, anyway, time hasn't hurt you much. At least you haven't gotten fat like me." Swain's eyes showed some wear but still shone with easy laughter. "My, *my*. It's good to see you, Johnny."

John felt some of his fear falling away, and was thankful for the grace. "It's good to see you, too, Swain." They shook hands, long and firm.

25

"Well, come on, come on in, it's too durned early to start working anyway." Swain ushered him inside and relocked the door. John took the deep breath of a man being offered a safe place of sanctuary in a foreign country.

"You look froze to death," Swain said. "Let's go to the back where it's warm."

"Guess I'd forgotten how cold it could get around here."

"Aw, it ain't cold yet. There's still plenty of winter left. I'll bet you we have snow this year. Maybe even an ice storm, heaven forbid. I've just got the feelin', cold down in my bones." Walking through the little store—the smell of after-shave and talc and soap, the sound of Swain's voice, long tubes of fluorescent light humming and blue-flickering off the rain-stained ceiling—John felt strangely light-headed. He put one foot unsteadily in front of the other, trancelike, as Swain led them behind the glass prescription counter at the back of the store. He felt like asking for water, but his mouth wouldn't open. Swain's voice came from far away: "We'd heard you were headin' this way. 'Course, 'round Tranquility everybody hears most every *thing* about every *body*, so I reckon half the town knew it, too. I asked Maggie when she thought you might get here. She said she'd managed to get in touch with you, but she wasn't sure if you'd get here in time...not sure when you might get here, I mean. Said you were way off in England or some such place..."

"Italy. It took me longer to get here than I'd hoped." John blinked and took a deep breath. He saw kindness in his friend's eyes. "I wanted...I tried to..."

"Yeah, well, Italy, that's not exactly right around the bend, is it?" Swain waved away his friend's unease. "A lot further away from this valley than I've ever been, that's for sure." He laughed, and motioned to two high stools. "Pull up a seat. My gosh, we don't get a lot of famous folk in here, you know. How about *this*—our own Johnny Allen, local boy made good. You did it, Johnny. You got outta here and really *did* it. I reckon you'd be about the most famous thing ever to come out of Lake County. And I knew you before you were wearin' long britches."

"I'm not famous anywhere other than here, Swain, I can promise you."

"Well, you've been in the paper more times than I can count, the Nashville *and* Memphis papers, and I've seen you on TV, too, for gosh sakes, way out there in Los Angeles. That's pretty dadgum famous as far as I'm concerned."

"So where's the soda fountain, Swain?" John wanted to talk about anything other than himself.

"Aw, that's been gone for a good long while now, Johnny. It just got to be too much trouble." Swain scratched at his graying crewcut.

"That's too bad."

The two of them looked at the place where the snack bar and stools had once been, now taken up with magazine racks and greeting card displays.

"Yeah. I reckon I do miss it, everybody hanging around all the time." Swain looked back towards the front windows and for a moment grew quiet. "Lots of the old gang is gone, Johnny. The square's not the same, with the big mall opening over in Williamsville." They watched the town stretching and yawning itself awake. "You knew old Task died, didn't you?"

"No."

"Yep, and Will Ingram is in a terrible way, all hooked up to tubes at the rest home. The family lost the place several years ago. Nora and the two boys tried to keep it going, but there's just not enough business anymore." Swain drew his gaze back into his own store.

"How're you doing, Swain?"

"Aw, fine, Johnny, fine. People have always treated me real good here, for a long time. 'Course, these days folks can get their medicine at lots of other places, too. Kinda hard for me to keep up with the big chain stores, price-wise I mean." His voice sounded tired. "I reckon the only truth in life that never changes is that *every*thing changes, Johnny."

"Nothing looks all that different to me, in some ways."

"Well, that's true. After all this time it's really the same old town. Still no traffic light, still no movie theater..." Swain grinned, and nodded back toward the magazines. "And of course, I reckon once we lost the best soda jerk in town, it was only a matter of time before we shut down the fountain."

"That's probably it, Swain," John said. "How's Louise?"

"Fine, doin' real good. She still puts up with me after all these years, somehow. House seems awfully quiet with Ellis gone. He's married, you know."

"Ellis? Married?"

"He is. Married a girl from college, sweetest thing, and they've got a four-year-old daughter."

"I'll be."

"Yeah, Lilly, our sweet Lilly. Look here." He picked up a framed photo from the countertop. Someone too old to be Ellis stood on a bright green lawn holding the little blond-haired girl's hand. John had the deep, disconnected feeling again.

"She's beautiful, Swain."

"Yeah. Thank God she takes after her mother." Swain looked at the picture with proud eyes. "Time goes by so fast. I'm a *granddaddy*, for gosh sakes. Sure seems like only yesterday, you strollin' in here every day after school."

"Sure does."

"Truth is, Johnny, I don't envy you fellers that jump and skip all over the place. I reckon I'm just old fashioned that way—still married to my sweetheart, comin' here to this same place every morning. I'm just not cut out for any other kind of living, more than likely. Life is simple, Johnny, but life is good. I wouldn't want it any other way."

"I can understand that, Swain. I really can."

"Yeah. There's a lot to be said for it, Johnny," Swain said. "We raised our boy here, and still go to church right over yonder." He pointed out the front window—just past the east corner of the square, John could see the cross-topped steeple pointing up into the sky. "That's *your* church, too, Johnny. You'd better come Sunday. Everybody would love to see you."

"I might do that," he said, knowing he wouldn't.

Silence settled on them. Then:

"I'm real sorry about your daddy, Johnny."

"Thanks, Swain."

"I know y'all have been through some hard times, every one of you." Swain paused, as if considering how much he should say. "Doc said he must have gone quick, painless, even. Maggie said he looked kinda peaceful when she found him, like somebody who'd just decided to lie down under a tree and take a nice nap."

"I'm...thankful for that."

"The funeral was real fine. I'm sorry you couldn't get here in time."

"Me too."

"Everybody did a good job." Swain again paused. "The new Methodist preacher said nice things. Big John looked real good, Johnny, real natural and handsome, like he always was."

"That's good."

"Yeah." Swain looked at the floor. "Well, anyway, I know everybody's gonna be so thrilled to see you. Have you talked to Joey?"

"Not in a long while."

"Well, we don't see him much these days. He stays pretty much to himself out there."

John felt almost too tired to say anything.

Someone tapped their car keys on the front glass.

"I guess I'd better get at it," Swain said. They stood, and when John stuck out his hand, his old friend reached around it and hugged him instead.

"How long you plan on staying?"

"I'm not sure."

"Louise would sure love to see you, if you could find time to come by the house, once you get settled...if you have time."

"I'd like that. I'll try."

"Lord in heaven, it's mighty good to see you, Johnny."

"It's good to see you, too, Swain. Take it easy."

"I'm gonna try, Johnny. I'm gonna try and do just that."

John walked back out into the winter wind, Swain's smile the only warm thing anywhere.

He drove to his sister's house.

The modest frame home sat like most in town, well off the small road with a large front lawn, and a backyard bordered by a wall of woods behind. Ellen would be in school by now, and he thought it best to try and catch Maggie one-on-one.

John felt an old uneasiness as he knocked on the door. He hadn't seen her in nine years, and then only for a few hours. But her eyes had looked weary and wrinkled at the corners even then...

He retained only a hazy memory of the service, held in the same old, cold funeral home he'd last been in when his grandmother died, near the end of his senior year in high school. This time the casket had remained closed, he remembered that; although everyone at the funeral home had done their best to make her look if not peaceful then at least presentable, his mother's body was too much ravaged. He stood numbly in a line while strangers he had suppos- edly known all his life pressed their hands into his and spoke things in a language he could not understand.

He remembered being at the graveyard alongside his sister and brother, in a kind of forced performance of unity, the three pretending to themselves and everyone else that they had actually been a well and whole family all along. A killer hangover grappled at his brain following his flight the night before, and to ease the pounding he had smoked a joint in the rental car on the way into town. This had not been wise; the whole affair left him feeling dreadfully exposed.

In his mind he had always pictured such a scene taking place beneath sullen skies, cold wind mourning in the bare branches, long black overcoats billowing out melodramatically from dark figures all huddled together against the rain and sorrow. But the skies that day had shone with inappropriate clarity—cloudless, brilliant blue, the surrounding hills blanketed by autumn. All this made the day feel even more surreal.

He held a nebulous recollection of standing there in his suit between his siblings, bloodshot eyes hiding behind dark glasses, wondering if he were supposed to be feeling something. If he felt anything at all it was a kind of shameful relief—not that their mother had gone, really, but that he would no longer have to deal with the nagging guilt of not wanting to be near her, of not helping her...saving her, somehow. He managed to remain precariously upright through the droning ceremony, supported by the miserable consolation of knowing he would never have to look into his mother's heartbroken, heartbreaking eyes again.

Looking back, the fact that he had managed to accomplish the trip at all—considering his condition at the time—now seemed nothing short of miraculous. Despite the sickness and fear he inexplicably found himself doddering at the edge of the pit that day, watching the gilded white box slowly sinking down. He stared into the wide, deep hole, doped and oblivious, feeling as little as he possibly could.

His father did not attend, not that anyone expected him to. John had nervously scanned the small crowd, prepared to run away if need be. Even so, he escaped as soon as the service was done. His own shabby appearance had unnerved everyone—or at least it felt that way to him then—and when the final amen died on the autumn wind John vanished as covertly as he had appeared. Steeped in shame, he crept from the little crowd, from his own brother and sister, driving quickly away through leaves that fell like swatches of colored cloth onto the windshield.

Before turning back toward the river and the city beyond he had headed out along the south highway. But he knew even as he headed toward Jessie's house that he would drive right by it, nothing more. Inside himself he knew it was too late. He had seen the casket sink, and then the sun. He would not find the courage to look into another face that day, much less hers...

"Hello, Maggie."

His older sister looked at him, and blinked.

"Sorry I'm late," he tried again.

Pushing a strand of gray-streaked hair out of her eyes, the small, determined-looking woman tilted her head as though considering whether or not he was an apparition.

"Don't look so excited, Sis."

All she could do was stand there, propping open the storm door with her hip. Something like relief and sadness and deep disappointment and joy passed quickly across her face like blown clouds.

"Well, maybe I should've had a parade lined up or something, in your honor," she said, finally.

"That would've been nice."

Almost imperceptibly, the corners of her mouth turned up.

"You need a heavier coat, Johnny." She sighed. "Come on in, before you freeze your tail off."

They sat on opposite ends of the living room couch. Along one wall cardboard boxes sat half-filled with decorations, and in a corner near the picture window the bottom section of an artificial Christmas tree stood leaning in its stand, its upper sections dismembered and strewn along the rug. Maggie stared at her brother with her mouth half-open, uncharacteristically at a loss for words.

"How's Ellen?" he finally asked.

"Oh, *fine*," she said. The delicate sarcasm made him wince. "She's a high school senior. She'll graduate in May."

"No."

"Yes. She's eighteen, Johnny. Life's been moving right along here." Her pretty but sad eyes opened in mock surprise. "Babies being born, kids growing up, divorces, people dying. My, oh *my*, it's been a real blast. Wish you could've been here. Sorry we couldn't all wait for you to get your life together." She looked at him and sighed, her eyes tearing, then leaned forward with her elbows on her knees. "Johnny, after the last few letters you'd sent, I thought when I called you about Daddy…"

"I'm sorry, Maggie. This time…I really couldn't get back in time. There just wasn't any way, with everything happening so fast. I really tried…"

"I think if you'd really wanted to be here, you could have been here," she said, looking at him hard. "He's in the ground now, and the ground's frozen over. Everything's been taken care of, as usual, by *me*, just like always. Joey's sure not going to do anything, he's crazier than an outhouse rat out there in the woods, and you're off God-knows-*where* doing God-knows-*what*. So I took care of it, Johnny. You don't have to be responsible for a thing."

"I'm sorry, Mags." He held out his hands, palms up.

Her voice cracked and she bit her lower lip but didn't take her eyes off his. "I'm a single mom, *again*, with two no-good ex-husbands, one who doesn't have the decency to pay what he owes to help feed and clothe our child, and I'm working my tail off trying to make ends meet every single month, and *nobody* takes care of anything in my life but *me!*" She squared her shoulders, and the years flew away and John felt ten years old, getting a no-nonsense talking-to from his big sister. She still looked like she weighed ninety pounds, and she still scared him to death.

"Sis..."

"Don't you Sis *me*, Johnny Allen." Her eyes again filled with tears, but she blinked them back. "And don't think you can just soar in and out of people's lives like some sort of bird, free as you please. And...take off that stupid jacket. You look ready to fly off again any minute."

"Okay."

"*Well?*"

"Well...what?"

"*Well*, do you want some *coffee*? Or do you have a *plane* to catch in the next few seconds?"

"I'm not planning on going anywhere for a while."

"Ha!" She laughed out loud. "Oh, dear *Lord*." She stood up and walked toward the kitchen. "I doubt you'll still be here when I get back." Then she stopped, took a deep breath, and turned.

"Johnny," she said, and hopelessly held out her arms.

He met her in the middle of the room.

"I'm sorry, Maggie."

"I know. I know."

They hugged each other tight.

"Daddy was so mean, and so pitiful, too, especially the last year or so. But he didn't have anybody else, Johnny. It was almost like he'd become a child again..."

"I'm sorry you had to do so much by yourself, Mags. I really am."

She lifted her head from his shoulder and looked him in the eye.

"Are you okay, Johnny? *Really* okay?"

"I'm okay."

34

"You *look* better. Way better than last time I saw you."

"I'm better, Sis. Still working on it. But way better."

Her look was hopeful but reserved.

"You're late for Christmas. For a whole bunch of Christmases."

"I know."

She sighed. "Come on in the kitchen, brother."

They sat and talked for a long time.

"He left what little he had to the three of us. There wasn't any money, of course. But the cabin was paid off, and he left us that and what's inside. I haven't had the heart to do much yet. Joey won't go anywhere near it." She rubbed her eyes, got up and took something from a cabinet drawer. "There's not a lot in there, and I left things pretty much the way they were. There's electricity and water, but no phone. I stripped off the sheets and washed them, but not much else. There isn't a key. As far as I know he never even locked the place." She handed him a worn envelope, with his name scribbled on the front in unsteady writing. "He left a letter for each of us. Here's yours. You can wait and open it later, if you want."

"Yeah." He put it in his jacket pocket.

"It was a good thing I went out there to take him some food that afternoon, Johnny. Doc told me later that Daddy had probably died sometime early that morning. When I found him he was halfway between the lake and the cabin, like he'd just been out walking. He could've laid there for days if I hadn't…"

"Yeah. Good thing you went."

"Anyway."

They sat still.

"So. Have you been to the gravesite?"

"Yes," he lied. "I stopped on the way in."

"Not many folks came. He didn't have any friends left,

35

to speak of. But it was a nice service. New minister, O'Neil's his name. Good man, and he said kind things."

This made John remember. "Maggie, is Preacher still alive?"

"Yeah, but not doing so good. He had a bad stroke, Johnny. Nearly killed him. He's fought back, though. His mind isn't always good. Ruth, bless her soul, takes care of him best she can, but he's mostly bedridden. The last time I saw her, she told me that as long as she's able, Preacher's gonna be in his own house. She just couldn't stand the thought of him in a rest home, Johnny. Said it would kill him, and her, too. A hospice nurse comes over a couple of days a week to help out, I think." Maggie watched John's face, then reached and touched his arm. "I know how close you two were. It would mean the world to him if you could go over there sometime."

"I'll try to do that."

"Are you really staying?"

"I'm...yes. For a while, anyway." He had no idea where he should go instead. "I'd like to sleep here tonight, if I could."

Her eyes softened. "That would be *wonderful*, Johnny. You can use the spare room for as long as you like, if you can dig your way through." She stood and took their empty coffee mugs to the sink, then turned to him.

"Is that the only coat you have?"

"I didn't bring much with me."

"Well, you'll need to get a bigger coat." She shook her head and headed into the kitchen. "No palm trees around here that I know of. This ain't La-La Land, brother."

At supper Maggie tried to keep conversation going. John remembered that silence had always made her nervous. But Ellen remained quiet. Tall and thin and pretty, she stared at her plate and pushed the food around listlessly with her fork. John watched her. Over the years Maggie had occasionally sent photos, whenever she had known where to send them. But he hardly recognized his niece now.

When his sister went to the kitchen for dessert, John tried breaking the uneasy silence.

"So, how's school?"

"You already asked me that, Johnny." She glanced up. "Why are you grinning?"

"I just can't get used to everyone around here calling me Johnny. I haven't been called that in a long time."

Before the silence could settle, she said, "Oh, yes. *Jonathan* Allen. Very impressive, almost...*aristocratic*." She practically hissed the last word through straight, clenched teeth.

"Yeah. Guess maybe I thought it made me sound smarter." He meant it to be funny, but the girl didn't even crack a smile. Instead she shot back—

"I read your book."

"Did you?"

"Yes. I did."

"What did you think?"

"It was good." She did not say this convincingly.

"Thanks."

"Hmm. Of course, I recognized things. Things others wouldn't. I suppose not everyone around here knew where some of the characters came from, some of the people and places you...*used*." She had a way of tilting her chin up at the end of a sentence, a slight but strong gesture, elegant in its subtlety, considering her age. He didn't know whether to smile or be afraid.

"Um, I suppose not," he said.

She aimed—"I guess a writer can just use any place or anybody they want to, just give them new names or whatever, and do as they *please* with it. Because most people wouldn't know, would they? I mean, most would just *assume* the writer was making everything up out of his or her head, wouldn't they?"

"I guess."

"But the truth is, people *do* know, the people a writer *uses*. Of course, if the people and places are far off and small and unimportant—in the greater scheme of things, I mean—then nobody would ever know they were real, or based on real, anyway. Nobody except *them*."

"I guess so."

"Well, it must feel pretty powerful, creating characters and making them do as you please. Does it make you feel powerful?"

"Not really. Maybe."

"Uh-huh. Because I would think it does. Make you feel powerful, I mean." She looked straight at him over the top of her glasses.

Unsettled, he cleared his throat and said, "Well, I guess every character in every book is based on somebody..."

"Momma can't get through it, you know," the girl broke in. "She would pick it up and start, but she could never get more than a few chapters in. Did she tell you?"

"No."

"Yeah. Never more than a few chapters. And then she'd cry and cry..."

Maggie swooped back in with a dishtowel in her hands. She wore the look of someone arriving at the scene of an accident.

"Ellen?"

"What?"

"Your uncle hasn't seen you in so long."

"No *kid*ding."

"Why don't you tell him something about school, honey?"

"Do you have a boyfriend?" John felt helpless, but gave a lame try.

Ellen rolled her eyes. "May I be excused, *Mother*?"

Maggie looked at John, then at her daughter, with an expression that indicated she had never before been addressed as "Mother" and wasn't quite sure how to respond. "Don't you want any dessert? I've got cobbler..."

"No, thank you," Ellen said. She leveled her eyes one last time at John. And then, with a kind of forced dignity, her nose held contemptuously high, she stood and walked out.

Maggie sat beside John and touched his arm.

"I'm sorry, Johnny. It's mostly my fault, probably. I've said things, I guess. She...she always just adored you, you know, when she was little. All the time you were away, she would ask and...you were her hero, really. I mean she was so proud of you, but when you would go so long without, you know, on birthdays and such. Maybe if there'd been an occasional card or something..."

"I know."

"And my gosh, the way she took to your book, you'd have thought she had the Holy Scriptures themselves always clutched under her arm. She kept it with her all the time after it came out. She's so *smart*, Johnny, and reads all the time. She started reading chapter books when she was *four*, if you remember. Ever since, I can't keep the girl in books. She runs through them faster than we can check them out from the library..." She stopped. "Why are you smiling?"

"I think that's wonderful."

"I *know*. She's a lot like you, Johnny, *just* like you, in some ways. She walks around reciting all that same high-brow poetry stuff you used to like. She's always been that way, too smart for her age, too smart for her own good, truth be known. She's about half snooty most of the time, and couldn't care less about those silly boys in her school. Top of her class, Johnny, valedictorian by a mile. Can you imagine? We've never produced one of those in this family before, have we?"

"Not hardly. It's just awesome, Mags. It really is."

Maggie smiled. "Yeah. Kind of unbelievable, really, considering Leonard's contribution to the gene pool. Anyway, thank goodness she's as smart as she is. God knows I couldn't afford to get her into college without the scholarships. She wants to be a writer, I think, but she's kind of secretive about it."

"Really?"

"Uh-huh. She's a strange little thing, so young in some ways, so old in others, like she was born out of time, out of place, somehow. Like you, Johnny. Mama always said you'd come into the wrong world, at the wrong time, born knowing too much, feeling too much." They both smiled now. "Anyway, don't take the way El's acting right now too much to heart. She'll get better. You two will have to get to know each other."

From the back bedroom defiant rock music suddenly shook the walls.

"She's still a teenager, though," Maggie smiled, "whether she likes to admit it or not."

"I missed her life, Maggie. A big part of it, anyway." He started to say he was sorry, but felt the words had become meaningless. "I missed everybody's life…"

"Johnny. You're here now. You're my brother, and Ellen's uncle. You're Joey's brother. And time can't kill that. Wound it, maybe, but not kill it. I've been so mad at you for so long, sometimes I couldn't stand it. But I've never once stopped loving you, or praying you would come home some day, safe. I knew you were…sick. We all heard from you so seldom, and it's really hard, especially for a child, to understand things…"

"I know." He wiped a lone tear from her cheek with his thumb.

"Oh, Johnny. I've been so all alone with everything… and so *angry*. I've cussed you up and down sometimes."

"Mags."

"He's a selfish, no good you-know-what, that's what I'd say, sometimes right in the middle of praying for you. I'd tell God what I thought of you, and ask him to take away all my anger, and sometimes he would and sometimes he wouldn't."

"It's okay, Maggie."

"No, it's *not*," she said, and the tremble in her lower lip started again. "It's *not* okay. And sweet Joey, he's never once said a bad thing about you. He's so proud of you, always talking about you and how good you've done. Not a bad bone in his body…"

John held her hand and let her cry. For a moment he felt like crying, too, but the numb emptiness rose up instead of tears, and he closed his eyes and heart against it. He knelt beside Maggie's chair and held her, letting the sorrow rise and fall. They stayed like this for a while, and it was better than words.

When her sobbing slowed, Maggie pulled back and looked into his eyes.

"You knew Jessie got married?"

The words sliced into him.

"Yes. I got your letter."

Maggie saw all the way into his soul. "I'm sorry," she said, and there was no logic or irony or judgment in the words, just understanding. "I didn't have any way of knowing if you'd get the letter or not, but I sent it to the last address you'd given me."

It had been a half dozen years ago. He had just spent a few days in a California jail for public drunkenness.

"I got it," he said. "Took me a while, but I got it."

"For the longest time," Maggie said, "she never stopped asking about you, Johnny. For the longest time."

He nodded, gave her one more hug, then stood.

"It's getting late, Maggie," he said. "Thanks for supper."

Johnny dreamed of spring, and of the old barn, and of the way her kisses tasted, warm and sweet like fresh things grown from a garden...

When he opened his eyes, the room glowed gray with early dawn.

Before the others woke he dressed, slipped quietly out of the house, and drove to the cemetery. He parked in the little lane separating two flat fields and walked toward the place where he remembered burying his mother.

Still the wet fog lay draped over everything. The sun seemed to have given up before fully rising and instead lay back down, covering itself under heavy blankets. A mournful mist hung so heavily that when he'd gone only a short distance John turned and could no longer see the car, or the little church beyond. At first he felt disoriented and small and lost. But he followed a line of headstones until he found hers.

His mother's marker was simple. Cold drops of moisture hung in the engraved letters: *Sarah Elizabeth Allen – 1925–1980 – From Her Loving Children*. He knelt and slowly traced his finger through the word *Children*. The water ran down the stone and into the brown grass.

The new grave was further down; his father lay at the far end, still part of the family but, it seemed to him, somewhat quarantined. The ground remained broken and upturned, wet clumps of dirt loosely packed down. The stone was very small: *John Phillip Allen – 1918–1989*. Nothing else. He had died on New Year's Day. John had missed the funeral by two days.

He toed the muddy earth but did not touch the stone. He closed his eyes against an empty grief, but no prayer came to fill him.

John knew his way down every back road and side street. He turned easily through places where he'd once ridden his bike, the places he hadn't stayed long enough to see the last time he'd been in town—the old high school, unchanged except for new paint around the windows and the back parking lot now pavement instead of gravel. The Methodist church. And most sacred of all, Miss Ruth and Preacher's house, which looked much smaller than he remembered. The white-framed house had been a safe place, when his own family's home had not. He drove by slowly, wondering, but didn't stop.

He avoided the street and house where he'd grown up.

Still the sun stayed hidden, the town covered in the cold color of wet granite. He drove as far as the north city limit, then turned and made his way back to the court square. Around he went again. Although he sometimes felt as if people were staring at him, he knew that in reality no one was paying him any attention at all. As he had for most of his life, John felt both conspicuous and invisible.

Finally, he pointed the car south. Just past the city limit sign the road became a highway heading into sparse country. He had last driven this road nine years ago; he had left the cemetery and, in the sanctuary of his rental car, finished off a pint bottle. This had given him just enough courage to drive past, twice, before turning like a coward and heading back across the river, toward the airport...

Now his face remained hard, hands more firm, but inside his chest a young heart raced.

Jessie's house.

A few miles out of town he saw it—the small ranch house, nestled in fog. At first look it seemed a deep sleep had prevented the place from realizing the passage of time. But as he got closer he saw the changes. The fields lay out behind the house, cold and unkempt. The fencing needed paint, and only a few head of cattle could be seen from the road. Looking at the place, a longing rose up, and he wondered if she was there, moving, breathing in the house. And as he passed he held his own breath, so as not to disturb the dream.

Turning back towards town, he realized his hands were shaking.

3

Jessie said a silent prayer of thanks.

Belle was able to eat a decent breakfast, and felt strong enough to stay out of bed for a while. The house always seemed less silent and empty to Jessie on mornings like this, even if all her mother could do was sit in the den and enjoy the warmth of a good fire. But these days were coming less frequently. So Jessie moved swiftly, dressing in jeans and an old sweater.

Tuck had cut and stacked plenty of dry wood behind the house, and Jessie brought in several armloads. Soon she had a nice blaze going. She tucked her mother into the old recliner with thick quilts and a pillow. This had been her father's favorite chair; he loved sitting near the fireplace, and now, whenever she felt well enough, Belle seemed to find comfort in it too. The wood-paneled room glowed and smelled of happy times. The two women talked a while, but soon Belle wearied.

"You go about what needs doing," she said. "I'll just rest my eyes a while."

Jessie's heart sank. She touched her mother's white hair.

Movement, somehow, gave Jessie peace.

She stripped the sheets and blankets off her mother's bed, and her own, and while the first of what would be several loads rumbled in the washer she smoothed clean bedding onto the mattresses. She cleaned the two bathrooms, and as always put extra effort into scrubbing the small one connected to her mother's bedroom. In the kitchen she washed and sliced an onion and a few carrots and potatoes, and started a stew on the back of the stove with leftover steak from the previous night's supper.

Each time Jessie passed through the den she glanced at her mother, who seemed peacefully asleep, though with the small, permanent frown drawn on her face in the last months by the down-turned corners of her mouth. And each time, Jessie would gently adjust the quilts, then stoke the fire before returning to her chores. After only an hour or so, though, Belle's pain drove her back into her own bed. Jessie helped her take her medicine and get settled, then closed the door on her darkened room.

Now the house felt deathly quiet. The chores served as a balm for Jessie's mind. Focusing on the tasks at hand helped to hold off the annoying self-pity attempting to sneak into her heart. These were feelings she would not allow. Each time the thoughts crept in, she would grit her teeth and curse beneath her breath such ridiculous weakness.

This won't do.

Jessie pushed all the more furiously into her work through the morning hours towards midday, dusting every room, jabbing a broom at the cobwebs along the baseboards and in the corners of the ceiling. But in her bedroom, straightening the top of the dresser, she made the mistake of pausing to look in the mirror.

The reflection was not as soft or forgiving as the one in the kitchen window, as if many years had passed since morning. Crescent circles lay underneath her brown eyes; up close they looked like the curled, lavender-and-cream petals of a lilac. There were fine lines running from the corners of her eyes and mouth. The lips were still full but now seemed colorless. Her hair remained sable-brown, but stray strands of silver could be seen half-hidden like birch trees in a dark wood. For one still instant, Jessie could not recognize herself.

A crease of light intruded onto the background, tearing the illusion in half. The bedroom door slowly opened. Tuck appeared in the mirror; the strange woman vanished. Jessie turned.

"Hi," she said.

"Hey." He took off his wide-brimmed hat and held it in front of him between the thumb and index finger of both hands, tentatively, as if he were about to ask her to dance.

"What are you staring at?" she asked.

"You." Tuck was tall and square and strong. He had a kind face that lately had not managed to completely hide a quiet sadness. "You look pretty," he said.

"Oh." Jessie tried to smile. "Well, take your coat off. I bet you're worn out and hungry. Let me fix you something." She came to him and took the hat and coat. Tuck reached to touch her face, and Jessie slowed her movement long enough to feel the strong reassurance of his hand. The words *thank God you're here* came into her mind, but instead she said, "There're some leftovers in the fridge."

"I'm not that hungry. Tired, mostly. Long shift." His voice was deep and soft. He sat in a chair by the window and began unlacing his work boots. "How's Belle? Ya'll get along okay last night?"

"Fine." Jessie said it almost too sharply; she had heard—or imagined she'd heard—the covert concern in her husband's tone, a worry she knew was not solely related to her mother. For the past few days there had been a quiet but sure tension between them. "We had a real good morning," she said, calming her voice. "She got tired, though. Went back to bed."

"You just stayed around here?" he asked.

"Yes. I cleaned some. Washed clothes."

47

"Oh."

"It's what I do pretty much every day, Tuck. I take care of Momma and I take care of this place."

"I just asked, Jessie."

"Well, I'm tired too."

"I know." He looked somewhat helpless. "I didn't mean anything by it."

"Yes, you did." She closed her eyes. Then: "I'm sorry, Tuck." She looked at him bent over his boots, a dark sweat stain running from the collar of his shirt past the middle of his broad back. *I do love him*, she thought, then felt strangely unfaithful for even having to think it. He had been there for her, time after time, through it all. In all their years together, he had never spoken a harsh word to her. His physical size and strength were tempered by an almost childlike gentleness.

Jessie knew he was unsettled about Johnny Allen's return, and she also knew that Tuck wasn't very good at putting his feelings into words. She wanted to comfort him, yet didn't know what to say, or how to say it. She felt a love for him akin to the warm depth of true friendship, a kind of trust she knew was rare. And yet for the past week both of them seemed unable to speak their hearts. *Why do I keep pushing him away...now, when we need each other most?* She reached down and touched his shoulder.

"Why don't you take a shower, and let me fix you something," she said. "You need to eat before you go to bed."

When his wife left the room, Tuck hunched forward with his elbows on his knees and stared solemnly at the floor. He opened and closed his big hands like someone trying to get a grip on something he could not hold.

Jessie barely picked at her food, and Tuck ate less than usual. When they were finished she stood behind his chair at the table and rubbed his shoulders. His broad back felt hard and strong through his shirt. He tried teasing her, the way he always did, because he loved the sound of her laughter, and she felt grateful for her husband's selfless effort to make her smile. But still a formless fear stood between them. They tried to act as if everything was normal, talking about this and that, but not about what was most on their minds, and soon a kind of heaviness seemed to press down onto their words like the cold air weighing over the land outside their window. Finally Tuck pushed back his chair and went to the bedroom to put on his boots.

Jessie could hear him busying himself with things out back as she washed the dishes. After a while he came in and walked up behind her at the sink, leaning down to kiss her on the cheek.

"I'm goin' on to bed, darlin'," he said. "I'm wore out."

She turned her face to him. He smelled like pinewood and cold winter air. "I love you, Tuck," she said.

He gently cradled her face in his two huge hands.

"I love you, too, Jessie," he said. "Everything's gonna be just fine."

Jessie stared out the kitchen window. Frost lay like fine fleece over the fields. She tried to control her thoughts, but could not. No matter how hard she shut her heart against the irrational feelings flooding through her, still they came.

The desolate landscape lengthened into the horizon like an abandoned graveyard; she imagined only bones beneath the soil, the barren ground beyond rebirth. She hugged her arms against the raw wind blowing through her spirit. All through the willful winter, no matter how many lights she turned on in the house, the weather outside confounded each room with gray gloom. She hated this season that never allowed the old house to feel fully warm, and she hated the night shift that caused her to sleep alone at night and her husband to sleep through the day. She longed for spring and the smell of blossoms in her mother's flower garden.

Jessie had little patience for self-pity. She had learned over time how to steel herself against any weakness of character that might interfere with responsibilities or duty. But lately she had not been herself. Time and again she had found herself uncharacteristically at the mercy of her fantasies.

She shook the thoughts from her head.

This...won't...do.

Looking out now into winter, though, the feelings pressed relentlessly in on her heart. She could scarcely recall long-ago summers on the farm, and things growing, and she closed her eyes, took a deep breath...picnic lunches out on the sweeping lawn beside the fields, and the sweet scents of honeysuckle and magnolia blossom everywhere. But when she opened her eyes again, the smells and colors vanished—the farm, like her mother's body, seemed to have been cut away a piece at a time, and Jessie mourned its slow dying, the pasture gone to weeds, the big work-shed empty and falling in. She wished for calves to birth, or at least eggs to gather from the henhouse. Most of all, she wished she still had Sky to ride through pristine pastures.

And in this one moment she weakened, surrendered, and allowed herself to gaze out over the subdued land, remembering...

His letters had come regularly at first. She kept them all, and for a long time they had been a sustenance. Much of their content she memorized, and after a while even without looking at them she could call the words up in her mind and see his face, and almost smell the sea on his words...

>...and the ocean... Oh, Jess, I wish you could see it, so endless and immortal, like a great living thing, older than time. Sometimes I'll sit by myself on the beach at

sunset, and watch the world easing into rest. It's so beautiful, Jess. The only thing missing is you, and the sound of your voice, your touch...

But with the passing of time each new letter seemed somehow more distant, less intimate, and his words would leave her more thirsty than before she'd drank them in...

...so much has happened... I've met so many interesting people...a group of writers loves my work...we all spent the night reading our stuff aloud, listening, helping... everyone says my work has great promise...tomorrow night some of us will build a bonfire on the beach...

And though she loyally kept the fire in her own heart alive, she felt their worlds slowly separating, the redundant, cycling seasons rolling mercilessly through her while he remained preserved in a place of constant summer...

...I'm sorry for not writing in so long...amazing pace... so much going on...someone is interested in being my agent...oh, Jess, this could be a very good thing for me...

For *me*.

Looking back, she wondered why it had taken her so long to realize the truth. But it had not been naiveté that blinded her; for a long time Jessie simply chose to believe. She believed in Johnny, and she believed in the power of their shared love. Long after her hope began to break, she steeled herself against this blatant deception and darkness. She simply did not have in her the hardness of heart required to comprehend such a level of selfishness.

...I know I keep saying it, and I know how disappointed you are... I promise I'll write more often...

calling is so expensive...it looks like it's finally going to happen, at least there's a chance...if they publish my book, Jess, I can send someone to help there, and then we can finally be together...

He had promised, again and again, and she had held onto his words with an unfaltering faith, certain of *him* even when she had become certain it was over, always believing, until the days turned to weeks, months, years, his letters more infrequent and frightening...

...I am not myself, sometimes... I can almost feel myself changing...do you remember, how many times I swore I'd never be like my father...and yet here I am...some nights it's as if some power is pulling me down, Jess, covering me...

His words frightened her, terribly, but when she prayed each night there was always within her a sense that love would triumph, no matter what. Even after her mind had come to accept Johnny's betrayal, her spirit refused to believe that the darkness would not be beaten; Johnny had been duped, his mind contaminated, but his strength would ultimately allow him to survive.

He would come for her.

He will come.

But the letters slowed, then stopped.

And life stopped, too, in many ways, replaced with a slow, sure dying. All that she had given him—her trust, her touch, her deepest self—had been stolen and discarded. The faith that had sustained her began falling away...

Jessie pulled herself back into the present, and stared out onto winter. Far across the broad, broken sea of furrowed ground, the once-comforting woods now loomed like a great fortress wall.

I feel like an unopened flower, she thought. And a memory possessed her, drew her again to a place outside of time, and she turned her face toward the outstretched palm of his hand...

She knew. He was near again, and she experienced the feeling as if no time had passed at all...a warm and humming thing within that had always calmed her, assured her that even when they were apart he was always no more than a few miles away. And she felt him now, as if his car might be driving by...

How can this be?

Jessie had watched her parents share something uncommon and beautiful. Both had lived out a mutual conviction that love at its purest and most profound was sacrificial—*Love is never selfish,* her mother said again and again. Jessie believed in this, and her own character had over time been sculpted by these truths. She had grown into a woman whose character remained grounded, practical, principled. She had watched her father keep fighting, even when the cancer had all but snuffed him out, and now her mother, too. And watching them, she had learned that faith and love were stronger than any pain.

And so, Jessie could never have merely settled for Tuck. She was incapable of compromised love; once decided, she had loved Tuck in the only way she knew how, completely.

I do love my husband, she thought. *Perhaps now more than ever...*

What was happening to her did not seem possible. She did not understand how a face, a *touch* more real than mere memory had invaded her peace. Some strange but essential part of her still held to the hope of an unresolved past, a separate time and place where love had first been forged.

How can there be two of me?

Now she realized that for a long time a hidden but still beating heart had been slowly withering away in her chest, the heart of a young girl who had never given up her hope for rescue, and who knew that without resolution some still-untilled interior of her soul might never fully flourish.

Jessie let go now, let herself remember a time when the wind carried song and soft-sang it everywhere, and the new spring held fragrant, expectant promise...bridling Sky, smoothing the blanket over his broad back and heaving up the heavy saddle, leading him out snorting, steaming and shaking his head, the cool air working warm life into the two of them, fields stretched out and waiting...then flying across spring heather and wild indigo, bellflower and switchcane blurring beneath them, leaning close over the strong neck with both their manes rippling out, power and freedom carrying her beyond the far hedges...

I have never pined for other worlds, she thought.
Only for him.

Everything Jessie saw—past and present, love and hate—began to blur, and she leaned against the edge of the sink, pleading to her God who in recent days had seemed so silent. She covered her face with her hands.

But only briefly.

This won't do.

Jessie went to the fireplace, poked the iron into the glowing coals until the flames reappeared, then added another log. She stared into the fire, listening to the ticking of the old clock, long enough to be certain Tuck was asleep. Then she walked into her bedroom, not bothering to be especially quiet; Tuck snored deeply, and she knew he would not stir. *A thunderstorm wouldn't wake him,* she thought.

She knelt and opened a bottom dresser drawer, and from beneath the folded winter woolens retrieved a small handkerchief. Unfolding this, she found the small silver key. Then to the closet, filled with her tired clothes. She pulled a little footstool out from the back wall, and standing on it reached into the far corner of the top shelf. Drawing down an old jewelry box, she cradled it in one arm and with the tiny key opened the lock, then slowly raised the lid.

Jessie took out his letters.

She would not have to lock it again. She put the handkerchief and key in the box and closed the lid, then slid the box back onto the shelf.

Gently closing the bedroom door behind her, she walked across the worn wooden floor and stood at the fireplace. One by one, she dropped the letters into the flames. The paper curled into gray, then black, then white ash that floated up on sparks and was gone.

4

John knew the way to his brother's place, which required backtracking to the old road and driving parallel with the river for several miles. Joey had lived there since graduating high school, as soon as he had married. Like the cabin, the fifty-foot mobile home sat back in the woods overlooking still, expansive reservoir waters.

The trailer sat on six short pillars of stacked cinderblock. The yard lay cluttered with random pieces of junk poking up from patches of brown weeds. More cinderblocks were stacked as steps up to the front door. John knocked, waited, then knocked harder.

The man who opened the door looked half asleep—unshaven, shirttail out, sandy hair sticking up. He squinted and pawed against the pale light like a bear coming out of hibernation. Then his eyes widened in disbelief.

"Shoot fire."

"Hi, Joey."

"Oh my...shoot *fire!*" His breath blew out in excited little clouds of frost.

"You gonna let me in?"

"Oh Lord...am I...oh, my, get *in* here!" He all but dragged his brother by the shirt collar. "Johnny," he said when the door was shut. *"Johnny."*

"Hello, little brother."

"Kick me *dead*. When did you get here?"

"Yesterday. I stayed with Maggie last night."

Shock spread into a smile and a stunned shake of his head. "You look great. Really great."

"You look terrible. You smell like a skunk."

"HAW!"

The same old crow-like laugh made John smile. "A skunk in a brewery."

"HAW! HAW!" The smaller man threw his head back and laughed between stained teeth, and his eyes filled with tears. "Man, it's good to see you!"

"Same here, little bro. You still cry at just about anything, don't you?"

"Shoot *fire*, Johnny."

The narrow interior was cave-dark and crowded with an old couch and a low glass-top coffee table sitting on worn, green shag carpet. A TV and some old stereo gear sat against the opposite wall on shelves fashioned from painted planks and bricks. The little living area opened into a closet-sized kitchen cluttered with dirty plates and beer cans. Two rooms lay down the adjoining hall. Joey sat in an ancient recliner in the corner, John near him on one end of the couch. John could see most of the entire interior from where he sat.

"Maggie said you were coming, bro. I was sure hopin' so."

"Sorry I missed the funeral."

Joey scrunched his face and shrugged. "Shoot, I understand. I only went so Maggie wouldn't feel alone. Was just a funeral like all of 'em, I guess." The smile slowly faded. "Still don't seem real, though."

"Yeah." John watched his brother rub at his eyes. "Been wondering what you looked like, Captain Hook."

"Oh!" Joey held his right hand up in front of his face. Only the thumb and little finger emerged from the stump. "You'd already heard, huh. Whatcha think?"

"Damn, Joey."

"HAW! Freaky, huh?" He opened and closed the two digits together. "Kinda looks like a big crawdaddy claw, don't it? Don't make you queasy, does it?"

"You're still crazy, little bro."

"Dang straight I am. This was the best thing that ever could of *happened*, Johnny. Now I get a check every month and don't have to go to that awful plant anymore, ever, for the rest of my *life*. I'm tellin' you, best thing that ever happened. Man, I hated that place." He stood and went to the refrigerator.

"Watch *this*." Joey held the can against his palm with his thumb, and, in a move that seemed to John physically impossible, effortlessly popped the tab with his pinky.

"How'd you *do* that?"

Joey grinned and winked. "Practice, bro. *Prac*tice."

"Little early, isn't it?"

"Naw! Have one with me."

"No thanks."

Joey started to say something, then shut the fridge door and returned to his chair. "Yeah," he said. "Maggie said you were tryin'."

"I'm trying."

"Well, I think that's good. *Real* good." The way Joey said it, one eye half-closed, it sounded both sincere and suspicious.

"Yeah."

"So, you don't drink at all? Not even *beer*?"

"Nope."

"You still smoke dope, though."

"No. Nothing. I'm done."

"Kick me *dead*." Something like awe passed across his haggard face. He took a long drink. "How long?"

"Closing in on a year."

"Naw!"

John shrugged.

Joey smiled. "I'm proud of you." He raised his beer. *"Real* proud, big brother!" His eyes misted in mid-toast. Then he chugged the beer and crushed the can with his claw.

"Man, I musta told everybody in this whole county about your book when it came out. I cut the story from the paper and took it to the plant, put it up on the big bulletin board in the cafeteria." Joey looked at his brother with wide eyes. "'Just take a look at this,' I'd say. 'This here is my big brother!'"

John saw Joey's face, just for a flash, the way he had always remembered it, looking hopefully up at him in admiration. He felt the sadness welling up, but smiled through it.

"You mean you actually read it?"

"Haw! Well, you know I ain't much of a reader. *You* was always the smart one. I was the one always gettin' into trouble, remember?"

"Please. Don't try that on me, little brother. You're as dumb as a fox. You've just always liked *pretending* you were stupid."

"Haw! Well, anyway, *yeah,* I read it. *Dang,* Johnny, it was somethin' else, really *somethin'.*" He headed for another beer. "Just between you and me, though, I didn't understand all of it."

"Me either."

Joey returned to his chair. "HAW! Where'd you learn all them big *words?*"

"Dictionary."

"Haw-HAW!"

John looked at his brother leaning back, toes wiggling in his dirty socks, and saw a young man grown strangely old. A distancing sense of loss fell on him, and he spoke quickly to drive it away.

"So. You like living alone?"

"Well, it ain't like I've had a lot of choice, is it?" Joey winked. "But yeah, it's okay I guess. I don't miss all that yellin' and crazy stuff, I can tell you that." He took a gulp. "She's already hooked up with somebody else, so I hear, over in Briarwood." He looked out the tiny window into the woods. "Glad to be rid of her."

"Yeah."

"Shoot, it's quiet here now."

"I'll bet."

"Only person I have to worry about is me."

"Yeah." John nodded. "Anyway…you look old, boy."

"HAW! Not as old as you, boy!"

"Did I tell you how *bad* you look? Man, Joey. You're not taking very good care of yourself. You're butt-ugly, as a matter of fact."

"HAW!"

"And you still laugh like a jackass."

"HAW-HAW-HAW!" Joey shook his head. "Shoot *fire*, Johnny. Where'd you get those sissy *clothes*?"

Later they sat in rusty lawn chairs on the crude deck built out from the trailer's back door. Joey had rough-framed two-by-fours around it, and tacked plastic sheeting across the open spaces along both sides as temporary walls for the winter.

"Been meanin' to finish this for a while now," he said. The open end pointing to the river was covered only with screen, but enough wind was blocked so that they could stand the cold for a while. John hunkered down inside one of his brother's heavy coats.

"What's wrong with *you*?" Joey stood in his shirt sleeves, though he'd at least slipped on his boots. "Gotten used to too much sunshine way out yonder, ain't you? Gone *soft* on me."

"Must have."

"Shoot, this ain't cold."

"Yeah, but you're the only one drinking antifreeze."

"Gonna get worse before it gets better, so they say."
Joey let out a long, steamy breath. "Spring's still a long
ways off."

They sat in silence and looked down toward the water.

"It's weird, Johnny."

"Yeah."

"Don't seem like you've been gone all that long, really.
Still, you'd sometimes go so long without callin' or
writin'...whole buncha times we all wondered if you was
dead or somethin'."

"I'm sorry about that, Joey, I really am. I never meant
to worry anybody."

"Oh, I know. Don't you worry about that. Shoot, we
was all so proud of you. Maggie, too—deep down, I mean.
She could raise a fuss now and then, but I reckon she was
more scared for you than anything else." He lit a cigarette.
"Things were kinda tough on her, especially these last couple of years. Once Daddy got sick, she did most of the takin'
care of him."

"You didn't see him much."

"Naw, I didn't wanna see him, and he didn't wanna
see me. We had us a bad break."

"What kind?"

"Oh, shoot, it was years ago. You were long gone, my
senior year in school. I was the only one left..." Ash dropped
from his cigarette onto his lap, and he brushed it off.
"Things got bad, Johnny. Even worse than you saw. Worse
than you'll ever know." He took a drag and leaned back and
got quiet. Neither felt like talking. The wind whined and
whistled against the plastic. Finally—

"HAW! Gotta tell you one, bro. You remember Wayne
Spader?"

"Yeah. He used to date Becky..."

"Miller, Becky Miller. He married her, and I never
have figured that one out, 'cause she wasn't nothin' but

pretty and Wayne is dumber than a sack of diapers. Anyway, he and Donnie Johnson—you know who Donnie is—were duck huntin' this past Thanksgiving. HAW!" He threw his head back and crowed.

"So..."

"So, they're down in the river bottoms off east of the bridge, and they ain't done squat all day, I don't think, not a dang duck in the boat more than likely, and anyway ol' Wayne is wadin' out into the shallows to get his decoys pulled in 'cause they're fixin' to quit, and Donnie's sittin' in the boat with Wayne's retriever, Champ—pretty chocolate lab, bro, *beautiful* dog. And so Wayne is out a ways, bent over gettin' the decoys together, and Champ is gettin' antsy and movin' around in the boat, I reckon, and Donnie ain't paying no attention... HAW! HAW!"

"So...*what?*"

"So the next thing Donnie hears—he's the one told me this—is a shotgun goin' off... HAW! And then Wayne is screamin' his head off and jumpin' around knee-deep in the water... HAW!" His face was now wet with tears.

"Joey, you idiot. What happened?"

"Champ stepped on the *gun*! *Fired* the *gun*, Johnny! Blew a hole the size of a bowlin' ball through the side of the boat and...oh, *Lord*...shot Wayne right in the *ass!*" Joey hugged his stomach, face bright red.

"You mental case..." John tried to say, but his own laughter cut off the words.

"Dear Lord! And the boat was sinkin' and they was half froze and Wayne's bleedin' and he thinks he's dyin'... shot by his *own dog*... HAW-HAW-HAW!" Joey's voice dissolved into helpless choking sounds, feet slapping at the floor. John couldn't remember the last time he'd laughed so hard.

"Doc said only a little of the shot got him," Joey finally managed, weakly. "Said that if much more had hit him that close up, it woulda blown his leg off for sure." He took a deep breath of air. "Oh, shoot *fire*! Whew. That's funny as all get-out..."

They both tried to recover, settling slowly into an uneasy quiet. Finally John said, "Don't you have a dog?"

"Naw."

"How come? You've always had animals around you, little bro. I used to say you'd end up having a zoo someday."

"Haw. Yeah."

"Seems like a great place for a dog around here."

"Well, I had a real good dog, Johnny, sweetest thing you ever saw. Mostly lab and shepherd, smart as a whip. His name was Bone. Real good dog."

"What happened to him?"

"He died. Last year."

"Oh. Sorry, little bro. Maybe you should get another one, a puppy."

"Naw," Joey said. "Dogs die too quick, Johnny. You come to love 'em so hard, raisin' 'em up and all. But then the years start goin' by faster, you know, dog years. A person comes to love a dog almost as much as a person, sometimes. Maybe more, even. They're easier to love, in some ways." He rubbed his stump against his chin. "Then they get old so dang fast, grow old right in front of your eyes, seems like." He shifted in his chair. "Life's short enough as it is, bro, without havin' to say goodbye over and over again."

The wind came up and the tall tops of the pines stirred, woke and whispered. Joey dropped his cigarette butt and ground it into the wood floor with the heel of his boot.

"It's cold enough to put bumps on a bronze frog. Let's go in, bro. I'm froze."

Joey found a package of suspicious-looking ground beef in the fridge; together they made hamburgers in a cast-iron skillet and shared a late lunch, eating with their fingers off

63

plastic plates. Joey picked up the meat and potato chips with his claw and stuffed them into his mouth, talking the whole time.

"Tell me about California."

"It's all right. Too many people, though."

"Yeah, but a lot of 'em are *girl* people. *Pretty* girl people."

"Overrated."

"Liar. You're a liar."

"You're a drunk."

"All right. So tell me the truth. Who's got the prettier girls, Tennessee or LA?"

John felt uncomfortable. "Oh, I don't know. Tennessee has a different *kind* of pretty. LA's got more of them. And some have a lot more money, fancier clothes, cars, things like that. But...well, anyway, they're just different, that's all."

Joey leaned forward toward his brother in confidence. "So, big brother, how many?"

"How many what?"

"Come *on*, bro. How many *girlfriends*? Shoot fire, you've been on TV and everything. I reckon you've dated all *kinds* of women, maybe even a few movie stars."

"Not so many. And no movie stars."

"You're a lyin' dawg."

"You are a beer-bellied hillbilly."

"HAW!" Joey drooped back into the chair and took a long swig, then wiped his mouth on his sleeve. A smear of mustard stuck on his stubble. "No kiss-and-tell, huh, big bro? You ain't gonna tell me *squat*, are you?" He reached into the pocket of his flannel shirt and pulled out an amber prescription bottle. It rattled when he shook it. "Don't guess you want none of these."

"No. And you don't look like you need them, either." John felt the fear welling up. He tried to keep things light. "What you need is a bath."

"Ain't a *need* thing, bro. It's a *want* thing." He popped a couple of white pills and washed them down. "Takes the hurt away, bro. Legal, too. Me bein' *disabled* and all."

"Joey, you moron."

Again they grew quiet, with only the wind making any sound. "I ain't been to the cabin." Joey blurted the words out. "I know the one. But I ain't been to it since Daddy bought it. Did you go over there yet?"

"Not yet."

"Well, I ain't been in it."

"Yeah."

"Maggie says there's stuff in there. But I don't want none of it." He grew sullen. After a minute he stood up and took a wobbly step toward the kitchen. "Whoa."

"Sit down, Joey. I'll get it."

"Much obliged, big brother."

"*One* more."

"One more." Joey sat heavily and blew air out, flapping his lips. "Shoot *fire*." He touched the thumb of his claw-hand on one closed eye and the little finger on the other. "Man. Did I tell you 'bout how we tangled?"

"No."

"Yeah. It was bad."

"You wanna talk about it?"

"Naw. Yeah. I just couldn't take it anymore." He took the beer from his brother and drank half of it down. "One too many times, bro. One too many times."

"Yeah."

"Maggie was married to that idiot, Leonard. You was long gone. I stayed out of the house all I could. But Mama was...sick. You remember?"

"Yeah."

"That was a bad kind of way for her to be, always lost inside herself like that. Sittin' all day in her bathrobe by the window. I couldn't hardly stand seein' her like that, Johnny..."

"I know. Don't cry, Joey."

"Well, shoot. That's a bad way to be."

"Yes. Yes, it is."

"Shoot." Joey wiped his face and leaned forward. "Johnny, you shoulda seen Daddy, lyin' in that coffin. I couldn't believe it. Even had a little smile on his lips, the no-good...like he was laughin' at us or somethin'." He narrowed his bloodshot eyes. "You know what I looked at the most, though?"

"What?"

"His *hands*. God, he had big hands. *Big*. They was layin' on his chest, fingers laced together, like he was about to pray or somethin', real peaceful almost. You remember those hands, Johnny?"

"I do."

"Yeah. Shoot, they was big as hams. And hard. I was scared to death of those hands, even with him lyin' in that box all gentle-like, foolin' everybody. He was strong. Remember how strong he was?"

"I remember."

"When he bought the boat, remember? And we'd go to the river every Saturday, the whole family. Man, that was so fun, when Daddy would pull us up close and we'd wade out and play on the sandbars... Sand Islands, we'd call 'em, remember that?"

"I sure do."

"And that time... I was real little, and got my foot hung on something under the water..."

"Yeah. You yelled like the devil. Scared us all to death. You nearly drowned."

"And Daddy was outta that boat and underneath me in two seconds." A faint smile. "Whatever was down there, he tore it up with those hands, by God, lifted it right outta the mud, big piece of metal or somethin', a whole car, maybe...like Superman..."

66

"Your foot was cut."

"Yeah. *Strong* hands. He would lift me and you up on his shoulders when we was little, just swing us up there like we didn't weigh nothin'.'"

John suddenly saw a picture in his mind. "When I was little," he said, "I could grab with both hands onto one of his fingers, and he'd hold me off the floor."

"Yeah," Joey whispered, both of them seeing the same thing in the faint, fading light. "His hands were *big*..." He looked at John. "They could hurt, huh?"

"Yes, they could hurt."

Joey's face darkened. "Tell you what, bro. I came in that house, and heard her screamin', and something just broke in me. I'd always been too afraid of him, all my life. But for some reason this time I didn't even think about it. I'd had enough, I reckon, grown up enough. I busted in their room and she was curled on the floor, and he was bent down over her with those big hands raised up, and I just laid in to him. I got in a couple of good ones, and I was cussin' and cryin' and hittin' him with everything I had. And then he got me by the throat. He got his big hand around my throat and 'bout lifted me off the floor and shoved me against the wall and squeezed..."

"Joey..."

"You shoulda seen his *face*, Johnny. He was *red*, even his eyes, like he'd gone all the way crazy, finally, like he was gonna kill me. And Mama's screamin' and I'm goin' out, man, everything's goin' black..." Joey's hands slow-motioned toward his face and shook as he lit a cigarette. "There was a lamp on the table, and I got hold of it some-how and broke that thing over his head, I mean *hard*. And Daddy let go and grabbed his face and went down and Mama was yellin', and I was chokin' but I kicked him in the gut over and over. 'If you ever touch her again I'm gonna *kill* you!' I said and I meant it, and I don't hardly remember all of it, but I musta kicked him a dozen times 'til he lay still and moanin'..."

John reached out and put his hand on his brother's shaking shoulder and said, "It's all right," but felt the words sounded thin and meaningless. Joey dropped his head and wiped at his face with the stump of hand, and all of it rushed in on John, every feeling there was to feel, all at once, and he wished he could stop it, stop it the way he knew how, the way he always had with the drinking, and the idea briefly entered his mind but he closed his eyes hard and shook his head against the thought. He just sat there with his hand on his brother's shoulder.

Once Joey caught his breath he said, "Mama called the ambulance, and Sheriff came, too. I said to Mama— 'He's leavin' this house, one way or the other, and you ain't talkin' nobody out of it this time, neither.' And they took Daddy to the hospital in Williamsville 'cause his head was bleedin' and shum broke ribs." His words slurred. He took a deep breath, his eyes drooping, as if the tears had drained him of life. "He never come back to the housh to live afer that. I used to lie awake...scared to deff...wonderin' when he was gonna come back. But he dint. He moved in to the cabin, lef Mama'n me in the house, jush like that. And I never said 'nother word to him, or him to me..."

The late winter day had ended without warning. The single lamp in the corner cast a weak yellow glow onto the fake paneled walls, and the gray through the small square window drained from blue to charcoal and quickly to black.

John sat still with his elbows on his knees, looking at his brother. He could not seem to move, because he did not know where to go. He felt sad, and lonely, too, but mostly scared, though of what exactly he wasn't sure. Soft sepia shadows smoothed the coarse lines of age on his brother's face, and John saw back through the fading years a boy who always cried the easiest and laughed loudest to cover up the hurt, and tried to make everyone else laugh, too. A face always transparent with truth, like an open window into his heart, a face often smiling but never quite free from fear. He saw a little boy, sleeping.

John lifted his brother's legs onto the footstool, then lowered the back of the easy chair as far as possible in the cramped corner until he lay partly stretched out. He took a quilt from the couch and draped it over his chest and legs. As he tucked it up under Joey's chin, his younger brother stirred and reached to lightly touch John's fingers.

"Hands…" he mumbled.

"Go on to sleep, little brother."

"Sumbeech had *big* hands…" Joey's eyes opened, frightened, as if he'd seen someone he hadn't expected. "Big…hands…" His eyes closed.

John let him settle, then walked to the door. Just before he stepped out Joey mumbled, "Wharyugon…"

"It's okay, Joey. I'm leaving. I'll come back."

"Oh." His eyes closed, then half opened. "Wishwun?"

"What?"

"Wish-*one*…Tensee or Calforna gurs?"

"Good night, little brother."

John drove to the cabin in deep darkness; he had forgotten how black the night could be, and a bleak alienation covered him. For so long he had lived in the city, among a million lights, another world where time all ran together, a skin-deep place over which the calm of night never fully fell…and now it was this truer night that felt foreign. The jagged veracity of his homelessness cut into him. He felt small and afraid.

The night held no moon or stars. The only light in the whole world emitted from the yellow headlight beams cutting a weak wedge into the snaking road ahead. He slowed the car and the crescent-shaped glow drew back, too. All he could see was the shallow semicircle of trees leering down, reaching out and joining their arms above, enclosing him in a black, tangled tunnel.

No, he thought.

The old panic, rising up. Beads of sweat surfaced on his forehead, lips, hands. His mouth felt dry as sand. And a deep voice crawled into his head—

Drink with me, boy...

John leaned closer to the windshield, afraid he might outrun the brief illuminated passageway and be swallowed whole. He felt an overwhelming dread, and with it the shameful reality of his own cowardice.

Time had not waited.

He had grown up in these woods but no longer knew them. Now he was as alone here as he had been everywhere else. He shrank from the familiar fear of things he could not see, afraid to keep going, afraid to stop...

And then, inexplicably, he found himself staring at the cut-through road ahead. He braked and sat there, focusing on the brief break in the wood line, and tried to deepen his breathing.

"Help me," he whispered.

He wiped sweat from his forehead. Turning the wheel, he followed a narrow, bending drive until his lights finally shone onto his father's cabin. The surrounding wood lurked in deep darkness on all sides, black and bare except for a few stray sycamore trees standing stark still, their pale bark the color of dead skin.

He sat with the engine running and the heater going, these and the pulse pounding in his ears the only sounds anywhere, staring at the pitiful thing with its black window-eyes fear-frozen in the headlights, a lifeless place so cold and empty it seemed even God was not there.

And the car and the cabin sat still, facing each other like wounded creatures crouched in the dark.

* * *

The next morning John sat across from his sister at the breakfast table.

"Joey looks bad," he said.

"I know, Johnny. I've tried to get him some help."

"It won't work, Mags. He has to want it."

"I know."

Finally John said, "I'm going to stay."

Maggie straightened. "Really?"

"Yes. And I need to go shopping."

"Um, o*kay*. What do you need?"

"Just stuff, food, cleaning supplies. I'm going to stay in the cabin."

Maggie blinked. "The cabin?"

"I drove by there late last night, on the way back here from Joey's. I didn't go in. But I've thought it over. I want to clean it up, you know, maybe stay in it for a while. I think...maybe it would be a good place to write."

"Oh. Okay."

"You know. Just take some time. I could use some peace and quiet..."

"And write a book..."

"Well, I don't know. Maybe. I need some down time."

Maggie's face struggled between smile and sorrow. "Well, I mean, it'll be wonderful to have you around...and you think the *cabin*..."

"I just want to go in there, Maggie. Clean it up. I think it's what I want to do. I don't have anywhere else...there's nowhere else I need to go right now."

"Okay." She squeezed his hand. "I've got some stuff here you could use. I'll help you."

"Mags, I need to go by myself."

Her eyes said she understood.

As her brother stood to leave, she said, "Johnny, Jessie

71

knows you're here. I saw her last week, before the funeral."
She looked at him closely. "I just thought you should know."

He felt something come alive inside his chest. He wanted to ask a million questions.

"'Bye, Maggie," he said. "I'll talk to you soon."

She smiled a small smile.

"Don't be a stranger, Johnny."

5

Though the skies remained dismal, John felt thankful for a new day.

The paved road that had seemed so sinister the night before now gently curved and twisted, finally leading to a gravel road that branched off for about another mile. The mostly dirt-and-gravel driveway dead-ended thirty yards from the cabin. His father had lived alone here since the divorce ten years before.

The weathered logs of the cabin walls blended seamlessly into the forest, half hidden on a sloping hill rising gently up from the river; through the bare trees the pale-pewter water below stretched out wide and still.

John got out of the car and approached the front porch slowly, like a man coming upon a wild, sleeping animal. Everything lay still and silent around him. He circled the cabin warily, stepping across rough ridges of frozen mud, wishing he had boots.

The side window was screened, opaque until he pressed his face to it and cupped his hands around his eyes. He did this only briefly, realizing he was looking into what had been his father's bedroom. Then he walked back to the front and stood still at the bottom of three wooden steps. The roof extended over the open front porch, upon which sat a well-worn rocking chair and an old wooden milk crate turned on end for a table. John put his right foot on the bottom step, then stalled, hands shoved down into the pockets of his thin pants, elbows out, giving the impression of frozen flight. He stood there like that for some time before stepping up onto the porch.

The rusty spring screeched and groaned when he pulled open the screen door. Then he turned the knob on the unpainted wooden door, gave a push, and stared into the shadows.

The main room was small and simple and square. What little light filtered in through the two small, grimy windows cast a dull pall. He grimaced at the familiar, stale smell of an empty life.

It took several moments before he felt safe enough to go all the way in, and even then he left the door half-open. A childlike fear followed him to the center of the room. The boards creaked under his feet. He turned in a slow circle.

The room was furnished with two old, wooden straight-backed chairs against one wall, and a tattered easy chair aimed at a bookshelf in the corner that held a small radio and lots of mostly paperback books. Magazines and empty beer bottles sat skewed on the low coffee table. At the back of the room a cast-iron pot-bellied woodstove squatted in sparse ashes scattered around its four clawed feet. Next to that sat another wooden chair; John imagined his father sitting there to stay warm during the long winter nights.

Above him, exposed log beams supported the low A-frame ceiling. John sensed something still unsettled about the place, a feeling that although in many ways the cabin had never been wholly inhabited by the half-life of his father, it had never been completely abandoned, either. A sudden familiarity entered into him; it seemed reasonable to think that if he walked to the stove and put his hand out, he would still feel its heat. For a moment he stood motionless, listening.

The main space opened into a tiny kitchenette with a small refrigerator and hotplate. The only other room held a single bed on a simple wooden frame, a nightstand with a lamp, a tiny closet, and a bathroom. He moved through the place, looking quickly without touching anything, avoiding details, barely glancing at the bed. Walking back into the main room he felt light-headed, and saw small puffs of frost from his mouth coming faster, shorter. He felt as if all the air in the little house was being sucked out, that he would faint unless he made it outside.

The screen door banged behind him like a gun. The earth lurched. John took a few weak steps and leaned against the wooden rail of the porch. Shutting his eyes tight, he took in gulps of frozen air and held hard onto the rail with both hands until the dizziness and sickness passed.

Finally he opened his eyes—the small clearing in front of the cabin surrendered into woods that sloped gradually down toward the river. He could see through sparse brush to the gray, wind-wrinkled skin of the water.

John looked through the trees and his breathing slowed. *In the spring,* he thought, *the woods will thicken and you won't be able to see the river at all.* He saw something shimmer on the water, then disappear, then again, in more than one place, light glancing off the silver surface in one spot, then another. Looking up, he saw the sun at long last burning its way through the miserable dreariness.

A movement caught the corner of his eye. It took him a moment to find and focus, but there—just at the far point where the woods released the still waters into the running river beyond, stood an ancient oak; a red-tailed hawk had just alighted gracefully on a high branch. He balanced, then wrapped his wings about himself like a royal robe. Big, old probably, with impressive, broad copper-colored tail feathers, the creature screamed, a sound both shrill and sad.

Almost sounds like a warning, John thought.

They watched each other. He knew the bird could see every detail, the tiniest movements, and he felt strangely vulnerable. The land and lake clearly belonged to the creature, and he held dominion, a keeper of what little law existed in these woods. The hawk decided which small creatures would live or die on any given day.

The man stared up, envious, as the hawk peered down from beyond earthbound limitations. John wondered how long the red-tail had called these woods his home. He wondered how often his own father and the hawk had sat and observed one another, warily, two old, cunning predators. Watching the exquisite animal waiting high above it all, patient and pure, John's head began to clear, and he gradually regained his balance.

He stepped off the porch, drawn to the faint glimmering of the lake. As he walked down through the twisted trail that had been cleared step by step over many years, he realized that somewhere on or near this path his father had fallen and died. The woods thinned again and he walked onto sandy soil mixed with rocks and tiny pieces of crushed shell. He touched the water with the toes of his city shoes.

The water went out deep and wide, embraced by woods, the reservoir reaching into the distance toward the waiting river. He picked up a stone and tossed it, and the sound and sight of the water rippled like clean memory through the haze in his head. He grabbed another, a flat one, and this time threw it sidearm. He watched it skip across, breaking the still surface a half dozen times.

John walked slowly along the banks, then turned and headed back, retracing his steps. Looking down he realized he had left no footprints on the frozen ground, as if no one had been walking there at all. He crossed his arms and pressed through the cold back up the slope.

He unloaded the sacks of supplies and food, and resolutely steeled himself against the deep desire to run away. Slow-emerging sunlight struggled through the windows, sending long streamers of dust to land in squares across the floor. The cabin brightened some, as did his spirits, and the frightened little boy inside him grew braver. Still, he was aware of the compulsivity in the way he unpacked and organized and cleaned, moving quickly, determined to stay one step ahead of the anxiety creeping around the corners of his thoughts. He finished unloading the car, then found the unkempt woodpile near the side of the cabin. A worn axe leaned against the stump of what had once been a huge oak. There was enough cut wood for a couple of days. He would have to chop more, and the thought of such a simple, exhausting job made him feel strangely hopeful.

He hadn't attempted such a thing in a long time, but it didn't take him long to get a fire going in the stove, using small pieces of kindling his father had kept in a metal bucket against the wall. Maggie had instructed the utility companies to keep the water and power on, and there were two large space heaters that would help warm the place, if needed. But he liked the smell of the burning wood. There was something comforting about it.

He tried to put things in some order. As the room warmed he rolled up his sleeves and plowed into the place. He used Maggie's vacuum cleaner and mop, and dragged the chair cushions and bed mattress out onto the porch for a beating. He scrubbed the kitchen countertops and sink. He threw out what little old food was in the fridge and cabinets and put in his own.

Opening the top corner cabinet above the kitchen sink, John froze—two fifths of whiskey, one bottle half full, the other unopened. His first thought was to empty the bottles into the sink. But he could not quite bring himself to touch them. He stood there for a few long seconds, staring. Then he shut the cabinet.

He didn't open the small chest of drawers in the bedroom, but instead opened his suitcase on top of it. In the little closet he found a few hanging clothes, and on a wall peg hung hunting gear—heavy brown-canvas jacket and pants, and a mud-caked but sturdy pair of boots. On the floor sat a half-full box of shotgun shells, and when he pulled aside some other hanging clothes he saw the long black barrel of the gun leaning against the back corner. He looked at it for a moment, then closed the door, leaving everything untouched.

By mid-afternoon he had filled five large garbage bags with trash and mopped the floors and put the sheets and quilts Maggie had given him on the bed. He dug at the corners of every room with a stiff brush and sponges, the dirt leading him panting around the baseboards like an animal in a cage, then started on the walls, wrestling with them, purging, scouring, releasing his fury into a bucket of soapy water. Sweat broke out on him, and he struggled to open every window despite the cold, letting the smell of cigarettes and booze and slow dying slip away into the watching woods. He recognized his mania but clung to it, as he had for most of his life, like a shield against the shame.

Finally, he gave in. As the light began to fail he sat on the floor with his back to the bare wall. Every muscle ached. He looked down at the red, raw hands lying in his lap...big and hard-knuckled, then shaking, and he couldn't stop it. The shuddering spread into his shoulders, and he pulled his knees up to his chest and drew into himself, into his own emptiness. The tears crept up on him, as they so often had during the past year. He had gone a long time without them, but the sure sadness surprised him often since he'd stopped running from it, just as it surprised him now.

John sat wearily on the top step of the porch. As the day ended, some color had returned to the horizon; the remaining clouds lay in shambles, low and lavender above the river like thin shards of colored ice. Bare tree branches above and around him grasped at the sky with morbid disinterest.

Soft light leaving the river little by little, the water and woods and sky all blending into one non-color...somehow all this resonated deep inside him, a new and old feeling, foreign and familiar. The only sound came from the lonely call of an unseen crow, echoing from somewhere in the rising hills. And the world glowed, slowly succumbing to winter's quick night.

Finally the lonely cold drove him inside.

He tried sitting and reading but could not get comfortable. He kept looking at his watch. Sitting by the stove he could get partially warm, but at last the straight-backed chair and deep fatigue convinced him to try the bed in the stark little room where his father had slept.

When he turned out the bedside lamp the pitch-black, vacuous silence encased and all but suffocated him. Unseen wooden beams above him creaked as if the whole weight of winter had settled onto the roof. He lay still on his back, entombed, wondering how he had managed to find his way to this stone-still place. Deafening darkness clanged in his ears.

He lay shivering under the blankets like a frightened little boy, unsure when or how sleep finally came.

He dreamed.

...and woke to his father's strong hand gently shaking him by the shoulder.

"Happy birthday, Johnny. You'd better wake up now. It's almost dawn. We're goin' huntin', remember?"

The boy's eyes opened and saw his father's face, clear-eyed and smiling, and all the longed-for feelings inside his new twelve-year-old chest burst loose like fireworks.

This was to be their day. Just the two of them.

"Yes SIR!"

Out of the covers and into the cold room, wanting to hold the day, all of it, knowing how quickly it might be gone...

Sharing the cold October morning, talking and getting things packed up, dressing in thick hunting pants and jackets, camouflage caps and shell vests, filling their deep front pockets with heavy shotgun shells, arming themselves like soldiers. Then into town, the Winston Diner, filled with the smells of bacon and eggs and coffee and cigarette smoke and the primal sound of men laughing, many outfitted for the hunt's opening day...for a moment, the old feeling briefly creeping in—the boy allowed entrance to this fearless fraternity and yet still somehow separate—but now, on the promise of this day, he did not feel afraid, side by side with his father, a giddy, blissful moment of belonging, shoulders straightening, head high, walking into this warm and heady place beside his father, Big John, all the men nodding, respectful, fearful even.

"Let's have some coffee, me and you," his father said. They sat in a booth on burgundy vinyl benches and held the steaming cups with both hands. The boy drank the bitter stuff but didn't make a face. "Mmm..." he said, just like his father, proud, proud, the feeling flowing warm through him...

Sitting side-by-side in the cold cab of the old truck, guns and gear and lunch stored in back, the engine complaining, complaining, but submitting and then the boy knew they were going, just the two of them, warriors, and nothing could stop them now. His father laughed, a deep, thrilling sound...

The cornfields, endless acres of them mowed from the middle out, making a wide, open swath between...

"Here," his father said, "with the sun at our backs. They'll come in fast, son, like arrows. We don't want the glare in our eyes."

The two of them tucked in tight beneath tall sunflowers and cornstalks, crouched and waiting, his father's voice calm and wonderful. "Just right. There's good corn on the ground. The birds will come, but we'll have to be still. Then listen, wait for me. We'll stand together and shoot..."

The hair standing up on the back of his neck now—he couldn't wait to finally shoot the 20-gauge, to kill his first dove. How proud that would make his father! And they laughed, waiting, well ahead of the birds, late morning opening up before the boy like fresh hope, the surrounding woods wearing soft, supple garments of purple and gold, autumn sky crisp and perfect blue, talking about things, good things, soaking up the precious time. Everything right, and the boy can't stop talking, stop smiling—

John smiled wide in his sleep.

—silently praying the day could last forever, endless as a dream, the two of them with their guns across their knees and the smell of wet earth and grain in the air...

No.

...his father reaching inside his vest, pulling out the bottle—

"Please. No." John, pleading into the black, cold room.

"What's the matter, Johnny?"

"You promised." *His heart could not believe it.*

"Aw, it's okay, son. It's just to keep us warm. You try some..."

But the day was already warming under the fall sun...

"Come on, it's your birthday! Drink with me, boy!"

Fire going down, choking...

The big man threw back his head and laughed.

"Please, Daddy. Don't..."—*out loud, white breath rising.*

"What's the matter, boy? Here, give that back. I'll have what you don't want..."

And slowly, a different kind of laughing, the hands growing bigger, slapping too hard on the shoulder, ducking in and out of the vest more and more until one bottle was empty, and out of nowhere a new one...never had the boy hated anything so much, their bond broken again by lies, the laughter too loud, his father's voice edged now with something steel-sharp, oozing out of him, words cutting...and with them that haunted look, those thirsting eyes...

The boy shrinking down, small, silent, trying to disappear. Then the gray-dart doves, wedge-winged and jetting into the opening, his father raising up and firing once, twice, three times, cursing, thunder jolting into the boy's bones.

"Shoot, boy!"

Up, foolishly firing at an empty sky.

"You have to LEAD 'em, boy! They're fast!"

Moving the long barrel but only seeing streaks, tear-blurred, squeezing the trigger, the force kicking into his shoulder and driving shaming water from his eyes...

"Get back DOWN!"

His father kneeling, reloading, guttural sounds, standing and firing again, explosions deafening, wincing under the weight of falling heavens, not safe, not safe...

"You moved! I told you to stay STILL!" The voice a coarse, shouted whisper, standing up, unsteady.

"I didn't move, Daddy."

Another swig from the bottle.

"You get back down and stay STILL, boy!"

"Daddy, don't..."

"Don't WHAT?" The big hands wrapping around the gun, staring down, other shots now sounding from across the field, and his father wheeling, shooting late.

"SEE? You're making too much NOISE!" More shots, thunder from everywhere, little lead pellets falling down on their hats like gentle rain, the boy cowering, covering...

"You AFRAID? You're worthless, boy. You're just takin' up space..." His father shoving in more shells, cheeks red and puffy like a man fresh from a fist fight, reaching for the bottle in his vest and somehow the boy stands, a fury lifting him, slapping it from his father's hand, hard, onto the ground, brown-gurgling like blood into the dirt...

"What..." black-empty eyes, big hand lifting up...

And again, blue bullets streaking across the opening, his father spinning, stumbling, a dozen cannon shots booming from all around, the boy crouching and covering his head. Then the giant shadow wheeling on him, kicking out, face full of rage...

"You ain't nothin'..."

"Daddy."

Down hard into the wet ground.

And the boot is on his chest, mud-caked and heavy as a tree-trunk, crushing, gun barrel lowering, searching, wavering, unblinking snake in his face...

"Don't..."

The face, terrible, terrible, contorting, flashing from madness to pain to great sorrow, anguished eyes suddenly lost, awful windows into a condemned place past pity, hovering from the shallow heavens, an angry god's face—first at the boy, then down at the gun, disbelieving, everything shuddering loose, collapsing under immense secret sorrow, backwards, two steps, falling, the gun hitting the ground, thunder shattering the tops of sunflowers and filling the air with seed.

"No, no..." a great tree falling, "no..."

"Daddy!" Coming up and to him, the big man pitiful, scrambling away, into the thicket of cornstalks on his hands and knees, "Daddy, it's okay, please..." But shame has turned away its terrible face, there is nothing else, nothing, small hands grabbing for him, pleading, reaching to hold him, "I love you, Daddy, please, no..." Clinging, sobbing, father, son, and holy ghost crawling in the wet mire...and his father's eyes for one moment clearing, black night lifting...

"Oh, my boy, my son..."

"Daddy!"

John woke shouting, grabbing hopelessly into the dark.

When he realized there was nothing but cold air around his arms he swung the sheets angrily away. The sweat lay like frost on his shaking skin.

Grief covered him. He held his breath and listened for any signs of life. Nothing, now, but stillness, and the lonely sorrow in it.

He sat at the edge of the bed and cried into his hands.

When there were no more tears he went to the wood-stove and sat, then stood, then sat again and wrapped himself in his own arms, the only comfort anywhere. But the cabin walls pressed in on him, and he was up and through the door, onto the porch, away. Leaning against the rail he filled his lungs and screamed into the night, a helpless, hollow howling, but whatever had been haunting him would not come out.

He did this for as long as he could, until the last remnant of rage in him died, and the winter night had carried away the last of his breath. The stars pulsed distant and cold.

After a long time, when the night had numbed his fingers and face, the man went inside and walked to the closet. He pulled out the hunting jacket and put it on; the brown canvas was stiff and fleece-lined, and smelled of woods and gunpowder. He found thick gloves stuffed into the pockets.

On the porch he knocked the dirt and dead leaves off the old wooden rocking chair. He sat and pulled the stiff collar up around his ears. The world settled back into silent sleep before him, and he watched stars fall and freeze themselves against the still surface of the river.

He rocked back and forth.

The cold did not cut through him as badly now.

6

Two dull days passed.

On the third day, while Tuck slept, Jessie pulled on jeans, jacket and boots and drove towards town. She didn't need or want anything the town had to offer, but she didn't want to be in the house, either. Belle's strength had not returned; over time she had grown weaker and taken more to her bed. Jessie often found herself roaming the still rooms like some silent spirit, lost and in search of something solid she could never quite touch. But now, as Jessie drove, at least some hope sparked to life in her when for the first time in forever the sun began to shine, glinting off miles of frostbitten fields stretching out along both sides of the highway. She could stand the cold, at least a while longer, if only the world had some color to it.

Even in the brighter light the old town square looked old and sick, the bandaged, blank-stare faces of the storefronts heaped side by side like casualties of war. She felt a heavy hopelessness pressing in, her world exhausted and done with living. One pass was enough; she escaped down Main Street toward the west edge of town. She considered the highway that would take her the twenty miles to the new shopping mall in Williamsville. But in truth she hated the concrete monstrosity now spread out over what had once been open fields. Her favorite stores on the square hadn't been able to compete, and had closed their doors. She could no longer sit and talk about things with the friends who owned or shopped in these places. Each time she walked through the new center she felt as though she might be in any town or city, any faceless place filled with nameless strangers moving up and down the aisles. There was nothing warm or welcoming about it.

Pulling into the parking lot of the town's only grocery store, circling, without purpose, Jessie felt a kind of despair bordering on panic. Pointing back out at the highway she considered turning to the right, which would take her a mile or so to the city limits, and to the left, back into town. She sat there with the truck running, unsure of where to go.

I have to keep on going, somewhere, she thought. *No matter how I feel, I have to keep going.*

She closed her eyes and summoned the strength that had brought her this far, but still seemed unable to make the truck move. Leaning her head forward onto the steering wheel, she took a deep, slow breath—faint, earthy, sweat, rain, sun, and somewhere woven in it the texture of her father's rich, full laugh. Jessie loved the truck. It felt like her father...

Her eyes startled open; someone had pulled up behind her and tapped their horn. Turning right she chose, or something chose for her. Jessie drove toward the old barn.

* * *

Belle lay staring at the ceiling, encased in her prison of pain.

She waited until she heard her daughter pull away in the truck. Tuck would be asleep by now.

The old clock chimed three times.

She had listened for a long time, counting the seconds, bracing herself for the living thing deep inside her to wake and come, tensing her whole body against the searing agony that threatened to make her cry out. Now, as the sound of the truck's engine wound away into the distance, she let out a long sigh that became a soft, suffering sound from deep within her, one she had never heard before. She prayed her same helpless prayer, but the fire rose up defiantly from her womb, abdomen. She slapped at the mattress and grabbed twisted handfuls of sheets like the manes of wild horses, turning her face down into the pillow, holding on as the merciless heat lifted her. She descended into the red-black and was covered by it, begging, until the wave weakened and receded, lowering her back onto the bed. Tears crawled down her cheeks. Her breath came out in small, suffering gasps. She let the secret moans move out of her with a grateful knowing that no one would hear.

She tried to lengthen her breathing, focusing now on the face in the framed print hanging on the wall across the room—the man with the long hair and calm yet tragic eyes. As she looked at him the braided agony within slowly loosened, and she mouthed the silent words, offering up thanks.

When the waves had ebbed enough she struggled to sit up. The sheets were wet beneath her. She pressed her right hand into her side, trying to hold herself in one piece, then slowly rose and made her way to the bathroom.

The cold tile floor felt good beneath her bare feet. *Wouldn't Dub laugh,* she thought. He had always teased her when she complained about her cold feet throughout every winter. It was true: she'd never liked winter, not one bit, with its stubborn, sleeping soil. She'd never been able to keep her toes warm, even after Dub gave her those wool-lined slippers one Christmas. But now she celebrated the feeling, so contrary to the burning waves of pain she dreaded. *Still alive,* she thought, the cool tingling against her soles somehow rooting her to reality, to the earthly truth of being among the living.

Even so, the woman Belle saw in the mirror was tired of the struggle, worn down with dying. Lately she had prayed each night that the next morning her daughter would find her in bed, peaceful, like someone sleeping, the taut pain gone, face relaxed.

Dying shouldn't take so long, she thought. *Why, Lord? What's your purpose in it?*

She had asked the same questions as her husband lay in the same bed, no more than a thin and brittle shell of himself. God had not answered her then, and he did not answer her now. But she had lived her life committed to a belief in something that existed above and beyond the pain of living. Though her suffering caused her to cry out the questions, her faith sheltered her from the silence. She could wait.

Still, she hurt for her child. *If I had the power to turn back the years I might do some things differently,* she thought. *Not for myself, but for my little girl.* She would have seen the hurt coming, perhaps, and done something about it, forbidden her to...*what?*

She bent and cupped her hands under the faucet, dipped her face into the cool water. *How could I have done anything?*—staring now at the skeletal stranger in the mirror. *Nothing can change love, or kill it, or even change its course.* A truth lived here, in this one unblemished place nestled deep in her heart—the place where she was still beautiful. She knew that if Dub were still alive he would not see her as wan and wasted; she would be beautiful to him, just as he had remained beautiful to her till the very end. Taking care of him in the last days was painfully difficult for Jessie, but never once was it hard for Belle to see, touch, nurture him.

Later, Belle would not look long at photographs taken in the last two years of her husband's life. "That's not him," she would simply say, without resentment. "That's not my Dub...not how I remember him at all." And so she could look confidently into the mirror, even now, knowing that beauty born of love remains timeless and unconquerable.

She let the water trickle through her fingers and drip into the sink, touching her tongue to the wetness of her palm, across the ridged texture of skin. The sound of running water made her remember...how Jessie would work so hard, uncomplainingly, helping care for Dub during those last, terrible couple of years. Belle had taught her well, growing up—*Sometimes life is full of rain, Jessie,* she had said, *but we get up anyway. Some days we have to choose love, whether we feel it or not.* And how strong her daughter would be, always smiling and trying to make Dub smile, too, doing all she could to lift his spirits. Jessie had never liked anyone seeing her as something less than strong, even as a child, always trying to hide her own sorrow. But Belle could hear from the bedroom, late at night after Dub was finally asleep, the awful sobbing through the wall, Jessie standing in the shower, crying.

Now, Belle wished to remember *everything.* The periods of peace separating her anguish were shortening, and each time the pain recoiled she sought out the pure touch and taste of life while she could, before the unrelenting tide roared back over her, possibly forever.

It's good, she thought, *that God, rather than me, controls time.*

Belle knew that all those years ago no one could have turned her own heart from its destined place. As she moved through the seasons of her life, wisdom put down deeper roots. Through the hard ground of duty a great gift began to emerge: by staying true—to promises, vows, commitments, to the steadying voice within—the dichotomy of self-sacrifice evolving into fulfillment began to take shape, gradually, like fruit faithfully tended. The sure shape of simplicity emerged; watered, fed and pruned, seed became bloom heavy with nectar. What had often through the years seemed bland and ordinary had in fact matured and borne the invaluable gift of peace upon Belle's nightly pillow, where somewhere in her dreaming the commonplace crystallized into the divine. The humble little house did not confine, but comforted—the sound of steady breathing beside her in the old spindle bed, the unfailing cadence of the clock, the tireless turning of the seasons across the land outside her windows—all of it complex in its simplicity, profound in its predictability. At some point she and her lover had come to understand that they as human beings had not been put on the earth for the sole purpose of seeking and satisfying all their worldly desires. Somehow, in the unfathomable mystery of faith upon which she entrusted her being, she had learned the most precious of secrets: true joy did not come from having everything she wanted, but in wanting everything she had.

But what about Jessie?

What would become of her daughter, of her grandchild, should God ever choose to bring one into the world? *Watch over her, Lord, and Tuck, too,* she prayed. Again the fear eased, and she knew the gift of faith would not fail her. She knew, truly, that Jessie and Tuck were meant to be. Oh, she had wondered at times, knowing how deep went the wound Johnny had left in her, when she was so innocent. *Love is almost too much for the young,* she thought. But she believed things happened by design. She believed.

Belle knew she was dying. In the cyclical reaping, sowing, and reaping Belle knew she had reached the end of her earthly time, yet held tightly to the unlikely truth that her death, like all death, would in some wonderful way become a beginning.

The old woman smiled.

And saw in the reflection a face impossibly beautiful, glorious, full of rich, hard-plowed harvest, vast victory, battered but unbeaten. Dub was gone, yes, but not forever, not for much longer, because love had outlasted everything, and she basked for one vital moment in the knowing that even as day descends into night all the world glows golden. Though she lamented that she would never see another summer, she rejoiced that she would also never see another blossom fall. Soon she would leave this world and enter one balanced on the eternal cusp of spring.

The woman clung to the edge of the sink, felt it coming, building far out to sea and gaining strength. She turned, took hopeless steps toward the bed, and as she fell time slowed, delicately folding in on itself like a morning glory at dusk. She pressed her face deep into the earthy smells of the old hook rug, the same one she had crawled on as a baby, and in this graceful gift of long and lingering stillness she felt the texture of fibers digging into her skin, the musty memory of it, the countless miles of steps woven deep within it, curling her into the shape of a baby. Wailing, rolling, she looked up at the picture, at the sorrowful eyes, and in them saw the image of a dove bearing away misery on its white wings, and heard, at long last...*love runs deeper than the pain, always...*

* * *

The old barn sat alone, deep back and unseen from the road.

The land had once belonged to her mother's uncle, and when Jessie was young Sky had been stabled here. She would come the few miles up the road from her house to ride and groom her chestnut stallion. Later, the barn had become a place of deep meaning in other ways.

Jessie knew the several hundred acres had been sold to some real estate company in Memphis, but as the years passed she tried not to think about it, a part of her dreading whatever disaster of development might be coming. But no one had touched the place in all that time. Now fields once plowed and producing lay cold and covered with weeds.

The barn sat hidden from the highway behind a shielding flank of towering pine. Rain had worn deep ruts into the dirt road, but Jessie maneuvered the pickup around and through as far as she could. She parked the truck a hundred yards off, close enough yet still far enough away. Even from what seemed a safe distance she moved tentatively—face leaning forward, hands gripping the wheel, motor running. Jessie felt like a child doing something terribly wrong, scared she might be caught stealing a precious object that did not belong to her, and at any moment might need a fast getaway. She felt almost too afraid to look.

The once proud structure reached up longingly toward a bright but still-distant sun. Much of the remembered red paint had faded away, the rust-colored wood now wrinkled like the deep-lined face of a weather-worn farmer. The towering point of its roof seemed to be leaning ever so slightly to its right, and Jessie wondered if it had always been that way.

Anger and loss mixed together and swept icily through her spirit.

The wide double doors were closed. She wished she hadn't come, that she had never seen the place as it now stood. She lowered her forehead onto the wheel. She wanted to curse or cry, but could manage neither.

Stupid, stupid, stupid.

Defiant, she lifted her head and stomped the clutch. But before she could shift something caught her eye—soft movement, the lightest touch of white against the brown wood-line to the left of the rear of the barn, standing delicately only a few feet into the clearing. Instinctively everything paused—woman, doe, fawn, heads up, alert, listening. The little one held near its mother's flank, mimicking her movements, ears stiff and muscles flexed, black eyes unblinking.

Jessie turned off the engine. Silence fell. For a few frozen moments the scene posed, stretched out like a painting. And then the two deer lowered their heads back to the withered grass.

Something in their silent trust lured the child in her. Jessie got out and left the door open. She walked slowly to the front of the truck and, facing the scene, lifted the heel of one boot onto the bumper and boosted herself backwards onto the hood. The two deer raised their heads again at this, but did not run.

Jessie pulled her knees up under her chin, watching.

The mother now and then raised her graceful head, keeping her body near enough to the young one so that both felt comfortable. The fawn occasionally looked up and flicked her ears. Lifting her own face to the sunlight, Jessie closed her eyes and let the warmth flow from her forehead down her cheeks and onto her neck, let it radiate into her clothes, insulating her from the frigid air. The light would be gone soon, and she wanted to take in as much as she could, in case it never came again. Slowly, something began warming inside her, too, a kind of stirring, deep down. And she turned her head toward the barn. She stared at the place for what seemed a long time.

My dreams were trapped inside that place, she thought.

After a while a strange weariness came over her. She felt like someone who had been determinedly pursuing life, never pausing to rest, and now had collapsed without warning and could not go one step more. She lay back on the sun-soaked hood with her hands behind her head and looked at the cloudless sky. A moment ago the fields fanned far out and all around her, but now she floated on her back, down, down, until the surrounding tree-line disappeared from her vision, and there was nothing but fathomless blue.

A jet almost too high to see was spinning a fine white thread across the center of the sky. Jessie wondered as she had since childhood where the people in that plane might be going, riding on a rocket to some far and foreign place.

My world is breaking in two, she thought, not really under-standing, the warmth beneath and above lulling her into timelessness, and her eyes would not stay open...minutes, hours...and it wasn't the sad, broken-down barn she saw now, but one full of life, and youth, soft hay beneath them, and the new tastes of love...

"When will you go?" she asked.

He lay on his back, still and quiet beside her, in the sweet-smelling hay.

"Two more weeks," he said.

She curled her body closer against him, his shoulder her pillow.

"Sometimes I can't bear to think of it, Johnny. The thought of it makes me feel too sad to...to even stay alive."

"Don't say that, Jess." He turned his face to hers, their noses touching. "It's hard for me, too." He put the palm of his hand lightly against her cheek; the girl loved it when he did that.

"I know." And they kissed.

Finally, "How long, Johnny? How long do you think?"

He smiled. "How many times have you asked me that?"

"Ten million."

"More."

"Tell me again. About where you'll be, and when you'll write for me to come."

The boy turned his gaze again to the high, pointed ceil-ing of the barn's roof; beyond the rafters everything arched into blackness.

"I'll go to the ocean."

"Yes."

"And as soon as I get there I'll take off my shoes and run across the white sand and straight into the water..."

"Cold."

"Yes."

"And it'll sound like..."

"Like the crashing of distant thunder..."

"On countless distant shores..."

He smiled.

"You know all this by heart, now."

"Yes."

He felt the warmth of her body contoured against his own. It made him feel whole.

"But Johnny." In the dim light managing to squeeze through the cracks in the walls, he saw that her cheeks were wet.

"It won't be forever, Jess."

"It will seem like forever," she said...

The far-off rumble of the jet seemed to take forever to fade, then hush away. Time vanished.

Jessie opened her eyes.

The gossamer strand had dissipated, as if God had reached with his hand while she slept and smeared the illusion into nothing more than shredded remnants of forgotten clouds.

Jessie sat up. She felt disoriented; the light landing on the fields looked different. The sky deepened toward dusk. The deer were gone, the woods still.

How long have I been here? She clenched her eyes tight against a foolish feeling of having somehow betrayed herself.

The wind roused, and she drew her jacket tighter around her. While she dreamed the sun had impaled itself on the high, pointed tip of the barn's roof, its bronze blood now pouring out onto the tops of the trees. She watched the shadows spill over the towering dam of pine and cedar and oak and flow slowly onto the fields like black water. Finally the shadow-tide rose to the front fender of the truck, then swept over and engulfed her and all that was left of the day.

Jessie slid down off the hood, shivering. *I hate the cold,* she thought.

Today, deep in the soil of her soul, it seemed to her that it had been winter ever since he left.

She drove away without looking back, promising herself she would never return.

Tuck stood in the kitchen as Jessie came through the door. She felt the quick surge of shame shatter into fear when she looked into his face.

"It's Belle," he said.

7

Belle stared at the white ceiling, waiting for the next wave of torture to crawl up and clutch at her soul.

She did not remember it, but someone had found her, and put her in her bed. Lying still, she could hear the ticking of the old clock making its steady way down the little hallway and into her room. By listening to this sound, she was able to authenticate her world, and her tentative time left in it. She had lived much of her life moving to the clock's steady music, its inexorable dance toward silence. As long as this companion heart remained beating, she would not be done; listening, she knew that for the moment there was still life in both of them. But even now a strange sense of disorientation suspended itself above her, a winged impression of time folding in on itself, so that she felt neither living nor dead, yet somehow understood that she was both.

She heard the clock's inner mechanisms groan, brace, then chime. And she counted silently along, lips barely moving—*five...six...seven.*

Belle had been born in this bed. And in this bed, forty years later, after countless days and nights of fervent prayer, she had conceived her only child. *We never lost faith, did we, Dub? Our faith was tested, to be sure. But we never stopped believing.* Jessie had come stubborn and squalling into the world here, too, in this very room, and the thought of it made Belle smile through thin, tight lips beaded in sweat.

97

Lying here now in the graceful pause between pain, beneath the heavy quilts made by her own mother, Belle stared at the fine crack running the length of her sky, just missing the tarnished brass base of the ceiling fan by inches. She had for so long looked up into this pale firmament that all of its details—the crack, the two small brown water stains, the wisp of web just visible in the far corner—had become imprinted into the essence of her being. Through childhood and its unspoken promise of immortality, through adolescent spring and sensual summer and the calming autumn of adulthood, the house and she had been betrothed and inseparable. Even after Dub was gone the house remained a living part of them both, with a true and steady heart. And though she had never spoken such an unreasonable thing, she had been afraid to leave the place, for fear that her very soul might wither and vanish like late-summer blooms from her garden.

Suddenly, the ceiling and the crack and the web and the lonely ticking from the next room, all of it held for her a divine beauty.

Perhaps this is the very first thing I saw, when they cut the cord and laid me in my momma's arms, she thought.

It's only right that it will be the last.

In the hushed room Belle prayed. Her parched lips formed silent words: *Lord, I know you must get tired of me asking. But if it be thy will, I'd sure like to live until spring. It would mean everything to me, Lord, just to hold an armful of my flowers, just bury my face in a bunch of blossoms and breathe in their beauty, Lord. I'd be much obliged...but thy will be done, not mine...*

And the wave rose up in her again. She focused all her strength on not screaming. She again saw Jessie's face staring out the kitchen window. *Oh, how it hurt me to see you there, little girl, way too still and staring out...*

98

"Momma." This time Jessie's face was real, inches from her own.

"Jessie." The weariness pressed down on her. *Sweet Jesus, you know your reasons. But Jessie's never had a full chance at living, in some ways, not even much family, both me and Dub only children, and with no child of her own.* Fighting to remain lucid, Belle reached and touched the angel's rose-colored cheek.

"Doc said I should let you sleep," Jessie whispered.

"Doc is an old woman."

Jessie tried to smile. She silently cursed her mother's enemy pain, but knew Belle would fight it tooth and nail, taking as little medication as possible. She pressed a wet cloth along the sides of her mother's neck, forehead, lips.

"Jessie—" Knowing the wave would come soon, wanting to warn her, "don't let them take me out of my house."

"Oh, Momma."

"You promised."

"I know. I'll keep my promise." The scene unfolding before her seemed so unreal. "You can rest easy."

"Well."

"Momma." The little girl inside Jessie felt helpless and afraid.

From her mother she had learned what it meant to be a woman, and a wife. Belle had taught her tenderness, and provided a safe place to feel. She had shown her how to fight without forfeiting her femininity. From her mother Jessie had absorbed much of her faith, too, and not just the shallow creeks of mind-faith but the deep reliance walked out on the storm-tossed seas of real living. But now faith felt shallow. Looking down at her mother she heard breaking everywhere, above and beneath her, the world all thin ice and falling sky.

Jessie pulled a chair to the edge of the bed. Taking her mother's hand, she leaned close down, gently, afraid of something precious flying away, because Belle had also taught her that love can be easily missed while life fleets away.

"Tell me again, Momma." Jessie could see the pain rising up, and wanted to whisk her mother away somewhere safe. "Tell me about you and Daddy."

"Child. Don't you ever get tired of this tale?"

"No, Momma. Never."

"Well, he was just about the most handsome man in the world, is all." Her voice, though hushed, seemed to strengthen as she spoke. "There wasn't much town back then, and most folks all knew each other, went to church together, the same church we've all gone to your whole life. The families all helped each other out with the farming or the livestock, whatever needed doing. And your daddy was flirtin' with me from the time we were both little." Her tone seemed to lighten. "I was nothing more than a girl, a young and silly girl. But by the time we started high school I already knew who I was gonna marry, and his folks and my folks, they all figured on it, too. There was just never any doubt in my mind. It was like God had planned it all out from a time before we were born..."

For one wonderful moment the old woman's face emptied of pain.

"Of course, Dub was so bashful. But I think he and I both knew from the first time we saw each other. The truth is, I never wanted to be anywhere else other than with him..."

As the red stream rose up hot in her, Belle closed her eyes and flew fast to her garden. The air flowed warm and rich and fragrant with nectar, and no day had ever been more dazzling. Living—the world was again living, breathing, buzzing with flight. The green was deep, the colors bursting, the low, lush pansies and arching orange lilies, crocus and chrysanthemum, and her roses, *sweet Jesus*, the roses had never been more bold, wine-crimson, cream, yellow as the summer sun...

Jessie felt her mother falling away, and spoke quickly, childlike. "Tell me about when I was born," she said, because she did not know what else to say. "About how it seemed I'd never be born..."

Belle held tightly to her daughter's cold hand, pulling herself back. She was ready to go, but not quite ready to leave her Jessie. "Oh, my, we thought it would never happen. We wanted you, prayed for you for so long, and it seemed God wouldn't answer. But the Lord had his plan." Belle looked into her daughter's amazing eyes. *She deserves true happiness, Lord.* "You had a head full of dark, curly hair the day you were born. The doctor and the nurses, everybody just oohed and ahhed and kept sayin', 'Look at all that *hair!*'" She reached up and ran trembling fingers through Jessie's curls. "And your daddy wasn't ever the same man after that. He thought you hung the very moon..."

"Momma..." Belle heard the voice from a million miles away, knew she was squeezing nails deep into her daughter's flesh, but she could stay no longer, her heart insisting on spring, air sweet and body light, and Dub there, too, more handsome than ever, reaching out to him with open arms, for the big bunch of blossoms in his hands, picked just for her...

"Tired, Belle?"

"Yes. But a good tired."

They sit together on the white wooden bench swing, near the garden. He holds her hand, and with the other he tilts up the glass and finishes his iced tea, the ice clinking together against his lips. He moves the swing gently back and forth with one foot, a gentle, long-practised rhythm. Birds sing.

"I'm so glad you feel better today, Dub. You seem real strong."

"I feel strong. Strong as an ox." He gives her a squeeze, though much of his strength is gone. "Wish I could help you

out here more than I do, my love. But you've done wonders. This might be your prettiest garden yet."

"You think?"

"Yep."

"The daffodils are beautiful. Not having a late frost helped."

They sit, their world quiet and comfortable. The sky is so blue.

"Dub."

"What, darlin'?"

"I know you told me not to. But I keep worrying about her."

"I know."

"She's so strong-headed sometimes."

"Ain't that the truth."

She elbows him in the ribs. "She loves him so. She doesn't know how to love any other way. But she's so young."

"No younger than we were."

"Yes. But that was different."

"How?"

"You and Johnny Allen are two different people."

"Johnny is a good boy. He has a good heart."

"But he's different, Dub."

"Yeah. I reckon he is. But he's not like his old man. Not deep down."

"Goodness, no. God forgive me for saying such a thing, but Big John Allen is mean as the devil."

"Mean men are more scared and lonely than anything else, Belle. Lonely in a room full of people, sometimes. Scared of living, mostly. All that bluster and threatening. Truth is, a man like that is usually afraid of his own shadow."

"Hmm."

"Anyway, Johnny means well by her. I truly believe that."

"I know he loves her. But I worry, just the same. He's a dreamer."

"That he is."

"Almost any other boy in this town, Dub. Most others, anyway. Every one of them would die to have her. They would stay around these parts, more than likely. Maybe even stay to work the land they grew up on, or open business in town."

"I know."

"And I know you two like each other. But Dub, Johnny's no more gonna stay around here than I'm gonna fly to the moon...and writing books, of all things. Who can make a living doing that?"

"Is that really what you're worryin' your pretty little head about, my love?"

"Yes. No."

"It might happen, Belle."

"It sure might."

"And if she does decide to go, that'll be her decision. Jessie's her own person, always has been. She's got her own wild streak, been that way ever since she was little, and you know that better than anybody. Once she starts rarin' up it's hard to get a bridle on her."

"I know. But, Dub..."

"My love."

"Yes, my love."

"I want her to stay, too. She's my little girl. But I don't want her stayin' because she thinks she has to help take care of me."

"Sweet ol' Dub."

"We've had her for eighteen years, Belle. Eighteen wonderful years, our only baby. But she don't belong to us anymore. Never did, really. She's God's own, and always has been."

"I know."

The chains holding up the swing gently squeak.

"But I think he ought to go on and marry her," she says after a while. "I'm just scared to death he'll hurt her."

"That's for them to decide. I think Johnny's heart is good."

"Then he ought to go on and marry her."

"Belle, marryin' ain't a human thing, it's a God thing. We can go through the motions, and the preacher can say all the words. And when it's over we can dance and have a party and slice the cake and sign the papers. But none of that's marriage. Marriage is…"

"Yes? What is it, then?"

"Well, it's beyond anything we could manage on our own."

"What in the world are you talking about?"

"I mean, if two people are meant to be together, if God really means for it to be, then it'll be. Ain't no power on this or any other world that can stop it."

"Well, my goodness." Her eyes open wide. "There's a lot of poet in you, my love."

"Aw."

"You're cute when you blush."

"Stop it, girl."

"Oh, Dub."

"Sweet thing, please don't start that cryin'."

"I can't help it."

"Well, then, come and lean over here."

"I can't help being scared for her, Dub."

"I know."

"Life can be so cruel and mean."

"Yes. Yes it can. But pain's part of it. Without the pain, I reckon we might take all the beauty for granted."

"Yes."

"All we've got is today, Belle. It's all anybody's got."

"I know."

"But we've got each other, don't we?"

"Yes. Yes we do, my love."

"And it's spring again."

"Like when we got married ourselves."

"Yep. And I can bring you flowers, a big ol' bunch of

wildflowers, and you can put them in water on the table, and they'll make the whole house smell sweet."

"Oh, Dub. I thought spring would never come."
"Her heart will know, Belle."
"Yes. Her heart will know..."

And when even the sound of the swing and colors and taste of cold tea faded away, and her eyes were forced open, the old woman moaned at the loss. Her pain cut so much deeper now that he was no longer sharing it with her. She longed for his strong hands and gentle voice.

But the room was real now, and the blade of pain twisting inside her finished body. And in her loneliness, as she had done time and again, she cast her eyes to the face on the wall, in all its incongruous passivity, those eyes of sad acceptance, of joy somehow still breathing, the eyes of someone who most deeply understood the heartbreakingly beautiful brevity of earthly life. And she called out from the airless core of pain, praying for arms to enfold her like soft, pink petals, white wings...

8

John had been in the cabin six weeks when the snow came.

Half of February had crawled tediously by. For the most part he stayed to himself in the cabin; over time the maddening quiet once threatening to drive him back to the city had become a kind of balm. But he also was aware of his tendency to isolate, and could not quite escape the feeling of impending danger always lurking within himself. The cabin and the woods had infected him, in ways he did not yet fully understand, with a kind of shared solitude.

And so he made it a point to share supper with Maggie and Ellen once or twice a week, though he had found himself going less frequently of late.

"How much money did you make?" Ellen had asked that night, before the snow had begun to fall. Over time the ice between him and his niece began a slow thaw.

"From the book?"

"Yes."

"Well, not much at first. Then it started catching on, and... I've never really taken the time to add it all up."

"But it was a lot."

"Hmm, yeah, I guess so. Everything's relative."

"Uh-huh. I'm sure that's true." She lifted her chin and looked at him as from a higher plane of intellect.

"So, do you have any left?"

"Some."

"Because I just wondered, what with all you've been through the last couple of years. Sounds like things got a bit...*expensive* for you..."

Maggie cleared her throat. "El."

Her daughter turned as though attacked. "Mom. I am simply asking *your* brother a perfectly *legitimate* question. He's a grown man. He doesn't have to answer unless he wants to." Ellen somehow managed to say this with an authority that kept it from sounding disrespectful.

Maggie looked helplessly at John, who had already surrendered.

"Johnny, did I mention that El is writing stories now? She reads all the time, of course, always has." Maggie pulled hard at the rudder, trying to turn the conversation. "She's secretive about it, though. Won't let me read much. Sweetie, maybe you could show John some of your work..."

Ellen seemed unaware of her mother's presence.

"I just wondered, Uncle," she said, deliberately slowing over *Uncle*, never taking her eyes off him. "A best*seller*, for goodness' sakes. One thing I read said maybe even a movie deal in the works."

He lifted his shoulders to get a better breath. "I made a lot of money. And I...spent a lot, too. But not all of it. This past year I've been able to convince my publisher that I haven't lost my mind. Not completely, anyway. They decided to give me another shot. Now they're waiting for the next book." He wilted somewhat under the bespectacled gaze, then managed, "So, yeah. I still have some money." He suddenly felt, as he had for much of his life, like the youngest person in the room.

Ellen advanced. "One critic didn't like it much."

"A number of critics felt the same way," John said.

"Uh-huh. One said it sure wasn't Shakespeare."

"He was right."

"I happen to love Shakespeare."

"She even memorizes it," Maggie said weakly.

Ellen ignored her. "Most of the people who didn't like it called the book things like 'old-fashioned' and 'sentimental.' At what point in time, Uncle, did words like those begin to be used in a context of negative criticism for literature?"

Their eyes met, and brightened.

"I don't know, El."

"It's tragic," she said, her face softening ever so slightly. "I think it's just tragic."

"I couldn't agree more." And he knew in that moment things were going to be okay between them.

Ellen allowed herself a small smile. "I've wanted to ask you this ever since I read the book. It's about Millie."

John tensed.

"Throughout the early part of the story I admired her strength. But when things went bad, she fell apart." Ellen seemed personally insulted. "I understand how much she loved Ned. And I could see how she'd given her whole self away to him, being so young. But when he left her she seemed unable to move forward. She pined like a puppy." Ellen's eyebrow's narrowed menacingly. "Why would Millie do that? She wasn't weak."

"Well, I didn't want to portray her as weak. I wanted her to be independent, and spirited."

"And you did, at first. But what happened to her spirit when Ned left?"

"Perhaps he took it with him."

"It wasn't his to start with," she said, almost laughing. "He held no ownership of her strength. She had it before they fell in love. By giving him such sway over her, you sucked the real life from her character. I understood her loss. But not her collapse."

"I guess." He felt foolish, yet challenged to defend the motives of someone real, someone he cared for a great deal.

"I guess she felt that without love, her life wasn't whole. Maybe not even worth living."

"Do you think that?" she asked simply.

"What?"

"Do you think, truly, that without love life is not worth living?"

John stared at his plate. Then—"Yes."

"I'll get dessert." Maggie left the room as if being chased.

Ellen, relentlessly, "Did you *really* believe that Millie, losing her first love, would suddenly curl up and *die*? I kept wondering to myself—does Uncle Johnny think life can be given up on so easily, without a fight?"

"She did fight."

"She fought for *him*. But not for her*self*."

"It was tragedy, El. Romeo and Juliet."

"No," she said flatly. "It was cowardice. Romeo and Juliet were victims not only of love but of their circumstances, and ultimately their own decisions. They finally felt they couldn't overcome what life had stacked against them. But Ned made choices—everybody makes *choices*. He gave away the gift because he was selfish, and his self-centeredness turned him into a fool and a coward. Millie had choices, too. But ultimately she lost hope because she had no faith." She pointed her fork at him. "No *faith*. You gave her a strength early in the book that had no base, no core."

"She had faith."

"She had false faith, faith that human love would survive anything. But it didn't run deep enough. It wasn't faith in the right *kind* of love."

He looked up, surprised to see his niece's sad smile.

"Johnny," she said, her tone suddenly softer, "you wrote one of the most beautiful books I have ever read. I cried again and again." Tears rose up. "It makes me want to cry even now, remembering how wonderful...how proud I was—I am—of you." In this moment the girl's mask of maturity fell away, her lower lip trembling. She used a paper napkin to dry her eyes.

The shift came out of nowhere, catching him by surprise.

"Thanks, El."

She tried to straighten, mascara smearing down her cheeks. "Oh my *gosh*, the story just broke my *heart*..." She paused to pull herself together. John marveled at how young she suddenly looked.

Finally she said, "But, Johnny, after everything fell apart for Millie and Ned, after life disappointed them, they gave up. Both, in their own ways. They had nowhere to turn for healing, because they had made idols of one another. And when they found each other again, found their happy ending, I didn't believe it. I wanted it for them, of course. But somewhere, deep in me, I didn't quite believe they *appreciated* it, much less deserved it. I don't know if they fully realized what they had been given."

"Do you think love can be earned?" He felt that the girl near him was somehow speaking truth from beyond her years or experience.

"No," she said. "It's a gift. It can be fought for. But the fight must be for the right reasons. That's the secret. Love— the kind between two people—isn't possible at all unless it comes from a deeper place."

"And that's where faith comes in."

Ellen smiled again. "That's where faith comes in."

He smiled back. "So you do believe in love, in its ability to survive. That we can find it again, even after we're sure it's lost."

"Yes, I do," she said. "I really do." She looked at him now as though he were the child. "But we don't find love. Love finds *us*."

Maggie, sensing it might be safe, appeared with plates in hand. She paused; her daughter and brother were touching hands.

"Oh," she said, her round eyes sparkling. "Who wants pie?"

"I'd better go," he said. They had sat for a long time on the couch, talking, the three of them now in full alliance. Ellen relaxed and actually snuggled against her mother's shoulder; John saw the teenage pretense fall away, and understood that mother and child shared a strong bond, one that had wordlessly helped them both survive. And somehow this made him feel all at once the detached loneliness of a traveling foreigner, and yet more connected to something than he had in many years.

"Maybe you should stay here," Maggie said. "If the weatherman is right, you won't be able to dig out of that place by morning."

"Yes!" Ellen pumped her fist. "No school! Bring it on!"

John smiled at how quickly Ellen could transform from woman to girl, and back again. "I'll be fine," he said. "I've got enough food to last forever."

They stood, and Ellen moved to his side. "So, Uncle, how's the new book coming?" She felt like the two of them now shared a creative bond.

"Good," he lied. Weeks secluded, and barely a word had made it to paper. Except for the letters, written for Jess, torn up, written again. "Worst part is the cold. I may never get used to it. I've been freezing ever since I got to town."

"Too long in the desert, country boy." Maggie said. "Don't worry. Spring will come. It always has."

They walked to the door.

"Johnny," Ellen said. "Belle Martin is much worse."

"Afraid so," said Maggie. Both women seemed uncomfortable. "Tuck found her on the floor two weeks ago, in a real bad way."

John remained silent. Ellen said, "She refuses to go to the hospital in the city."

111

"Hospice comes several times a week, I think," said Maggie. "She's not expected to live long."

"That's too bad," he said.

Ellen narrowed her eyebrows, but kindly. "You haven't contacted them?"

"No."

The girl nodded. "Probably best, right now."

"I know Dub and Belle always thought the world of you," Maggie said, and then hesitated. "Let me get your coat."

When her mother left the room, Ellen touched John's elbow and drew close. "I saw Jessie in town last week," she said. "She asked if you were still in town."

He didn't know how to respond.

"She asked it...casually," Ellen said. "I told her you were staying in the cabin." Maggie's footsteps made Ellen hurry the last whisper—"She didn't say a word at first. Just looked at me. Then she said goodbye, and left."

"Well, if you're stubborn enough to drive back out there in this mess, go ahead," Maggie said, opening the door. The porch light illuminated the first glimmerings of wide, white flakes floating down.

"Oh, my," Maggie said.

"Silent and soft and slow..." said Ellen.

"...descends the snow..." John finished, and he and the young girl exchanged knowing smiles. Maggie looked from one of them to the other.

"Longfellow," Ellen explained, face glowing.

He hugged them both and drove away.

* * *

John dreamed.

He and his father sat in rocking chairs on the porch. Winter had drained all the blood from the landscape, turning the world the color of dirty ice. His father rocked

112

silently, staring straight out toward the river. He wore a black suit and tie, and with stolen glances Johnny realized he had never seen his father dressed like this before. He felt an almost overwhelming sense of joy. He wanted to jump up and embrace him, but could not move; he longed to tell his father how good he looked, how proud he was of him, but he could not make a sound.

Trapped like this, he watched the man begin to change, his face aging, the light in his eyes dying to darkness. Johnny gripped the arms of his chair so hard he could feel splinters cutting into his palms.

"It's about time you got here, boy," his father said, leaning in close, and then Johnny saw the shotgun propped against the rail. He tried to move away from the fear and the stench but couldn't move, couldn't close his eyes, forced to look at the face now gaunt, glaring.

"I'm thirsty," the tongue slithering out, poised to strike, a cracked, draught-dry hissing—*"Thirsssty..."*

But Johnny couldn't rise, his body bound to the chair with long leather straps, belts, his father's belts, round and under and over, a choking cry soundlessly rising up in him. The old man reached out as if to strike but didn't, and Johnny saw a bottle nearly swallowed up in his raw and red-knuckled fist. His heart pounded in his chest.

"Drink with me, boy," the face said with a voice like distant thunder...

John sat up, gasping.

The bedside clock showed 3:08 a.m. He had slept only fitfully for many nights. Now he had been jolted awake by another nightmare.

It had taken him weeks to adjust to the cabin's isolated silence. A part of him longed for the quiet, but he had forgotten how to be still. His mind restlessly paced, darting this place and that; he found it difficult to read, even harder to write. He wanted to be left alone, yet often felt he would die of loneliness.

Now he lay back onto his pillow and stared into the blackness above. The wind prowled at the door, tested the windows, moaned under the eaves. He pulled on his heavy socks and shuffled in to sit in the dark by what was left of the iron stove's warmth. He thought of stoking the fire, but after a few minutes the cold drove him back beneath the heavy quilts of his bed. Finally, he drifted off.

This time he was shaken awake by a softer silence. Sunless, soundless light glowed into the room. There was no hint of anything living, of even the earth turning. Something in his spirit knew. He was out of bed and onto the porch.

John stared out onto the glimmering surface of an alien world so overwhelming he held his breath, eyes wide at the wonder of white folding into seamless white. A snow this deep was somewhat uncommon for these hills. He had not seen a sight like this since he was a little boy.

The snow clung to everything. It had come down wet and sideways in the overnight gusts, sticking even to the sides of trees. Limbs of cedar and pine hung heavy with it. The flocked forest inclined toward the lake, endless white disturbed only by jagged gray-brown bark and branches, and juts of rocky earth and shale occasionally yawning their way to the surface. Far out across and beyond the reverent river there was now no land, sky, or line drawn between the two, all shocked whiteness without horizon.

A lonely sound echoed. John looked up to see a single goose, separated from his group, flying beneath the domed, milk-glass sky. Once out of sight, a final call resonated throughout the luminous world. Then everything stilled again to stunned silence, all creation gone deaf, and, for a moment, God himself mute.

The stuff was so deep it took him a while to clear a path, but the steep pile of dry wood under the tarp now made his raw hands and sore muscles seem worth the effort. He got the potbelly stove burning, and as the cabin warmed he cooked a big breakfast, the kind his mother might have long ago prepared in celebration of a no-school snow day—eggs, bacon, toast and coffee.

He ate like a man starved, wishing inside his humming head that he knew how to make biscuits like hers.

The woods splintered with the roar and sputter of an unmuffled engine, and the lunatic screams of his brother. The sounds were so alien to the serene setting that John found himself temporarily bewildered. He went to the porch. About sixty yards away, up the dirt road, Joey had the four-wheeler skimming sideways across a sheet of silver, his war cry piercing the shallow sky. He came to a sliding stop in front of the porch; the fat tires threw snow onto the steps.

"Mornin', bro!" Joey's face shown from beneath a red-and-white Santa hat, eyes wide as Christmas morning. "Want a lift?"

"No."

"Aw, come on! You're stuck here for a while. That sissy rental car of yours ain't goin' nowhere. You don't wanna starve, do you?"

"I've already eaten."

"Well, let's go for a ride, anyway."

"You are out of your mind."

"What's that got to do with anything?" The look on Joey's face and the tone in his voice made John suddenly realize with a glancing blow of sadness that the question was literal, and completely sincere.

"Be right there," he said, and went inside to bundle up.

After a while, John lost count of the number of times they nearly died. He hung on to his brother's waist, the machine roaring beneath them. Their shouting shook the stillness, ripping a gash through the quiescent forest.

Neither wanted to stop, until finally Joey got the four-wheeler turned too much sideways. The tires slammed into a fallen tree trunk, sending both men flying through the air. They landed howling and wrestling. John finally got the advantage, pinning his brother's arms into the snow.

Joey suddenly went limp. A look came over his face—young eyes, frightened, the look of someone who has been too suddenly awakened from a dream.

John rolled off and the two of them lay on their backs, white puffs huffing up from their mouths like smoke from twin stacks of a locomotive. Silence gradually pressed in around them.

"You okay?"

"Yeah." Joey sounded like a little boy.

"Are you hurt?"

"Naw. I'm fine." Joey lifted up onto one elbow, the snow up to his armpit. "You?"

"Every bone in my body is broken," John said. "You moron. You haven't changed at all."

Joey looked hard at him; snow melted on his forehead and dripped into his eyes. He stared at John as though trying to recall who he was, and then he said, "You have." He got up and walked away.

John pushed up to a sitting position, and watched his brother labor up the ridge toward the stalled four-wheeler.

By the time they reached the cabin they were wet through and nearly frozen. There was not another hoot in them. Joey pulled in front of the porch and sat still with the motor idling. John moved gingerly up the porch steps, then turned.

"Come in," he said.

"Naw."

"Joey, come in this cabin."

"I'm goin' home." Joey pulled the soggy Santa hat down over cherry-colored ears. The middle three fingers of his right glove flopped limp and dripping over the handgrip. He kept looking down and said, "Hey, bro."

"Yeah?"

"Sorry about...when..." He raised his head. "Shoot *fire*, Johnny. You look just *like* him, sometimes. Kinda freaked me out, that's all."

"Joey."

"It was fun, big brother," Joey said, and rumbled off. John watched the vehicle bounce up the slope toward the road at the top of the ridge. His little brother grew smaller and smaller before vanishing into the whitewashed air.

John spread his soaked clothes on the floor near the wood-stove to dry. He dressed and sat in a straight-backed chair, inching his frozen feet as close as possible to the stove without setting them aflame. He felt exhausted and wonderful and afraid.

After a while he grew restless. He stood and walked to the front window, risking a glance at the coffee table as he passed; his notebook and pencils lay there unused, as they had for weeks. An old, empty dread pressed in.

All his life he had been at war with himself—calm on the surface while inside all conflicted emotions, spiritual and carnal, pious and profane, never sure moment to moment if he was running to God or from him. For as long as he could remember, tireless thoughts had spun spider-like inside his head, weaving webs of contradiction. But even as uncertain as everything else in his life might have seemed, once he had discovered books, and then writing, it was as if he had finally found his center. No matter how lost he became, the act of putting words to paper allowed him to see, if only faintly, a kind of distant hope that his existence might have in it some purpose and meaning. By purging himself in this way, he found he could slow the thoughts enough to keep them from driving him insane.

As a young boy, when the air inside his home grew edged and dangerous, he could hide in his room and create stories that would teleport him away. Writing filled him by emptying, tapping the toxicity into imaginary worlds where no one could be hurt. He had discovered a voice for his mute despair, discovering a language that in some mystical way bridged the duality of life and made sense of his secret soul.

Years later, when he had traveled far away only to discover that the darkness had followed and was with him still, there had at least still been the writing. The words breathed life into people, places, into *him*. In the clamoring chaos of the degenerate world around him there had at least existed one hovel of hope, a place where seclusion made perfect sense. Even at his worst, some sanctuary remained in the paper and pencils, and in the bottle always within reach, weapons cocked and loaded against the loneliness.

But now, with the silence surrounding him and time at last for uninterrupted creativity, he could not seem to create. The one thing that had always brought him a sense of shelter now left him exposed. And exposure momentarily blinded him, and created thirst. *I will not drink,* he thought. But in this moment he allowed himself to imagine such an unreasonable thing.

John Allen understood that his life up until now had been a sort of prolonged childhood, an extended period of immaturity during which he honed irresponsibility into an art form. His drinking helped fulfill a predetermined destiny of self-sabotage. Eventually all the safe ports—the friends, lovers, associates—had closed their harbors. Still, this did not seem tragic to him. In a strange way feeling lonely was the most familiar, and therefore most comfortable, of any emotion he had ever known.

At least since I left her...

He could have gone anywhere. He had always dreamed of the ocean, but more than anything he had wanted to just get away, as far away as possible—from his father and mother, his home, from what he feared might be his own dark destruction. Over time, it had been easy to convince himself—and Jess—that if his dream had a chance of ever taking shape, it could best do so in a place built on fantasy. His romanticized image of the coast seemed grand enough to hold his ambition, vast and alien enough to conceal the immensity of his rage, a place so adept at makeup and tricks of light that any immigrant might effectively cover up the black-and-blue hues of his bruised soul and blend easily into the surroundings. And for a while, after the improbable success of his book, the whole thing seemed to have finally come true—he was suddenly desired, and, he thought at the time, validated.

None of it had lasted, of course.

She's the only real thing I have ever known, he thought. After Jess, everything and everyone else had been little more than a false attempt at connection. He had spent years trying to draw water from the shallowest of wells, and grown thirstier still. Now, he had come back to face what he believed to be the source of everything—hope, sorrow, meaning. He would have to at least try; until he knew whether or not she was real there could be no new books, no more passion. Jess was the girl against whom he had judged all other women—their looks, voices, touch. None had ever come close. He believed only Jess could save or kill him. In his mind, the vacancy of passing time had bestowed upon her the impossible powers of divinity.

I'm always making gods. Out of everything. Out of everyone.

He felt cold. Surrealism again surrounded him—a feeling of being yet not being who and where and what he was. He shut his eyes and shook from his head the stubborn image of a mean, unshaven face full of fear. He pressed his cheek into the cold window, his breath making fog-ghosts appear, vanish, and reappear against the glass.

You're just takin' up space, boy...

And there was little thought or purpose as he turned and went to the bedroom. He sat on the edge of the mattress, then slowly stretched out and lay looking at the ceiling. He closed his eyes—

Go away.

—then opened them. He did not know if a minute or an hour or a whole night had passed, but the room had grown dark. Turning on the lamp, he opened the drawer of the bedside table and pulled out the envelope he'd put there on the first day. His fingertips tingled as he slowly turned the wrinkled paper in his hands.

He returned to the chair by the stove, to the smell of wet wood and denim and melted snow, and opened the letter from his father.

9

Tuck sat still as a mountain on the loveseat under the living-room picture window.

Night had long since fallen, but the moon shone from a cloudless sky and lit up the endless acres of glassy snow. Frost on the glass soft-framed the portrait; he could see clearly the line of trees at the far end of the main pasture, and the white-topped fences running the length of both sides. He had tended to the cattle, what few were left, regretting now that all of them had not been sold off before the storm came. The scene held a familial beauty for him, yet filled him with an unsettled spirit. His wife was in the next room with her dying mother, and old Doc. He wished he could take all the ache from that room and carry it on his shoulders far away, so far it could never touch Jessie or Belle again. He would do that, without pause, if only it were possible. The house, and everyone in it, had been too long in pain.

The old clock struck ten times.

Tuck rose and walked to the mantel, his movements almost involuntary. He took the key ring from his jeans pocket, then opened the round, delicate glass door on the front of the clock. His hands were big-knuckled and calloused, made for work, but with great care he inserted the small brass key and wound the mechanism, just as he had done every night at the strike of ten since Dub died.

He had never asked Belle; this seemed the natural way of things, the handing down of an ancient rite. Tuck took over the responsibility humbly, gratefully. Each night before leaving for work he made certain the house had a strong pulse. He considered this act more sacrament than ceremony. God had granted him inclusion to a hallowed place, graciously answering years of prayer. But more than that, Tuck understood he had been awarded stewardship of this family's safekeeping. He felt blessed.

Belle never said a word to him about it, nor he to her. But their eyes met the first time she saw him carefully turning the key with those big, gentle hands, and she had placed her hand on his shoulder. In that small moment they both knew—Tuck was accepting leadership of the house. He had become guardian of the home's heartbeat.

Now he closed the glass door and stood at the mantel, listening to time ticking steadily away. His heart was haunted with unsettled feeling...a lurking, persistent fear. The cancer had been killing Belle's body and Jessie's spirit for far too long. But that wasn't the only thing gnawing at his mind. Tuck struggled with the sense, as he had for many weeks, that someone or something had thrown open a section of fence and let loose chaos into the calm order of his family's life.

Tuck had loved her forever. The memory of falling in love— they had both been only children, always together at church, with quilts laid out on green grass and food and children and laughter—was a precious prize he kept in a safe and sacred place within himself.

They had known each other for most of their lives, played together countless times as little children, but something on this day changed him in a brilliant moment—the sun glancing off her face, the angle of her chin, the high cheekbones beginning to redefine the round contours of a youthful face, a languid light landing just right on a smooth neck the color of cream. Nothing before or since had ever been more beautiful to him than was her face that day.

He did not dare dream of ever winning her confidence, much less her affection. But from that moment he had died to himself and sworn his soul to hers—not in any way by possession, knowing he could never possess such a creature—but through a personal pledge to her protection and wellbeing. While Jessie bucked against the fences of a world too confining, fierce and full of fire, with never enough pasture once she began running, he would remain steadfast, feet planted firm and deep like the roots of an oak. His life belonged to her, though most likely from a distance, she being royalty and thus untouchable. But his purpose for existing had been defined: nothing would ever harm Jessie, as long as he lived.

He dedicated himself to this role uncomplainingly as they grew up, watching her from across classrooms and at church, reveling in those moments when she would grant him the priceless privilege of her smile, sometimes even offering up the song of his name from her lips. He surrendered easily to the fact that his life was no longer his own.

Still, it did not seem unusual to him when at sixteen Jessie had fallen in love with someone else; in a way, he had always assumed it would happen, though the truth of it, painfully played out in front of him and the rest of their tiny town did indeed crush him, slowly, in those teen years when life lay heavy enough as it was. This feeling, though, had less to do with Tuck's opinion of himself than with his reverence for Jessie; no matter how badly his own heart might be broken, he would honor whatever choices she made that might keep her own heart safe.

Strangely, it did not seem to Tuck that all was lost; he knew from experience that life was uncertain, and love unsafe. He had learned that daring to love—*truly* love—

carried with it great risk. He believed that his charge remained essentially unchanged, his duty clear: he would gratefully exist just outside the beautiful bounds of Jessie's universe, as observer if nothing more. He would not interfere. But he would watch closely, from a safe distance, tirelessly committed to making sure she remained unharmed. He would pray daily for a miracle. And he would do this for years.

Then, somehow, the miracle happened.

It came more than a year after Johnny had come home for his mother's funeral, without contacting Jessie. Tuck knew this, because many people in Tranquility talked about such things. And a year, Tuck thought, seemed long enough. He had gone to Jessie's house, and stood at the front door with his hat in his hands.

He courted Jessie with an infinite patience. Over the next months he tried to listen, more than anything, to whatever she felt the need to talk about. This seemed to help her, Tuck thought. And he was content to listen to the sound of her voice for as long as she would let him.

And so Tuck had a good while to mentally rehearse in his mind what he would say to her, once the time felt right. Day and night he practised the words in his head. He did this carefully, prayerfully, knowing that the words he used would carry upon them the weight of all his future, words that would of course never match Jessie's beauty, but might somehow, by the grace of God, manage to express his devotion.

And so Tuck waited, prayed, and waited some more, all the time loving and respecting her as best he knew how, which for Tuck came somewhat naturally, love and respect in his mind being more or less synonymous.

Finally, the day came. They had walked several miles on a fine early afternoon in April, beyond the cleared fields and along the woodline to a grassy knoll where they often picnicked. Tuck spread out one of Belle's quilts in the shade of a wild persimmon. They talked for a long time, as always, only this time Tuck's heart pounded even more than usual. And then without thinking he had reached and taken her hand, and she had stopped in mid-sentence to look right at him. Forgetting every single word he'd ever imagined himself saying in this moment, he looked at her dumbly for what seemed a lifetime. And Jessie had waited, patiently, kindly, and finally had squeezed his hand and tilted her head. This freed his heart to speak.

"I've loved you my whole life, Jessie," he said. "And I'll love you forever, if you'll have me."

Jessie had stared straight into his eyes. Her face became calm, and, though Tuck would not have thought it possible, even more beautiful.

There was no hint of waver in her voice when she finally said—"We'll have each other, Tuck. Forever."

Tuck knew, of course, that he had not been Jessie's first choice. And all along he would have sacrificed his own desires if doing so might have somehow shielded her from ever having to experience the pain that ultimately brought her to him. He knew what unrequited love felt like, and did not wish it on anyone, much less Jessie. Still, he understood her wounds, and she his. Once God had joined them, together they forged a lasting trust.

Never once throughout the six years of their marriage had Jessie ever shown signs of regret, of being anything less than satisfied. But Tuck understood. He did not waste time resenting the past; he knew that the wedge driven into the solid ground of her heart happened long before he had been offered residence there. This was something he could not change. And though a part of him mourned, quietly, that he might never be all that she had ever longed for, still he gave daily thanks for having been given even a taste of something so clearly divine, a thing so precious as Jessie...

Tuck started from his daydream, turning as Jessie came out of her mother's room. She quietly closed the door behind her. He crossed the room and gently took her arm. They sat on the loveseat in the cool moonlight.

"She's quiet," Jessie said.

Tuck felt frightened by her pale face, the snow-covered fields reflecting onto it a lifeless light. "I wish you'd get some sleep yourself." He took her hands and warmed them in his own.

"The spells are coming more often," she said, lifting her face to him. "I'm so scared, Tuck."

"I know." It was all he could think to say. Seeing his wife in pain was almost more than he could bear. He tried to have her lean onto his shoulder, but she straightened.

"I'm afraid if I sleep, she'll go without..." Her voice broke.

"I know."

"...without saying goodbye."

"You can't stay awake forever," he said. "At least let me get you something to eat."

Tears came, and Jessie relaxed into the sturdy strength of his shoulder. "Oh, Tuck."

"I'll come and get you if anything changes," he said. "I'm worried about you. You need to rest."

She looked up into his face. "Tuck, I can't. How will I...without her?"

"I'll be here, Jessie," he said. "I won't leave you."

"I know," she said. "I know."

"Belle is going to a better place. A place where she won't have to hurt anymore."

"Yes."

"I know it's hard to see her suffer," he said. "I can't hardly stand it myself."

She eased back and placed her palm against his cheek. "Sweet Tuck," she said. "I know you love her."

"I do. And I love you, Jessie." He felt he would break in two.

She tilted her face and looked deep into his eyes, two vast pools of kindness, and she knew that for as long as he lived, if she let him, he would cherish her. The world, and all things in it, would change. But Tuck would not. She held onto his big arm and prayed with all her might that God would, somehow, let her love Tuck as much as he loved her...

She jerked to her feet the moment the bedroom door creaked open.

"Jessie," Doc said.

"Momma?"

"Jessie?"

"I'm right here."

"Good. You be strong."

"Oh, *no*. I don't know..."

"You be strong, Jessie."

"I will. I'll try."

The old woman could barely whisper. She looked crushed into the sheets beneath the weight of a burdensome body, the light of life all but gone out. But a new calm covered her now, the pain drained from her face. Jessie leaned in close, desperate to harvest what remained.

"Tell me again, Momma," she whispered.

Belle never missed a beat.

"Tall, and handsome, and strong. I knew, the very first time I saw him. He would bring me fresh-picked flowers..."

"And you knew. You just knew."

"I knew."

"How did you know? Tell me again."

"A woman knows. It has to just...happen."

"And if it happens..."

"Jessie. Come close."

"I'm right here."

"*Listen...*"

"Momma, please..."

"Listen. Your *heart*..."

"What, Momma? I can barely hear you..."

"Your heart will *know*."

The old clock struck eleven times.

The slight warmth of the breath against her ear all but vanished. Jessie felt their wet cheeks pressed together, both of them still hanging on to living, and because she could think of nothing else, she said—

"Please stay."

But Belle's eyes had seen someone other than her daughter now, and widened. Her mouth opened in breathless surprise. And she lifted her arms from the bed and held them out into the air, as if accepting a gift.

"Oh my," she said—

"My *love*..."

10

Johnny,
If you're reading this I'm dead.

A full day and night had passed since John had first read the letter, but still he shook his head in befuddled resentment. Few people had ever seen beneath his father's rough exterior into the more complex person John knew. His father had been a voracious reader, and vivid thinker, at least when sober. And yet, Big John had been a man at war with himself. His potential had been wasted, his life thrown away.

From the sloppy punctuation and shaky hand, John knew the man had been drunk while writing. He almost put the letter back in the envelope, but couldn't, combing slowly through it again, afraid he might have missed a hidden clue in the dozen or so times he'd read it before. In a way he could not understand, reading the letter again and again seemed to force breath in and out of his father's lungs, keeping him barely alive, giving John at least a glimpse of something lost.

I hope you get this. I can't be sure but I believe Maggie will find you sooner or later. You know I'm not much with words but I wanted to put this down just the same.

129

I did a lot of bad things in this life and truth is I'm alright with this life being over and done with. I'd do some things different if I could I guess but a man has to look back on his life and take what's been given. My own daddy always told me and you've heard me say it a thousand times—A man makes his own choices, and a man's always got options. I made mistakes that's for sure but don't we all. The real truth is I'm a sinful man but maybe more than that a coward. Only a coward kills himself like this, slow, but I don't see me stopping now, I've come too far and this looks like the way it will be for me and if I wanted to stop I would and everybody trying to make me change can go to hell.

Anyway I want to say I'm more than sorry for what I did to hurt your mama and what I did to hurt you kids too. Maybe things could have been different but they are what they are now and the only thing I can do is say I'm sorry. Most of what I done I wish I could take back but I can't and no man can but Jesus ate with sinners and I'm counting on him asking me to his table soon. Maybe he will and maybe he won't. All I know for sure is that a husband and a father has responsibilities and I did not do enough. I did not do near enough. I loved you though even if I never said it and I loved you kids and I loved your mama too though I know you won't believe that. I just couldn't stay sober I guess though sometimes I tried. Truth is I'm not sober now either. That's no excuse I know and it might be that God won't forgive me and you won't either but I have to live with what I am.

I want you to have my shotgun. It's a nice one, 12-gauge pump you might even remember it [here John felt a cold shudder run down his spine]. *I'm sorry for having to tell you this I sold your 20-gauge that Springfield double-barrel and I'm real sorry for that sure wish I hadn't. If I could take back what I did I would. I made my mistakes and lots of them. I am afraid I don't have much else to give. You kids can do what you want with the cabin, burn it down for all I care.*

I won't ask you to forgive me though I have prayed you would but the truth is I loved you when you were born and every day after and I love you now and have missed you my son. I miss your mama too though I doubt you will believe that and I can't say I blame you. But I do hope Jesus saves us at the end if we ask and I'm asking him and I'm asking you. I have told Maggie all this and I ask her and you to tell Joey, poor little Joey I love him too.

Daddy

John folded the paper. The words left him weak, again. He stood and walked to the front window and looked out. The snow had stopped falling a day after beginning, and much of what had covered the open ground had already begun to melt. But the skies had stayed stubbornly colorless and cold, and nothing moved on the melancholy land. John could not get to town even if he wanted to, and there was something comforting in knowing this. He felt again glad that he had no phone in the cabin, that his brother and sister knew he wanted time alone. For a while the storm provided a reason for solitude.

The paper hung like a dead thing in his hand. He felt convinced his father had written the letter as part of his plan for suicide. But at least it hadn't ended that way, or so it seemed, and he was glad for that. He liked to think that his father would have never really gone through with such a thing, though he himself knew too well that suicide, like healing, is often a process rather than an event. The way it all turned out, he could now choose to believe that his father would not have shot himself. But another part of him, the unforgiving part, wondered if the old man had planned on using the shotgun—his legacy—to do it, and this brought back the full cruelty of one half of his father's soul. He stood at the window all afternoon, staring out onto the hushed white world.

Night seemed to rush up and overtake the light before the day was fully done. John went to bed early, and lay on his back listening to the sound of his breathing and the beat of his heart. At last the dark depth closed around him and he drifted up and off the mattress, to the front porch and rocking chairs...

"I reckon you don't believe me," the man said, and his voice was deep but kind. *"But I can't change that."*

"I want to believe you," the boy said.

They wore hunting clothes and their guns lay across their laps.

"Well, it ain't about what we want. It's about what we've got. A man's always got options, son. I've told you many times, it's wantin' that gets us in trouble. A man can be at peace until he starts wantin' something."

"I'm glad you're here, Daddy. I like it when you're like this, when we're together like this."

"Me too, son," the man said, rocking, sober and serene. *"Let's you and me just sit like this a while."*

The boy felt wrapped in a kind comfort he wished would last forever. A warm wind moved in the trees.

"Maybe he won't come back, Daddy," the boy said at last, and he meant it with all his heart. "The mean one."

"Maybe not, son."

"I hate him. I hate that man, Daddy."

The man rocked and watched the woods. His hands lay big but gentle on the gun.

"I hate him too, son," he said. *"I hate him too."*

The next morning John stood and lobbed stones into the smooth water. The sun shone strong with expectation, and a few birds stirred hopefully to song, but their music broke against the bright cold.

He had hiked several miles through the woods, around dwindling patches of snow still shielded from melting by the dark canopy of heavy pine. Somehow he knew where he was going, an internal compass pointing him through a place untouched by change. He emerged at the curved point above the wide waters stretching out to the wall of trees beyond. From the water's edge he could see the calm reservoir finding its fuller meaning out into the river.

The cold did not bother him much anymore, and he stayed for hours, sitting in dry spots warmed by the sun whenever the chill soaked too much into him. The day passed by him all too quickly, like the dream of a lover, the sun slowly slipping through the trees toward the waiting water. As it sank, thin clouds spread long and low beneath both sides of its flame, sheer softness stretching out along the horizon like feathers. John watched the great burning bird hover on crimson wings, settle gracefully onto the river's silver surface, float there, then submerge.

A bold moon lit his way home. It shone through bare branches and threw angles of light on the ground all around him, highlighting sparse, blue-white patches of leftover snow huddled beneath the trees. The forest had over time become his friend again. His movement through the trees had a natural rhythm now, and he could pass through the stillness as inhabitant rather than intruder. He realized he had not had another panic attack since that first night driving to the cabin. Fully exposed, he felt safe.

"Thank you." He spoke it out loud, to himself, the woods, the stars.

The steady pace of his stride, the immediacy of his thoughts, all now hung more comfortably around him like the old hunting jacket. As a boy he had hunted these forests and fished these waters, and on this night, all these years later, the boy in him could again inhale the richness of it— moss-covered earth, damp leaves, the sleeping but living river, cold-bracing pine needles and juniper and somewhere, far off, the reassuring smell of burning wood. His legs had grown strong and young, his gait sure. The icy air woke him. John became aware of an elusive, whole-souled serenity he had all but forgotten. The woods, water, moon, the sharp sting of ageless winter in his lungs…

I'm not afraid.

The thought thrilled him.

He had learned fear early on, as a boy. When his own family had foundered with little faith to anchor it steady, the woods had always saved him. The trees and wind. The sound of far-off leviathan barges on the water.

I'm not alone.

Remembering.

I am not afraid. And I am not alone.

He stopped dead still, listening to the night…his own breathing and the near-silent sound of creation was all he could hear. And it was enough.

For most of his life he had watched the rest of the world as from a distance. And even when his body grew into adulthood, in many ways his heart did not. He had peered secretively out on the world and wondered—to the extent that there was any wonder left in him—at his all-too-temporary place in the universe, wondered how many other distant countries there were, how many cities filled with people living and loving each other, how many miles it would take to travel closer to anything that looked even a little like home.

But he had almost forgotten. Long ago, the woods had been a sanctuary. The one world where he could silently scream and be heard. And tonight, in this unchanged, forgiving place, he felt something. For the first time in many years a feeling began taking shape and making itself known, a thing long asleep and thought dead now rising up, stretching, moving toward the light at the open end of a tomb.

He began walking, and the movement again freed him.

For so long another kind of darkness had tried to snuff him out. He had run from home, from himself, but no matter where he hid the dogged loneliness followed the fresh scent of shame and found him. And no amount of success or notoriety or booze or world-lust could make it go away, at least for long.

But here with the immortal moon and stars hanging clean above, he allowed himself the frailest faith.

Perhaps he *could* be loved.

This was not a thing he hoped to fully believe, much less understand. Up ahead in the clearing he could see the faint outline of a curtain of woodsmoke airbrushed onto the night sky above the cabin. Something in his step moved him toward the small beckoning windows ahead, and he all but ran the last few yards.

A sound with both laughter and sorrow in it came out of him; hope flushed and flew when his boots hit the steps. He looked at the rocking chair, then turned and gazed down through the woods into the moon-polished water. Lifting his arms, he grasped at the heavens as if to gather God back into his empty heart. But whatever had touched him seemed to have vanished as swiftly as it had appeared.

But I did feel something.

The night air now carried only a cold scent of seclusion. John lowered his arms and stared into his empty hands.

He brought in wood and stoked embers into new flame. Boots off, feet stretched out at the stove, again and again he stood and paced, then returned to the chair.

Tomorrow, Ellen would come to visit. And he would show her the letter he had written to Jessie, the one sitting in the drawer now for days. He would ask the unlikely sage what she thought about it all, trusting that a young woman's heart, still innocent, would know more truth than his own.

* * *

Ultimately the decision had been his alone. But Ellen had helped, though he again wondered at his willingness to accept the counsel of one so young.

She had come early the next day with fishing poles and a picnic basket.

From a high bank they cast in little fly lures, all wrong but all she had, and they laughed and reeled in their lines and cast again, cold wind snapping at their collars. Ellen was more a girl now, pony-tail pulled through the back of a baseball cap, dappled sunlight highlighting a splendid splash of freckles across her nose.

"You have lost your mind," he said.

"Don't be such a *ba*by! It's not *that* cold."

"I can't feel my fingers any more."

"Some mountain man *you* are. Suck it up, Uncle!"

Though they quickly knew the brightness of the day had lured them prematurely into a false spring, they lasted as long as they could, not expecting a single bite. They shared memorized verses:

"How about this," he said. *"But when his fair course is not hindered / He makes sweet music with the enamell'ed stones / Giving a gentle kiss to every sedge / He overtaketh in his pilgrimage / And so by many winding nooks he strays / With willing sport to the wild ocean..."*

She laughed, turned to him, and taking in the quick breath of someone about to leap into deep water said, "How about this—*This afternoon has bled its life away / In reddening*

136

circles from the sun's raw wound / And I have watched it die without regret / Or loss. All things end, of happiness / And hurt; in order to begin again."

John lifted an eyebrow. "That's not Shakespeare."

"No, silly."

He smiled. "El. It's yours, isn't it?"

Ellen dropped her eyes; the smile blushed cherry-red across her cheeks, and memory moved though John swift and silent as shadow. In this moment he realized that Ellen was the same age now as Jessie had been when he left her all those years ago.

So intensely had he held onto this image of her, young and vibrant, that only now did he see how many years had passed, how lost and deluded a man can become who dares sleep his life away.

Then, in the way she had of suddenly transforming, Ellen pushed her glasses straight and opened her wide, wise eyes: "But if it's Shakespeare you want—*Then let me go and hinder not my course / I'll be as patient as a gentle stream / And make a pastime of each weary step / Till the last steps have brought me to my love; And there I'll rest, as after much turmoil / A blessed soul doth in Elysium..."*

And then elegance turned into squeals and sounds of splashing as the lake came alive.

"Johnny!"

He laughed and watched—jeans rolled up above her sneakers, feet dancing, a little girl blissfully unaware of coming womanhood, reeling in from the frigid water an astonished little bluegill no bigger than her open hand, glittering gold and silver in the waning winter sun.

"You're afraid of hurting her again," Ellen had said later, after listening to him for some time without speaking. They sat near the woodstove warming their bare feet and eating their planned picnic sandwiches. "But the truth, Uncle, is that she's hurt already. Like you, she carries a wound that won't heal."

"I know. But what right do I have to barge into her life? I'm tired of destroying things, El. I didn't come here to hurt her. I came here to make amends, to make things right. After all that's happened, if I could just talk to her, ask her forgiveness, tell her how sorry I am, face to face..."

Twice he drove under the cover of darkness past the house huddled on the hill, unable to shed the feeling of trespass, until finally he pulled off the highway's shoulder and opened the mailbox...

"It's something you both must do," she had said, "if either of you ever hope to fully heal."

Holding the envelope in his hand like a ticking time bomb, wavering...

"This way feels...cowardly."

"I don't believe this is about cowardice, Uncle. I think Jessie should have the right to make this choice on her own. If she doesn't want to see you, she can choose otherwise. But at least this way the decision will be hers alone. You've never left her life, Johnny. She's moved on, but not away. Neither have you."

"That's true."

The wise eyes had glowed girlishly in her delicate face. "Then you'll have to risk it."

And he let go, closed the box and pulled away, pursued by an ancient shame...

"Is it selfish? The risk isn't mine alone."

"Love," Ellen had said, "is *fierce*. True love is never safe, Johnny. Love is the riskiest thing there is."

That night, after driving to Jessie's house, again John could not sleep. He stared into the dark and tried to put the thoughts out of his mind, the doubt and growing guilt. But now it was done, for better or worse, and he could not change it. She would find the letter. The connection had been made, and he could not turn back. He would live with whatever happened, and hope she could, too.

11

The house had lost all hope.

Jessie moved through the rooms like a sudden stranger. There had been so much to do about the funeral, and the responsibilities had temporarily suspended her above the surreal fiction playing out below. For a while this helped her function, as she set her strength upon the tasks at hand. But now Belle had been laid to rest, and the house felt vacant without her. There had been life in it once, and life in her mother and father, and now there was nothing but the ominous realization of just how quickly life can abandon a body, and desert a home.

Jessie had for so long focused on the daily tasks required in caring for her parents that only now, with both of them gone, did she realize just how much these responsibilities had imbued her with a sense of purpose. In the days and nights since Belle's death, Jessie had found herself struggling against a spirit of pointlessness. The truth of this new reality fell in on her again and again, and each morning she would wake and allow herself rare moments to lie very still, listening to the hollow tapping sound of the old clock in the next room.

Now she stood in the living room at the picture window. Outside the somewhat warmer air had melted much of the snow but left a soggy mess behind. *If only spring would come,* she mused. Winter waned, yet each time she thought it dead the wounded thing uncurled its talons and clawed at the earth. Of all years and seasons, this one had decided to fight, clinging into early March.

When spring comes I will tend to Momma's garden. The thought brought her more sadness than satisfaction.

Tuck had returned to his regular work schedule, and the nights now felt even more miserable. The house felt oddly obsolete, a cathedral full of relics. People from the little country church would stop by with meals, offering their love, people she had known all her life. And Jessie would smile, brave and strong as always, thankful for their kindness, yet strangely disconnected from their compassion.

She longed for Tuck to return each morning. He had promised to fight even harder for a day shift, though he said it would take a while. But for the time being he could only keep her company for so long before sleeping, and the day would stretch itself out before her with an endless emptiness. She had never been able to adjust her own internal time clock to his. And yet, two warring parts of her always grappled when he had gone to bed, one remorseful, one relieved.

Unexpectedly, a thought entered Jessie's mind. Since their marriage she and Tuck had fervently prayed that they might have a child of their own, and yet for six years those prayers had seemed ignored. Jessie had never given up; she found hopeful comfort in knowing that her mother had herself been over forty when her only baby was born. But now, with the house so still and soundless, thoughts of a baby to care for came into her with new ardor.

Tuck, she thought, *I wish you were awake, and here with me.* Jessie stood silhouetted in the pitiless light. *I wish this old house didn't feel so empty. And I wish I didn't feel so alone...*

Tuck slept. The house stretched and its old bones creaked. Jessie walked from room to room, touching things, sitting, standing, moving again. In the living room she stood at the mantel, her fingers lightly touching the smooth, curved wood of her father's clock. She loved and hated the thing now. The sound of its ticking reminded her of both love and loss.

Looking out the windows made her long for something, and not looking out made her feel caged. She stood in the middle of the living room, lost.

Later she walked to the end of the long, winding drive that led to the highway, as she did every day. Had she not been so dispirited, she might have noticed the first green shoots of daffodils emerging from the ground around the base of the mailbox post. But her mind was still cloaked in winter as she stood at the box near the road, hands idly shuffling through the small stack of afternoon mail.

Then she saw the envelope.

The other mail fell to the ground.

Her legs became unsteady, and for a moment she felt she would have to sit down, right there in the gravel at the edge of the highway. With one hand she steadied herself on the mailbox post, and with the other she clutched some dreaded hope hard against her heart.

Deep breaths. Elation and anger, shame and sorrow and longing. The fields and the hanging clouds and the ground beneath her fell away into flat, toneless nothing.

No stamp or address, but she knew—the handwriting was as recognizable as if they'd been exchanging secret notes in class the day before. There was only her name on the envelope, what he always called her—*Jess*. She realized he had been there, his hands this close, and the intrusive truth stalked and shook her. A kind of pitiful rage filled her. She wanted to destroy the letter, make it not exist. She felt humiliated and exposed. Her hands shook as she hurriedly folded the envelope in half and crammed it into the front pocket of her jeans.

She bent and watched hands no longer belonging to her gather the fallen mail and, as if to turn back time and make everything go away, put it back in the box. This made her feel even more idiotic. Her body turned and walked back toward the house. Tuck would be deep asleep. But still she felt watched, that at any moment she could be caught, accused, and ruined. Her heart pounded with indignation. She drew cold air through her clenched teeth and shook her head against such weakness.

This won't do. I'll go inside, and wake Tuck and tell him how much I love him, make him hold me...

But a stranger seemed to be controlling her now. She did not dare even glance toward the house. Her secret self burned its way to the surface of her face, and she no longer felt the cold. She passed the watching windows in slow motion, holding her breath, continuing into the bare square of ground where the grown-over garden ended, and kept going toward the fields.

The muddle of emotions coiled and twisted inside her as she pulled the envelope from her pocket. She increased her pace, seeking distance. The strange feet betrayed her, breaking into a run toward the trees.

The wind whipped at her and she crushed the letter in her hand. She aimed her rage at the wall of trees ahead and charged toward them, through the fallow fields of waist-deep broomstraw. The cold wind forced tears from her eyes.

When she reached the woods she wanted to just keep going, but her breath was gone. She bent with her hands on her knees and sobbed the air in and out.

Here in the merciful shadows, her hurt hidden from the spying eyes of the house, she lost herself. Frantically she wheeled, searching, and chose a limb—many had broken off when the snow fell—and as she picked up one long and heavy, the envelope fell away. With the crooked weapon she savaged the nearest tree trunk, animal sounds rising up and out of her into the hooded woods. She swung the gnarled thing two-handed again and again until it broke apart, then scrambled for another and set her whole strength into it until the rough bark rubbed her frozen fingers raw, every living thing subdued and hidden from her wrath.

Finally she fell, no longer able to lift her arms. On her hands and knees she clawed at the emotionless earth, curses crowding out her crying, until the dizziness dropped her onto one side. Water from the cold ground soaked into her clothes.

She was unaware of how long she lay like this. But at some point the internal roar relented enough for her mind to return to reality—there was a house, and husband, and life still living on, though from her place on the ground she could see none of it. She took a few moments to lie still, breathing in the wetness pressed against her face.

She sat, then stood and stared at her scratched and bleeding hands. She did not know where to wipe them, or how she would hide the wet parts of her clothes or her wild, matted hair. She blinked until some focus returned, looking down for the envelope, and saw it lying crumpled and half-hidden in a brown bed of leaves. For one moment she thought of killing it, shredding and burying it, but instead stooped and picked it up. She flattened it against her stomach, folded it twice into a small rectangle, then shoved it deep into the front pocket of her jeans.

Walking back toward the house, she smoothed herself and lifted her head. Everything up ahead—the low brick house, the empty clothesline stretched across the backyard, the weathered workshed—looked normal, but her sense of time and place had been altered. She had no idea how long she'd been away, or how old she was, or what strange man might be sleeping in the bed that had been hers since childhood. Feet touched the ground—she could hear the sounds—but she could not feel anything that might prove the steps were her own. If Tuck had suddenly appeared at the back porch, his arms held out in question, she would not have been able to respond, or walk any faster, or say anything that would help him. By the time she reached the barren garden all she could feel was a dull edge of fear.

And the house sat still, unsuspecting of the coming storm that threatened to tear it loose from its foundation, lift it up, and sweep it forever away.

Tuck dreamed.

For several hours he had stared at the ceiling and prayed for rest, but the train-roar memory of the big machines at the plant echoed in his head more persistently than usual. An aching worry had stubbornly refused him any peace. Jessie had been kind and loving all through their shared meal, but Tuck knew her well. *Maybe better than she knows herself,* he thought. He felt her pain more deeply than his own. He could shove down his own sadness, far enough at least to stay strong for Jessie.

Lord, please protect her. She doesn't deserve all that's happening to her.

Tuck knew what lonely felt like. *She needs me more than ever now,* he thought. He watched a tiny black speck of spider crawl across the ceiling, and the thought of Johnny Allen flashed again through his mind. He clenched his eyes against a sickening anger, but it would not subside. Tuck could not clear his mind of the resentment toward a man who had no right to interfere with his wife's happiness. The joyful balance of his home had been upset, yes, and maybe even his own future. But more than anything Tuck felt a threatening rage rising up at the thought of Jessie in pain. For weeks the look in her eyes had been almost too much for him to bear. Every instinct made Tuck want to end her suffering, by whatever means necessary. Pictures of violence invaded his mind. *Forgive me, Lord. Take these thoughts from me.*

Tuck forced his mind into saner images, and pictured Jessie's smile. This calmed him. He didn't know how much time passed, but finally he had drifted off...

...and saw Jessie standing in an open field. Spring bloomed everywhere, a warm wind rippling her long white dress into a gentle dance around her ankles. She appeared close enough to touch and yet just beyond his reach. She smiled, but the smile held a remote sadness. When he called to her no sound came from his mouth, but she reached out her hands to him, trying to connect.

Suddenly a deep foreboding filled him, a knowing that Jessie was in danger and unaware, and he wanted to run to her but couldn't move his legs. And then the woods transformed, dark, winter-bare, moving into a dense circle behind her, so near now that their skeletal arms linked and spread across the remaining separating distance, covering Jessie in shadow. Still she reached for him, but her smile faded. He shouted her name but his voice was lost in the wind, and she could not hear him. He watched her slowly turn away...

Tuck sat up straight, blinking. For a moment he did not know what part of day or night it was. He looked at the bedside clock—he'd only been in bed for a few hours. As tired as he was, he knew he would not sleep. Despite the continuous cloudiness and the heavy shades pulled down over the windows, too much light seemed able to find its way into the room.

Later, Tuck would be unable to recall exactly what had drawn him from the bed to look out the window. But an uneasiness lured him across the cold wood floor, where he raised the shade and opened the wooden blinds...

Although a man of solid stance and calm temperament, Tuck now admitted to himself that in the whole season of his marriage, and the time of courting prior, he had always done battle with what felt like an enemy too nebulous, a foe too formless on whom he could never quite get a good stranglehold. Tuck knew he could never defeat an opponent he could not see.

Through the years he had never held hostility toward Johnny; no mortal could be faulted for succumbing to Jessie. Back then, with high school graduation and all its possible ramifications looming, he had accepted that she would go with Johnny. Tuck's heart had been in a constant state of grieving since the day he'd seen Jessie and Johnny holding hands at school; everyone knew they were dating, that it was serious. But as time moved forward he had felt it ignoble to allow rival jealousy to taint his fond feelings. Jessie had clearly chosen, and he would honor her choice.

Still, there had been nothing dishonorable, it seemed to him, in waiting. Mere human circumstances could not deter destiny. If what he felt toward Jessie was as authentic—perhaps even ordained—as he believed, he could wait things out. In this he secured a clandestine hope. And, as things turned out, perseverance proved sufficient.

Not once since marrying Jessie had Tuck allowed himself to be deceived; he knew the heavens had bestowed on him a gift greater than he deserved or could ever hope to fully comprehend. And he was wise enough to see that she had at least to some extent finally been drawn to him more by a spirit of recompense than passion. But she had come to him nonetheless. He had determined long before that if she came, however she came, it would be enough. And so he took what love she could offer, knowing that even a portion of her heart was more than he had ever truly expected her to share with him.

Now, peering out between the slats, something began edging its murky way into his mind. As he caught sight of her—only a flash, like a bird flying across the field, away from him—a shift occurred. Long ago he had promised to protect her from harm. And he had never seen her run quite like that, as though something or someone, real or imagined, was pursuing her. He wanted to save her, but did not know how. He slumped in the chair by the window for what seemed forever, until he finally caught sight of her heading wearily back.

He dressed, and met her in the living room.

"Jessie?" The look on her face, pale and half-alive, made him feel afraid.

"What?" she said, in the dazed voice of someone waking.

"What's the matter, Jessie?"

"Nothing."

"Jessie..."

"I'm fine." She tried to smile, her head tilted up in that way she always had when trying to gain leverage, but Tuck saw no power in her now. Her clothes were dirty. There were pieces of leaves in her hair. The love that bound them together would not allow deception; their eyes met, and Tuck knew.

Johnny.

She tried. She placed her hand on his cheek. "It's okay, Tuck. I'll take care of this." His eyes broke her heart. *My dear, sweet Tuck,* she thought. "I'm tired. I'm going to lie down, in Momma's room. Go to bed, Tuck." She found no strength to say more.

Tuck stood speechless and bewildered. A thousand thoughts rattled around in his head, but he couldn't get a good grip on any of them. He wanted to take back whatever control had been lost, but in truth he had always been in awe of her, and in this awful moment felt overwhelmed. Paralyzed, he watched her turn and leave the room. He heard the sound of Belle's bedroom door closing.

Tuck knew that trying to live a life of faith did not make life a predictable thing. And he knew that every man was responsible for his choices, and that any given choice might change the course of a man's life. He knew from experience that God's voice, however one might hear it, could be trusted far better than a man's own thinking. But as he sat on the edge of the loveseat by the picture window and tried to pray, a white heat kept scorching the prayers from his head.

After a while he stood. In the hallway he took his coat and hat from the closet, then closed the front door quietly but firmly behind him.

It didn't matter exactly what had occurred to throw her into such a state; Tuck knew who had caused it. Though he had never been able to see very far into the complicated maze of her feelings, he knew that Jessie was in pain. And this would not stand. For Tuck, it was not so much an issue of ownership—since Jessie was not a thing that could be owned—as it was a matter of honor. Jessie's honor.

He gripped the wheel with hard hands and drove toward the cabin in the woods.

12

"I reckon not," Joey said.

His younger brother had made it as far as the porch for the second time, and it seemed to John that if he was ever going to get him inside the cabin, now might be his best chance.

"Come on, Joey. There's nothing in there."

"Big bro, I'm fine right here on this porch."

"Well, I'm not." The midday sun occasionally managed to break through curdled clouds, but its light was ashen, aloof. The wind had them both huddled at the railing, hunched down into their coats. John said, "I'm going in. You do as you please." He used his older-brother voice, lined with a hint of sarcasm.

"Well go on, then," Joey said, and John did, pulling open the squeaky screen door, and with his hand on the knob of the main door he added—"You chicken"—and went in.

John went to the woodstove, opened the grate, and prodded at the coals with the iron poker. He had his hopes up this time. And sure enough, after a minute or two he heard the screen door whining open.

"Good Lord. This place is ugly as sin." Joey stood with his claw still touching the doorknob, ready to run.

"Close the door, you idiot. I'm trying to warm us up."

"Shoot fire, Johnny. There ain't nothin' here, hardly."

He slowly closed the door against the cold. "Is this all he had? What do you do all day and night, stare at your dang belly button?"

"He had lots of good books."

Joey snorted, and stepped gingerly toward the fire. "Yeah, the old man always had his nose in a book, when he wasn't yellin' or kickin' somethin'."

Joey quietly followed his brother into each room.

Together they looked at what few relics remained of their father's past. Joey stayed mostly quiet, and seemed relieved there wasn't much in the way of memorabilia. There were no photographs, except for one of the three kids, framed and sitting on the dresser. Maggie looked no more than ten, John a couple of years younger, Joey around five, all standing arm in arm in their old backyard on a fine spring day. John marveled at how blue the sky looked back then, even in a faded old snapshot. Joey glanced at it, head tilted, then walked away.

As the time wore on some uneasiness passed, but John could tell the brief tour had left his little brother unsettled. They sat a long time by the woodstove, talking more of life ahead than of the past.

"When are you headin' back, Johnny?"

"I'm not sure. There are things I have to do first."

"Yeah."

"This might sound weird, little bro. But sometimes I wonder if I could just stay here."

John didn't expect the reaction.

"Stay? Are you out of your cotton-pickin' *mind*?"

"What?"

Joey's eyes widened with hope. "Shoot fire, Johnny. Lord knows I want you to. I'd give anything to have you close by." Then doubt moved like a cloud over his face. "But why would you wanna stay *here*? Of all the places you've been to and could still go...mercy, Johnny, sometimes I think you're really *crazy*."

"Why does it sound so crazy?"

"Bro," Joey said, shaking his head. "You've said it yourself, ever since you was a kid. You don't *belong* here."

Something inside John fell. "I was born here."

Joey looked right at him. "You was born here, Johnny. And I reckon a part of you loves it here. But ever since you was little...it's like you didn't quite *fit*."

The truth of it landed on him hard, something he already knew despite the quiet hours spent trying to convince himself otherwise. "I'm older now, Joey," he tried, but his heart was already beaten.

Joey put his misshapen hand on his brother's knee. "Johnny. What would you do? Live in this cabin?" His face held a resigned sadness. "Already you've started holin' up by yourself all the time. Maggie says you don't come by that much any more. You could write your books, I reckon. But what else? Lord knows I'd love havin' you close, and Maggie and El would, too. But Johnny, nothin's changed here." Joey shook his head. "You ain't sat still for long in your whole life. Shoot fire, look at you. You need to shave, and get your *own* clothes." He frowned. "It's weird, big bro, if you ask me. I'm just not sure this place is good for you. It's good for some folks, real good. Because they belong here, they're like a part of it, and the land and the river a part of them, too. Some folks stay here because they want to, 'cause it's what they love. Some of us stay here 'cause we're afraid to go anywhere else. But either way, we're dug deep in, planted here. It's home for us, good or bad."

"It's good," John offered weakly. "It's...simple. You don't know how good it is here."

"Well, I do and I don't." Joey looked through the glass. "These woods are the only place I know."

"These woods are a part of me, too, Joey. I didn't realize until I came home how much I'd missed it here, the woods, the changing seasons..." John searched for the words. "Nobody's chasing after life. They're just living it."

Joey turned to his brother and smiled. "Well, that's true. There's a bunch of folks around here who wouldn't want to be anywhere else." Then his eyes grew sadder still. "But you're not *them*, bro. You ain't never been, even when we was little kids. Shoot, none of us never knew where your head was, way up in the clouds all the time, and no use tryin' to get you down from there, either."

John's eyes filled, remembering. He felt too tired to say the words out loud—*I don't belong anywhere.*

"You're a dreamer, Johnny. And dreamers don't settle good, not in one place, and not for long."

"Everybody has dreams," John said.

"Yeah." Joey turned back to the window. "But some of us know better than to believe they can come true."

By the time noon had come and gone, Joey was getting antsy. John realized his little brother had at some point decided not to drink when they were together, and he couldn't help smiling at the gentle gesture. But Joey would be needing a beer by now.

Joey cranked up the four-wheeler, hesitated, then yelled over the engine to his brother on the porch.

"Hey, bro!"

"Yeah?"

"Don't think I wouldn't *want* you to stay. More than anything."

"I know," John said.

He watched his brother disappear over the hill.

The door hadn't been closed ten minutes when John heard the truck. Through the little side window he saw it stop.

When the man got out, everything crashed in—shame, foolishness, failure, an unreasonable but overpowering sense of betrayal. The knock on the door startled him into reality.

"Tuck," he said. The big man on the other side of the screen blocked out much of the light behind him.

"Johnny."

"Come in."

Tuck opened the screen door and stepped inside. He did not offer his hand. He took off his hat and held it at his side.

"It's been a long time, Tuck."

"Yeah, it has."

The two men looked at each other, and right away knew there would be no need for small talk.

"Come in and sit."

"No, I don't believe I will. I won't be stayin'." Tuck looked around, his face set. "I've been in here before," he said. "When it belonged to old man Pierce."

John didn't speak.

Tuck returned his gaze.

"We knew you was comin', Johnny. Word gets around fast here."

"Yes, it does."

The two men stared at the unlikely, older versions of the faces they had remembered.

"Well, I'm not much for words. I'll just tell it straight." Tuck pulled back his square shoulders a little. "I want you to stay away from Jessie." He waited for a response, but didn't get much. "Jessie is my wife now, Johnny."

"I know." A strange feeling came over John, and he almost said, "I'm sorry."

"Her daddy and momma are both gone." Something like helplessness passed across Tuck's face. "I'm what family she has left now."

John remained silent.

"I don't know what you've done"—John knew as Tuck said this that he didn't yet know about the letter, perhaps, and the barest ember of hope glowed—"but you stay away from her. You stay away from both of us. That's what I'm here to tell you, Johnny. Do you understand?" Tuck's voice was calm, firm.

John considered, but only briefly. "I'm not sure I can promise you that, Tuck." He saw the muscles in the big man's jaw clench. "I had hoped to talk to her. There are some things I need to say."

"You listen, Johnny Allen," Tuck said, low and tinged with menace, and hearing his name spoken like that made John remember...the dark-eyed face of his father coming into him so hard he had to blink it away. "I'm only gonna say this once. You leave Jessie alone. Don't try to see her. I can't make you leave Tranquility. But I can watch after Jessie, and I will." He hesitated. Then, "She don't wanna see you, Johnny."

"Did she tell you that?"

Tuck blinked. "She don't wanna see you," he said. And he turned without warning and opened the door. John moved to the screen door and watched him go, boots heavy-shuffling across the porch boards and down the steps. Tuck reached the ground and turned.

"I'm a Christian man," he said, almost apologetically. "I got nothing against you personal, Johnny." Then his tone toughened. "But hear me good—her name is Jessie *Tucker* now." The big man squared his shoulders. "If I ever come back out here, it won't be to talk."

Tuck got in his truck and pulled away.

13

Jess,

I've started this letter more times than I can remember. I've been writing to you my whole life, it seems, ever since we started passing notes in school. And I've never stopped. I just stopped sending them, finally. I probably won't send this one, either. But I have to write it just the same.

First, please know how sorry I am about Belle. Your father, too, of course. I struggled more than you will ever know with Belle's funeral, not knowing what to do. I wanted to be there. I really loved your parents. They always treated me like a part of their family, and me just a teenaged punk always sniffing around their house, latching on to their only daughter. It felt so wrong not being there to see Belle laid to rest. I couldn't help think-ing how our parents are now all gone, mine and yours, barely in their seventies, my mother even younger. How I wanted to be there, Jess. But I knew it would be wrong, after all this time, to intrude on your life that way. I'd made a choice long ago to leave family, both my fami-lies. And once a man does that, it can be too long a road back. Life doesn't wait. So I stayed away.

After a while, after I'd been gone for longer than I meant, each passing day somehow made it harder to return. It's almost like we get so far away, so lost, that the distance just can't be traveled anymore. I've learned in the past year or so that all this thinking is about shame, a shame I've carried a long time, since I was a little boy. Knowing this has helped. Maybe I won't have to keep making the same mistakes over and over again. But time is beyond my control. I can't go back. I've hurt so many people. I've hurt you most of all, and in that I've all but killed myself. And that's how my life seems to have gone, where the road seems to have taken me.

I'm here in Dad's cabin, and I've stayed this time a while because I need to see you, and tell you some things. And so I'm stuck, really, between knowing I should not contact you and knowing that I can't leave until I do. Maybe the reason I never mailed so many of those letters in the past was because deep down I knew I had to see you face-to-face. But I don't know how to do it. I don't want to interfere with your life, Jess, just speak into it, if only for a moment.

I have not come back to ask for your forgiveness, because I don't deserve that. And I haven't come back to try to explain anything, to blame the drinking or anything else. But to stay sane I do need to tell you I'm sorry, so sorry, Jess. And more than anything I need you to know I haven't come back to cause you any more pain. So I'm now fighting a battle within myself between what's best for you and your life, and what I seem compelled to do in order to move forward in mine. I've been selfish my whole life, Jess. Am I being that now? I don't know. Maybe. But I can't seem to leave Tranquility. I've started to a dozen times. But I can't go, not yet. And I can't bring myself to mailing a letter, either. I'm not even sure I should.

I'm going to say this, at least say it before it breaks me, and hope it's not my selfish shame talking. If I've found the courage to send this letter, and you're reading it now, know that I am going to the barn every afternoon from this point on. I'm going to sit there until the sun sets. For how many days I'm not sure. Just until I know.

If you don't come, I'll understand. I won't pursue you or cause your family any more harm. But this is all I can think to do. I want you to have a choice. Whatever you choose, I will live with that.

Johnny

Jessie sat on the edge of her mother's bed and read it for the third time. With each pass something new surfaced in her, a different but no less mournful muddle of emotions, and each time what she considered as the reasonable resolutions to which she would lend her allegiance fell away, transformed into fresh turmoil.

She didn't cry. She would not give him that.

Her own heart broke for Tuck. She'd heard him drive away, but felt no desire to talk to him, or to stop him, even. Part of her was glad, the part that could not imagine having to lie to him, to move through the coming days in shrouded secrecy. But she could not completely shake off the other voice, the younger one within, the one grieving what would soon be the final act of a faint but not-quite-faithless fantasy.

She had not been able to muster the strength to move from her mother's bed for some time. But now she stood and folded the letter, went to the closet, pulled out the footstool, and put the letter in the empty jewelry box. She walked to the bathroom, turned on the shower, and slowly undressed.

In the mirror stood a tall girl, more daunting than beautiful, with still-strong angles to her face and fine curves to her body. She reached her hands to her stomach and lightly touched the tips of her fingers to alabaster skin.

She studied the girl's face—striking but perhaps too stern, the eyebrows dark and pointed, strong but stubbornly decisive. The brooding eyes had not been domesticated by age—large, dark, wet-black as molasses. Around her high cheeks fell abundant, undisciplined curls. The chin often thrust itself forward in a kind of protective defiance, but today did not; the features seemed softened, almost defeated. Her skin had winter-paled to porcelain.

In that moment she called on the last of her weary hate...for him, yes, and for herself, and perhaps even for God, if she looked honestly into the glass at the truest reflection of herself. But none of this could stop it now, could hold back the torrent of spirit emanating from a deeper place, an essence of memory clear as new morning, of spring and a barn...

"When will you go?" she asked.

"Two more weeks," he said.

"For how long, Johnny? How long do you think?"

"How many times have you asked me that?"

"Ten million."

"More."

"Tell me again. About where you'll be, and when you'll write for me to come."

"I'll go to the ocean."

"Yes."

"And as soon as I get there I'll take off my shoes and run across the white sand and straight into the water..."

"Cold."

"Yes. And salty, with the smells of countless other countries carried on its breeze."

"And then."

"And then I'll roll up my britches as high as they'll go, and wade out into the surf."

"And it'll sound like..."

"Like the crashing of distant thunder..."

"On countless distant shores..."

"You know all this by heart, now."

"Yes. But Johnny."

"It won't be forever, Jess."

"It will seem like forever."

"I'd take you if I could."

"I know."

"I'll start classes, and work the rest of the time. Remember our promise?"

"Yes." She let him wipe her tears with his fingertips.

"I'll have to find work first. My old man's run through most of what should have been mine..."

"Johnny."

"I can't stay here, Jess," he said, his voice suddenly taking on the dark sound that always made her feel uneasy. "I won't. Sometimes I can't stand it. Sometimes I'm afraid of what I might do... I swear, Jess, sometimes I get so angry I could kill him..."

"Please, Johnny. Please don't." She laced her fingers through his hair, stroking, soothing.

After a while this calmed him. Then—"Anyway, I'll find work, live where I have to." He turned and looked into her wonderful, merciful eyes. "It won't be easy, Jess. I have so little. And it's no way for a girl to live."

"We both dreamed of college, Johnny."

"I know, Jess. I'm... I'm awfully sorry for the way things have happened."

"It's God's will."

He grew silent again.

"Johnny."

"Hmm."

"Then what?"

He took a deep breath, as if to chase the miserable images from his mind. "Then I'll have a place, our place. And it won't be much, but it'll be all ours. By then you'll be able to come. I'll have enough money..."

160

"Yes. Yes you will, Johnny. Nobody writes as beautifully as you. Nobody."

"We'll go there, to that stretch of beach where the water first curled up over my toes." He laced his fingers into hers. "And I'll hold your hand, Jess, just like this. And that's where we'll be married."

"Yes. With our bare feet in the sea."

"Yes. Just you, me, and the preacher, barefoot in the cool sand."

"Barefoot in the cool sand."

He touched his lips lightly to hers.

"That's it," she said softly. "That's our dream. The one we share."

"The one we share."

"And we'll live happily ever after."

"Yes," he said. "Ever after."

"And until then, this will be our place."

"Yes."

"I'll come here when I'm missing you so much I can't stand it, Johnny. I'll come here and just sit." She stroked his hair. "I will love you forever, Johnny Allen."

"I will love you forever, Jess Martin. And I'll be here with you. Always."

And his arms were strong around her. He pressed into the vital warmth of her, away from the world, from pain, from reality, burying his face into the merciful blackness of her hair. And she was his, he knew it, had always known it, she belonged to him fully, the one thing that made him feel whole...

"Wait," she whispered. And he did, as always, though he knew she couldn't stop him and knew she wouldn't even try, because there was something sacred in her word, as sacred as their love, fresh as spring morning after the rain. "Wait..." and he did, holding her without forcing, honoring, understanding that the thing they shared was more perfect than any passion,

the spirit of their love more powerful than flesh, the only thing the boy had ever known that flew above the pain, above and beyond the reach of time itself.

"Wait..." And she took the fury from him, all of it, and drew it into herself, all his loss and loneliness, his restless heart. Again she saved him from his fear, from himself. And her whisper was neither request nor command but only truth, the one sure truth he had ever known, would ever know—that any violent intrusion would shatter the illusion, waking them both from a divine dream.

"Wait."

"Yes. We'll wait, Jess. We'll wait..."

"Until you come back," her breath warm in his ear.

"Until I come back." And again he knew she had saved them both, because there was somehow something more precious in the waiting, more holy, even. Now both knew death could be defeated. They were life's essence to one another, and once joined they would live forever.

She nestled her head into his chest and the two of them drifted away, the hay making soft noises under them, their eyes closed and everything else falling away, only the cracks of light and the shuffle of hooves in hay and horses snorting in their stalls...soft streaks of sunlight stretching across and bending over them, and spring giving birth outside...the humming of horseflies, the tapping of wasps wafting against the rafters. They dreamed the same dream, belonging to one another completely, sanctified and sure, for as long as forever turned out to be.

They would wait...

Jessie stared at her body. All pretense had been stripped away. Her authentic beauty—her truest self—had remained half-buried for years, a fertile but unfulfilled spirit that had never fully broken through the ground. She had hidden her heart like the box in the closet, hoping against hope that it might over time be forgotten. And now she had returned to find it still there, estranged but essentially unchanged. Life had seemingly led her into a closed corral, her spirit trampled under heavy hooves.

To Jessie, the face in the mirror looked more astonished than anything else. *This won't do,* her mind insisted to her heart. *I'm a grown woman.* The chaos within her did not seem possible, this cruel and foolish timelessness of love.

She had thought this door to her past closed and nailed shut. Once decided, her love for Tuck had never been one of compromise. Her union with her husband had felt whole and unimpaired, and she had accepted it as nothing less than a blessing from God. None of what was now happening seemed real. How could she allow such a thing? How could God?

There was no choice she could make without loss. Whichever way submission came, either her soul or heart would be sacrificed.

Momma, she thought, then spoke the words, tentatively— "Oh, Momma. I need you. I don't know what to do." Then, as it had all her life, Jessie's sorrow sparked to anger. "Why now, God? All Momma wanted was one more spring. One more *spring!*" She slammed her fists on the edge of the sink and shouted at the mirror, but her voice broke into sobs. She felt too tired, finally, to fight. "If only you were here, Momma," she said, with the voice of a frightened little girl. "I miss you so much." And she could not stop crying. "I need you. I don't know what to do."

She stepped into the steaming stream and let the water fall onto her, warm and weeping, the sorrow washing out and over her on tears no one would ever see.

14

For the fourth day in a row John waited at the barn. The previous two days the remains of winter had been unwaveringly wet and spiteful, confining him to the car, where he sat staring past the barn into the woods. But today warmer winds had begun breaking up the clouds. What little was left of the dirt road had washed out into calf-high ruts, and he had to park close to the highway and slog through red mud the quarter mile around the shielding tree line.

The great, lonely barn leaned against the muddled sky. John moved closer, stepping over abandoned farm equipment rusting in the dirt, and looked up the tall wall of gnarled wood to its peaking roof. It had been an impressive, practical barn in its day, not huge but built for horses and hard work. He glanced again at his watch, then peered through the just-cracked doors into the damp shadows. He had not yet been inside; it did not seem right to go without her. But with each passing day he realized she might never come. And so he decided now to go in alone.

Overgrown scrub made moving the double doors difficult, but John lowered his shoulder and pushed one side open. Stale, abandoned air met him. Light fell in on a lifeless tomb.

He walked a few steps in, his eyes adjusting to the colorless gloom—four stalls, two to each side, a wide berth down the middle, and what had been the tack and feed rooms further down. The far end of the barn had long ago been piled high with hay, but now what remained lay shrunken and matted, depressed with age. Once all this had vibrated with living—snorts and scraping hooves, buzzing flies, heavy scents of animals and feed. But now the place felt black and damp as a lifeless cave.

John stepped, very slowly, almost to the back wall.

He saw draped over the rail of the last stall what looked to be part of an old bridle; he reached and touched it. The leather felt dried and hard.

Then he knew, without hearing or seeing, and turned.

She stood silhouetted in the doorway at the opposite end of the barn, blurred by the brightness behind her. He could not see her face. Shafts of light came through the cracks of the walls and illuminated beams of swirling dust, animating the air between them, flashing down across the dirt floor and bending themselves up the sides of the stalls, giving the illusion of the place lifting itself toward rebirth.

His hand rested on the rail.

She did not move as she spoke.

"His name was Sky. Big. Strong, but sweet. He never liked anybody else riding him, though. He was all mine; I was the only one he trusted. You remember, don't you? You rode Doone."

John felt frozen to the dirt floor. And the place was stilled by long silence, both listening for some secret the shadows might share. But then words flowed from her, droning and dreamlike before he could move.

"I would have come to wherever you were, Johnny, however far, however sick you were, I'd have come, without asking why. I would have packed my bag and been gone from here, left everything I've ever known and made my home wherever you said home should be, no matter what."

"Jess…"

"*Don't* speak to me." Her voice shook the shafts of light.

He took a step.

"No."

He stopped.

"I might have been afraid, but I would have come, Johnny. Because my love was stronger than the fear. And I was never so afraid of love that I couldn't do anything, fight anything, go anywhere in the world to have it. I believed you felt the same way. So I waited. I waited for the letters, and when they stopped coming I waited for a miracle. I prayed that you were safe, and when we heard you were in trouble I prayed you wouldn't die." She paused. Nothing dared stir.

"I never gave up. But time went right by me, and time never cared if I gave up or not. When I heard you'd come to town for your mother's funeral, and that you hadn't come to see me, then I finally mourned you. A little at a time, all that turned to anger and I hated you, Johnny, I hated you as much as I'd ever loved you, maybe more. I hated you with my whole heart."

The words flowed with a strange, steady calm, as if she had rehearsed them in her heart for so long that they now moved seamlessly from her mouth, as natural as breathing. Her hands made fists at her side.

"So much time went by and I was so tired, I just stopped feeling anything. I swear my heart all but stopped. Because I just got to where I couldn't feel anything at all. And that's the worst kind of dying, slow, a heart breaking little by little, just barely beating enough to keep me alive when I wanted to die, but not enough to ever share with anyone else. And that's when I finally knew. I finally knew I wouldn't come after you, Johnny, though I'd started to a hundred times. I guess by then the anger had grown stronger than love, or at least what I remembered as love. I couldn't remember being filled with love anymore, and I just felt empty. You robbed me, Johnny, season after season, until there was only a small part of me left. Nobody should ever give away that much of themselves. And no one should ever give themselves the right to take it."

Her hands unclenched, then fisted again, and from within the light her dark head seemed to lift.

"Now you've come back. And seeing you, something's come to life again, only it's not love, Johnny, it's the hate. You're a coward, a weak coward, and you had no right to come back here out of nowhere and make me *feel* again. You were hungry for the world, Johnny, but *you* were my world, and I was only hungry for you. And now you come riding back and crash into things with no regard. What were you expecting? Something from a story, like one of your books?"

She paused again, but he had no voice.

"Did you think you could come back and sweep me up and we'd live happily ever after?" She tried to laugh, and it was the saddest sound he had ever heard. "I lived on your promises for a long time. I fed on the meaning of them— your face, the memory of you telling me how beautiful I was, how your heart could never belong to anyone else, that your heart would be mine forever and ever. I lived on those moments, played them over and over in my head until finally they faded and I stopped believing."

She took her first steps, slowly, and as she moved the bars of light rolled up her legs and chambray shirt, neck, face, eyes, thin shards illuminating brief glimpses between wide black. She drew only a few feet closer, stopping safely three stalls away. One bright blade cut across her lips and cheek. Her eyes remained in shadow.

"Your turn," she said.

For one heartbeat he thought he would be unable to speak. He had listened as pain poured out of her, but it was he who felt emptied. But here she stood, half-phantom, and he did not blink for fear she would vanish. He opened his mouth and said—

"I'm sorry."

She remained still.

"I...don't know." He knew if he could not speak she would fly. "I lost myself," he said.

"You lost more than that."

"Yes." He squinted, desperate to see her eyes. "I always planned on coming for you, Jess. Always. All the letters were true. It's just that...something happened. I fell in love with a dream."

"So did I," she said. "But love's not a dream, is it Johnny? Love is real, as real as the wind. You don't have to see it or touch it to know. Love's something that we take for granted, like the air around us, and yet the whole time it's keeping us alive...sometimes just barely alive."

He searched for words.

"I can't blame the drinking or my family or anything else. Something snuck up on me, caught me not looking. And the longer it went, the deeper down... I don't know how it happened, really. I kept thinking I would fix things first, pull my life together and then come for you, but the more I went into that world the more lost I became, until I was something I couldn't let you see."

"I would have come to you. No matter what."

"You can't imagine," he said. "I changed..."

"I didn't," she said, shifting, her mouth disappearing, eyes briefly flashing. "I would have been there for you."

"You would have hated me, the way I was. You wouldn't have known me."

"You were a coward and a fool," she said, her voice more remorseful than angry now.

"Yes," he said. "More than you'll ever know. But not anymore. Not today. I didn't come back to hurt you. But I had to tell you, had to at least try. I don't expect forgiveness. But I can't live anymore until I say it." He felt himself shaking. "Something happened to me, Jess. I lost who I really

168

was, lost everything true. I felt like I'd wandered too far away, too far to ever make my way back. I wasn't the same person..." In his mind over the years he had rehearsed countless versions of this encounter, and said clear, meaningful things to her. But now every word from his mouth felt meaningless. "I did it," he said. "All of it. Nobody forced me to change. But over time, something took over, another part of me..."

John saw her stir, and knew at any moment she might be gone.

"I never stopped loving you," he blurted. "In my heart, what was left of it. I know that's useless to you. But that's what time did to me. I thought the whole world, the one I remembered, must have stopped, waiting for me to get back. I know how crazy that sounds. But everything had collapsed in on me, just fallen in, and I kept thinking, tomorrow I'll get better."

He felt weak and foolish, but it didn't matter now. This might be his only chance.

"I kept saying to myself, tomorrow I'll clean myself up and go back," he said. "I'll escape all this. I'll find myself and I'll find my way home. I'll come back and nothing will be any different, the real world, the true world, just as I left it, and I'll be okay. I won't have to be ashamed anymore. I'll explain, and she'll..."

"You're too late, Johnny."

There was little life in her words. And everything within him buckled, hope falling finally away. She faltered but then the words came full out and all his life, their life, descended into dust. She did not move forward, and he knew the jagged beams of light between them would not be passed through.

"I'm married now, Johnny. I waited, until I couldn't wait anymore. Tuck was here. Tuck was always here, and he never ran away. And I didn't want life passing me by all alone. Time fleets away," she said, her voice breaking, "and love, too."

And then she turned toward the door and his heart flew up, he reached and would have died to be able to touch her, just touch. He took a step but she stopped and so did he, and half turning she said—

"Sometimes sorrow kills us, and sometimes sorrow makes us stronger. This isn't a story you can just write your own ending to. Life is not a *book*, Johnny. We make our choices and take what living brings us. Life is not for cowards. And neither is love."

Then, after endless years of waiting, imagining, he found himself unable to act, to move, to speak, his soul turned to stone. He stretched out his hand but there was nothing he could do, reaching into a dream that no longer existed, once real but now no more than swirling beams of dust.

She turned and disappeared into the light.

The shaking had finally calmed by the time Jessie got home.

She parked the truck and walked into the house, straight to the bedroom. Tuck was still asleep and didn't stir when she entered. Jessie sat in the chair by the window. She stared at the bulk beneath the covers and willed him awake.

His eyes opened. He sat up.

"Jessie?"

"I've just seen Johnny," she said simply.

He blinked hard.

"I wanted you to know," she said, trying to control her emotions.

"What..."

"I went and spoke to him. I told him everything was over, that I was married now. I told him."

"Jessie."

"It's okay, Tuck. It's all right now. Johnny was only

dreaming, that's all. And he needed to be told. I hope... I hope you will forgive me."

The big man was off the bed. He came and kneeled, his hands on her knees.

"I'm not mad at you, Jessie," he said. "I wish he hadn't... I wish he hadn't done it. He had no right. It ain't right he made you go through it..."

"It's okay now, Tuck," she said. But his eyes made her feel like dying. She did not know how to comfort him.

"No more," Tuck said, but there was no power in it.

"No more," she said. And she reached and put her cold hand against his face.

* * *

That night John did not sleep.

He no longer felt afraid of the silent darkness all around. The nights were becoming his friend, and sleep less necessary. He had been in the cabin for more than two months and had accepted tenure; what was left of his father had become a part of him, their shared spirit of fierce loneliness now inhabiting the place. John sat and absently poked at the soft-hissing fire in the woodstove like a man who had done the same thing for years.

After a while he stood, went to the bedroom closet, and got the gun and the box of shells. Days before, he had found rags and oil and cleaning rod, and had begun wiping away the neglect, swabbing out the barrel, lubricating the action and parts, polishing the hardwood stock. The slow, methodic work with the gun—pushing the oiled rags through the bore and out the muzzle, years of fouling coming gradually clean with each new pass—had given him a sense of centering calm.

Now he wiped off the excess and racked the pump, smooth and easy. The 12-gauge looked and sounded the way

171

he remembered it, new and powerful, a hero's gun held firm in his father's granite hands. With his thumb he shoved one, two, three, four shells into the magazine, pumped to chamber one round, then pushed in a fifth.

He went to the porch. A three-quarter crescent moon lay on its back, staring down from the starless sky like the heavy-lidded eye of a cat, yellow-jeweled in a black face. It hung there, watching, unblinking, glowing into the thin clouds around it as if encased in ice. John held the gun in both hands at his waist, and the smell of timelessness lay on the damp porch and out into the slumbering woods and under the nails of his oil-stained fingers cradling the stock, giving him a partial peace. An owl offered its eerie, echoing hoot.

And in this moment John came to accept whatever fate waited. He would stay, not so much out of any determined purpose but instead for lack of knowing where else to go. He had seen her now, or at least some ghost of her, and both of them had survived. Both had proven to themselves and to each other that if nothing else there was at least flesh remaining on the temporal spirit of their dreams. He had heard her voice, and for some reason felt neither hopeful nor defeated.

He would not run away, not yet. He knew she had done the only thing she could, in the only way she knew how, and yet he would not believe she could leave it at that any more than he could. He hoped with what hope remained in him that no one would be hurt, but one way or another his re-entry into her world had now occurred, setting his future destiny into inevitable motion. He had come too far into a land that no longer knew him and yet was somehow essential to him, a separate time and place from which his only escape lay in a resolution, whatever that might be.

"You know what to do, boy."

Fear spoke inside him with ever-increasing dominance. Though he again stood on native soil, it had frozen over, forever, and his roots would no longer put down. His life was without mooring. He belonged nowhere.

"You're just takin' up air. But you don't have to live like this..."

Tomorrow and each day after, he would go back until he felt satisfied that the thing was finished. He knew that one last, vital part of himself remained there, at the barn, and even here, in this place hidden deep in the woods.

"A man's always got options."

Standing there, he felt somehow less alone. The cool air settled into him with quiet conviction. Somewhere in the distant night a dove mourned, and the owl warned small living things to lie low and out of reach.

Behind him, John heard the creaking of an old rocking chair.

15

She met him at the door as if he were her own lost son.

"Johnny!" she said, and he held her frail body gently, fearing she might break in two.

"Johnny, Johnny Allen, get in this house where it's *dry!*" March was more than half-spent, but the skies held little promise. Another day of miserable cold rain had set in, adamant in its defiance of an unwilling spring.

"Hello, Miss Ruth," he said. They held onto each other's arms and tilted back for a better look. Her eyes glistened. "Oh, how big and handsome you are. Gracious. And growing a *beard*? Mercy, how it makes you look even more like your daddy." A brief sadness passed between them, but she quickly regained her smile. "It's wonderful to see you. We knew you were here. What in the world took you so long to come visit?" But she wasn't scolding; John gratefully breathed in the grace.

"It's good to see you, Miss Ruth. You look absolutely beautiful." John noticed she had done up her white hair with a mother-of-pearl comb and worn her Sunday best, as if all for his visit.

She scrunched up her nose and giggled like a school-girl. "Oh, Johnny Allen, still the charmer, I see! You know good and well I'm a shrinking old woman."

"No ma'am," he said firmly. "You were beautiful the last time I saw you, and you're beautiful now." And she was, too, in his eyes, though he also felt the same sense of loss he'd experienced with nearly everyone he'd met since coming home. Time had been more kind to some, less to others. But though the ravages of age and care-taking had slowly eroded her face and body, Miss Ruth's spirit still shone.

"Come in, come in," she said, taking his elbow and moving him toward the living room. "Sit. How about something to eat?"

"Oh, no thank you."

"Don't be shy!" She laughed. "You have a seat in this chair and wait right here. My goodness, you used to come in here and eat half the cookies in the jar..." She took a few cautious but still-brisk steps into the little adjoining kitchen. "...and drink up all the milk, too!"

She emerged after a minute with a platter of cookies and a glass of milk.

"Chocolate chip and peanut butter, remember? After all these many years Preacher still has to have them, whenever he's up to it. It's by God's good grace alone I can still make them for him." John took a cookie and the milk. The old woman's face blushed with memory. "You two used to sit and dunk cookies in your milk, together out on the back porch, didn't you? Lord, how the two of you would talk, and you not more than a sapling."

John didn't know whether to laugh or cry—the chair, the antique end table with lace doilies and glass figurine birds, the framed photographs of her and Preacher, young and smiling. Again, the strong sense of time arrested, days and days gone by without variation and yet also without him, a man who long ago moved out of frame just as a beautiful photograph was taken.

"My, my," Ruth said, shaking her head. "Who could have imagined? It seems like only yesterday you were barely knee-high to a grasshopper."

He bit into the cookie and a million flavors rushed through him, and he felt himself surely shrinking into the chair, clothes hanging big and baggy and feet lifting off the floor to dangle. Here, again, in this warm, welcoming place where he had often come to feel safe.

"Let's visit a spell before you see Preacher." She sat on the end of the couch nearest his chair. She did not lower her voice, even though her husband was only in the next room of the tiny house. "I told him you were coming. Johnny, he may not know you. But he might. He's had a decent morning. The nurse, sweetest little thing, was in early, and Preacher felt good enough to sit up in his wheelchair. That's a good thing. He's not always able to anymore. The days run good and bad now."

"I'm sorry, Miss Ruth," he said.

"It's the strangest thing," she said, dabbing at the corners of her eyes with a handkerchief that seemed to appear magically in her hand. "He can still quote whole passages from his beloved King James like nobody's business, just sharp as a tack, I mean to tell you. And then some days he...he doesn't even know who I am. *Sweet* Preacher."

"Yes, ma'am."

"You knew him at his strongest, Johnny, his best. I've watched him falling away from himself, from me...sometimes he has no idea what year it is, doesn't know one day to the next if he's a little boy or an old man." Her eyes brightened with something that looked to John like both melancholy and joy. "But I guess the truth is that's how God sees us, anyway. Young, old, it's all the same to him. And wherever Preacher goes back in time, I know the Lord is going with him. Sometimes, Johnny," she said, "I wish I could go with him, too."

"I'm so sorry, Miss Ruth," he said again. "I know how hard this must be."

"No," she said, straightening. "Sad. But not that hard. When two people give their hearts, it's for rain as well as sunshine, bad times as well as good." She smiled, and years faded. "Preacher and I made a promise, a long time ago." She said this with such simple and dignified finality, John felt tears coming.

"He's a lucky man," he said.

"There's not a lick of luck in it, Johnny," Ruth said. "Preacher and I were born to be together. Till death do us part. They're not just words." She looked at him with clear eyes. "God puts people together for a reason. Everything—" her gaze almost made John squirm—"everything happens according to God's plan. There are no accidents in this world. There's purpose in it all, Johnny. Even in the pain."

"Yes ma'am."

The old woman's eyes were soft and filled with love. "You know I've never been one to mince my words, Johnny."

"That's true."

"There aren't many secrets around here, you know," she said, folding her hands in her lap; they looked like little broken birds. "The whole town knew you were coming, and that you're staying in your daddy's cabin now. I see you grinning, Johnny Allen. It is almost funny, isn't it?"

"Yes, ma'am."

"Well, once you got famous—now don't *smirk*, you're surely the most famous person *I've* ever known born out of this valley—once a person gets their picture in the papers, I guess they give up their rights to privacy."

"I guess."

"But I just want you to know, Johnny, how proud Preacher and I were to follow those stories about you, about our little Johnny grown up and become a big-time author. And oh, Johnny, what a wonderful book. I just loved it." Her smile turned almost coy. "Of course, some of it got a little... well, *feisty* for my taste. But it had considerable beauty in it, Johnny. Considerable beauty."

177

"Thank you."

"I only wish Preacher had been in better shape. But he was able to read it, mostly, and on more than one occasion said how much it pleased him to see God using you in such a way."

"That means a lot to me, Miss Ruth."

"Well, you know Preacher always said you were going to make a powerful warrior one day. You've always had a good heart, Johnny, a *special* heart. Gracious, Preacher thought the world of you. He always said that for a young feller you had such a powerful appetite for the Word, always asking him questions, wanting to know what he thought of this and that scripture." She paused. "He always thought you might even follow him into the pulpit one day..." She dipped her china-thin chin a bit, and aimed her gaze. "We heard about all the other things, too, Johnny, when things got hard for you. Preacher said you'd gone to your own 'distant country,' like the prodigal son. He said that darkness can gain a foothold on the most noble of men."

John swallowed, and tried to nod.

"We prayed for you when you left home, Johnny Allen," she said. "And we prayed for your family, through it all."

"Thank you."

"Johnny." She seemed at a loss as to her next words. "I hope you know... I pray you understand how your daddy..." She spoke kindly, as if to a child. "He didn't *mean* some of the things. He didn't always know what he was doing. A lot of the time, he wasn't his true self." John saw her take a short breath, considering. Then, "And at the end, your mama wasn't herself, either. Both of them lost their way. That wasn't who they truly were. But our God of grace knew them, all along."

"Yes, ma'am." He felt like running away.

"Just like you, son," she said. "Sometimes we lose our way. Some of us get lost in such a way that we can't find our way back. Preacher always believed your daddy to be a good man, underneath, and there for a while Big John would come and sit with Preacher, talk to him. But finally he quit coming." She dabbed again at her eyes. "Jesus loves us all the same, Johnny, sinner and saint. And Jesus loved your mama and daddy, too. He doesn't love us any less when we're lost. He might even love us more..." She hesitated, perhaps perceiving she had said too much. But there wasn't a hint of anything coming from her other than affection. "The important thing," she said, "is that you chose the road home."

He tried to nod.

She stared at him, saw into him, and suddenly he couldn't keep from looking down at the floor. He wished he had cleaned up more, at least put on a nicer shirt, shaved. He ground his teeth, trying to control the emotions heaving at his insides, wanting very much to be held in her arms. But he sat very still. Tears glistened in both their eyes. Ruth just let him sit for a moment, then stood.

"Let's see how he's doing," she said, then disappeared down the short hallway. In a moment she returned, motioning him to follow. "He's good, Johnny," she said. "Come see him."

John stood in the doorway. Preacher sat slumped in a wheelchair, rolled up close to the window, his face tilted toward an imagined sun.

Ruth walked John up close and sat him in a straight-back chair.

"Preacher," she said, soft but firm. "Johnny Allen has come to see you."

The white head turned. The deep-furrowed face worked at focusing. And Ruth lightly touched John's shoulder, then turned and left the room, closing the door behind her.

Of all the changes John had seen since returning home, this one was most profound—the raven-black hair had turned sparse and wool-white, the rock jaw now loose and half-hanging. John lay his hand on the old man's skeletal shoulder.

"Hello, Preacher," he said.

The old eyes of power squinted and then widened.

"Johnny?"

"Yes, sir. It's me."

A withered hand reached. "My Lord," the old man said, the voice that had once shaken the stained-glass windows with awesome authority now weak and rasping. Preacher touched the bony fingers of one hand to John's sleeve. The other arm lay in his lap like a dead, twisted branch.

"Johnny."

"It's good to see you, Preacher. It's been a long time." John had no idea what else to say.

"Time," the old man said, and then grinned at some secret joke. *"Time."* The once-steely eyes were smoky blue with cataracts, obscured by drifting, feathery clouds. Then, as if a breeze had suddenly lifted, the haze thinned and the old man's gaze locked with John's. "What've you been up to, Johnny? You behaving yourself?"

"Yes, sir."

"Good." The barrel chest now seemed collapsed beneath an orange wool sweater, as though someone had kicked it in. "What a blessing. The Lord has brought you here. How long has it been?"

"Sixteen years."

"Sixteen years." Tears appeared like melting snow. "My, my."

John could barely speak. "I've sure missed you, Preacher."

"I've missed you, Johnny. Never stopped praying for you. Never."

"I appreciate that, Preacher. I sure do." John saw the old eyes fade and the head turn again to the window. Cold rain

180

peppered the glass. "I'm about ready for some warm weather, Preacher." He tried to sound cheerful. "How about you?"

The shrunken face did not move. *"And the parched ground shall become a pool, and the thirsty land springs of water: in the habitation of dragons, where each lay, shall be grass with reeds and rushes..."* This took all of the old man's labored breath.

Preacher suddenly brightened.

"Spring has come," he said. "Look out there, will you? God's beauty is bursting forth. I'm getting married, you know. *Behold, thou art fair, my beloved, yea, pleasant: also our bed is green...* This is going to be *some* day, Johnny."

"Yes, sir."

"I've been so nervous, couldn't sleep last night, can't stand this waiting." He paused to reel in a hissing breath between remaining teeth. "I had to get up at the crack of dawn and work in the garden all morning, just to keep back the jitters."

John squeezed the old man's hand. Preacher's face showed alarm.

"Do I know you?"

"Yes, sir. I'm John... Johnny Allen."

"What *time* is it?"

"Three-thirty."

"Oh." The eyes calmed, but only some. "Still, I'd better get myself cleaned up. Can't get married smelling like a scarecrow." He smiled. "Have you met her, my Ruthie?"

"Yes, sir, I have. She's a beauty, Preacher. A real beauty."

"That she is, son." The old man winked, then closed his eyes. "I'm deeply blessed," he said. His chin slowly lowered onto his chest.

"I've been wanting to come see you for a long time," John said softly, not sure if the old man was awake. "There've been so many times through the years, times when I'd think about you, and remember things you taught

181

me." Preacher didn't stir. John leaned forward in his chair, closer to the old man's face. He watched him like this for some time before speaking.

"I've meant to come see you ever since I got back to town, but for some reason I just never could. I think maybe I was...afraid for you to see me now, the way I am. Time slips away so fast. I guess I always felt I'd have plenty of time for everything, time to come home, to the people I loved." His words quavered with grief. "You were always here for me, Preacher," he said. "When I was little, when it wasn't safe for me anywhere else, I always knew I could come to you. I knew you'd love me, no matter what. You and Miss Ruth would take me in. And we'd laugh together, and everything would seem okay. This was the one place where I felt I could be myself, Preacher. The one place where I didn't feel scared. The truth is, Preacher, I don't really know what happened to me...to my faith. My faith used to be strong, strong enough not be afraid." He wiped his sleeve across his face. "And lately, it's like that old fear has come back, worse than ever. I'm afraid of what's happening to me, Preacher..."

The old man groaned a rattling, morbid sound, and then his eyes flashed open so sudden and clear it made John jerk back his head a few inches. But the eyes were both wise and kind. "It's not faith you're lacking, Johnny," Preacher said. "None of us have enough faith. It's not *faith* that casts out our fear, son, but *perfect love*..." And then his eyes again closed, and everything about his countenance became still as death; it seemed to John that the old man had stopped breathing.

"Preacher?"

"Yes?" The pale face turned. "Oh, it's *you*." The voice hardened. A semblance of strength dug new rows in the old man's deep-furrowed forehead. "Are you sober?"

"Sir?"

"I told you last time. Don't come into this church drunk again, acting like a damned fool."

"I'm...not drunk, Preacher." Fear and shame rushed through John's heart.

The smoky old eyes bore in.

"I have no fear of you, Big John. You may be able to make everyone else cower, but you'll not do so to me." He inched closer, color coming back into the glare. "Your breast-beating will not intimidate *me*, Big John Allen. Unclench your fists, reach out your hands! You know you are loved, John, you know it. You have tasted the very blood of the Lamb. *But now, after that ye have known God, or rather are known of God, how turn ye again to the weak and beggarly elements, whereunto ye desire again to be in bondage?*"

John's eyes were locked into Preacher's now. "I can't..."

"Your bondage is already broken, John. You just don't see it. You hold the key to your cage—*And, behold, the angel of the Lord came upon him, and a light shined in the prison: and he smote Peter on the side, and raised him up, saying, Arise up quickly. And his chains fell off from his hands...*"

"I am a sinful man," John heard someone say, the voice not his own.

Preacher nodded. "But aren't we all, John. *We should not lust after evil things, as they also lusted. Neither be ye idolaters.* Each of us will find ourselves in the wilderness sooner or later, Big John. *Neither let us tempt Christ, as some of them also tempted, and were destroyed of serpents...*"

"I've tried, Preacher."

"You've relied upon your own power!" For a moment swagger overpowered infirmity, and the old man straightened as much as his time-bowed back would allow. *"There hath no temptation taken you but such as is common to man: but God is faithful, who will not suffer you to be tempted above that ye are able..."* His gaze bore in hard as ice. "God *loves* you, Big

John," he said. "And there's not a blessed thing you can do about it."

And then a breaking tenderness, reaching up, touching John's cheek, and when the hand pulled back there were teardrops trembling on his fingertips. Preacher stared in wonder.

The old eyes widened.

"Johnny?"

The younger man came to himself. "Yes," he said, breathing again.

"My *God*. How long has it been?"

"Not...not all that long, Preacher."

The dried lips cracked into a smile. "Where've you been?"

"Traveling."

"Hmm. See anything worth seeing?"

"Not so much."

"Maybe you weren't looking in the right places."

"Maybe not, sir."

Preacher turned his head to the window and world beyond.

"And now you've come home. *And he arose, and came to his father. But when he was yet a great way off, his father saw him, and had compassion, and ran, and fell on his neck, and kissed him...*"

John struggled not to sob.

The old man again grew silent, then sighed, and sat slumped and dispassionate in the way of dying men.

"*My days are like a shadow that declineth...and I am withered like grass...*" Preacher stared out into the gray, grieving sky.

Finally the old man turned and touched John's coat sleeve.

"I know where she *hides* them," he whispered conspiratorially.

"Sir?"

"She thinks I have no *idea*, but I've *seen* her." The dry lips cracked into a grin. "She thinks I'm asleep sometimes, but that gal has to get up pretty early in the morning to fool ol' Preacher." He cut his watery eyes toward the door and pulled John closer down to his mouth. "Bottom drawer of the dresser, left side, all the way to the back. How about it, Johnny?"

"What..."

"Come *on*, don't be a *sissy*. If you get them, I'll *share*."

"Okay." John whispered now, too.

The old man nodded and winked. "I'll keep a look-out." His face shone with mischief. John knew he could not refuse, regardless of the possible consequences. He went to the antique bureau and knelt on one knee; the drawer creaked when he pulled.

"*Ssshh!*" Preacher's eyes were wide.

John froze. "*Sorry,*" he mouthed, squatting down, the old bed between him and the door, an accomplice now too deep in crime to turn back. Slowly this time, he got the drawer open enough to reach in. Smooth cloth gave way to crackling plastic. He felt eight years old and terrified.

"*Yes*, boy!" The white head palsied with excitement.

John drew out a cellophane bag of multicolored jelly beans. They gleamed like precious stones.

"That's it...*easy* now," Preacher whispered, the point of his tongue tapping impatiently at his upper lip. "Close it back, now. *Hurry!*"

John came and sat. The plastic popped and crackled like fire; he was sure Ruth would catch them any minute. The old man cupped his one good shaking hand.

"*Lemon,*" Preacher said low, reverently. "The yellow ones are best. Pick me out some *lemon* ones, Johnny-boy... *that's* it, wonderful, *wonder*ful..." He chewed between a few good remaining teeth; the jelly beans made little clicking sounds rolling around inside his mouth. "Mmm..." he

185

hummed, eyes half-closed. John watched him—tasting, *really* tasting.

"Well, go on, *have* some," the old man said, and John reached into the bag and drew out bright jewels. Their colors defied the dreary day.

"I remember," Preacher said. "You like...the *red* ones."

John felt his jaw drop; he was genuinely astonished. *"Yes,"* he whispered. "Cherry. I like the *cherry* ones." He put some in his mouth.

They tasted like joy.

The old man smiled, a tiny, unashamed rivulet of drool working its way down his stubbled chin. John smiled too, desperately, at the taste of immortal summer, the two of them momentarily reborn. He felt tears on his face, and this time did not bother wiping them away. Celebrating, lamenting, for a long while looking out the window, two boys restlessly waiting for the rain to stop. John wished they could stay that way forever.

After a while Preacher reluctantly found his way back into the broken body. "You know, Johnny," he said, his words again weighted with weariness, "in all the time I've spent on this earth, I think the only thing that's surprised me much about life is how quickly it passes us by." His voice deepened, and he leaned toward the world outside as if from the edge of a high pulpit. *"For all flesh is as grass, and all the glory of man as the flower of grass. The grass withereth, and the flower thereof falleth away..."*

"Yes, sir."

"All men are grass," the old man said, and his good hand pawed once at his emaciated chest as if he could not believe his heart was trapped inside it. "The whole thing's run by me like I was standing still." His head slowly swiveled, eyes glazing and then clearing, back and forth through space like a human time machine. "What's the old hymn?" A strange sound began forming deep in Preacher's chest, and John realized that somewhere song was being sung in the old man's soul—*"We fly forgotten as a dream..."*

Preacher looked up. "It doesn't seem *possible*, Johnny."

"No sir, it doesn't."

"Listen, one day you'll see. It's just so *fast*. Enjoy it now, while you're still *little*. Take it all in, Johnny—*all* of it. What a holy privilege, just to be awake in it, breathing it in, watching creation unfold itself anew each morning. My *God*, Johnny. Can you just imagine what heaven must be like? Through grace we are recreated, like the seasons, son, *eternally* recreated. Oh, what a *glorious* world..."

And then he was gone again, to the window. He sat like this for several still minutes, and John sat silently with him. Cold crept in through the panes.

Preacher turned—"Do you have the ring?"

"Yes, sir. I have it."

"Thank *God*. Hang on to it, for the love of Heaven!" He rubbed weakly at his chin. "I need a shave. What time is it?"

"Still plenty of time."

"Good." Eyes clearing—"Johnny, I had a talk with your daddy yesterday. He won't talk to hardly anybody anymore, but he'll talk to me, by God."

"Yes, sir."

"You know what I told him?"

"No."

Preacher reached, and for the first time his grip felt like iron. "I told him I *loved* him."

"I'm glad. I'm glad you did that, Preacher."

The old man smiled. "Have you met her? My girl is the sweetest thing ever walked the earth. Sweetest thing. *The beams of our house are cedar, and our rafters of fir. For, lo, the winter is past, the rain is over and gone...* A woman's heart is the most mysterious of things, young man. But only God can arrange it, *bless* it. Everything else is dust." A thin smile fought to the surface of his face. "Love makes us young, and grows us up, too. *The flowers appear on the earth; the time of the singing of birds is come...* You'll see soon enough, Johnny—Love will sweep you up and change you, ruin you, *save* you if you let it. But *watch* for it. God's got somebody already planned for you, Johnny. Don't let her get by you. Love makes us *young.* But there's only so much time..." And then his strength was gone. He turned away and this time would not turn back. The white head drooped gently forward.

Without thinking John stood and quietly returned the bag of candy to the drawer. Then he bent and scooped up what was left of Preacher and laid him in the bed. The old man felt light as a bag full of fallen leaves.

Preacher slept.

The rain wept at the windows.

A long and still moment hung over them, John standing at the bedside. Finally, he pulled his chair up close and sat. He leaned forward with his elbows on his knees until his face was inches from the old man's. And very quietly, as if sharing some great secret, John said, "I don't know what to do, Preacher. I was hoping you could tell me what to do." And then what was left of his heart surrendered. Silent sobs shook him. "I guess I came so you could save me," he said, "or tell me how to save myself. I always thought you were the one person in this whole world who wasn't afraid of anything. You weren't scared of life, or of my daddy, even. You had something I wanted, Preacher. You had courage. And you had love. Maybe they're the same thing, in a way. You and Ruth had faith, and each other, and that was more than enough. That's the kind of love I want more than anything in the whole world. And I guess I thought that after all this time I'd come see you again, and you could tell me how to not be so afraid. How to love without being afraid." John covered the old man's hand, brown and wrinkled as walnuts, with his own. "I wish you could tell me, Preacher," he said. "Tell me one more time who I really am..."

And though he could think of nothing else to say something held him there for a while in the darkening shadows, the room washing away, until all he could do was lean down to the old man's ear and whisper soft as rain...

"Congratulations, Preacher. She's a special girl."

Just before closing the door behind him, John heard a stirring, and turned to see the old man staring straight up at the ceiling, smiling—

"Prettiest church I've ever been in," he said.

16

Change was coming, and the whole world knew it.

John woke and felt morning melting subtly onto the cabin. The air still hung cold but with more life in it, and the light coming in did so playfully, reflecting off the ceiling and walls, chasing out the heavy hues with clean shades of yellow. The sunshine gathered in shallow pools on the floor and rose up the walls.

He lay listening. Humming. Fluttering. The cautious emergence of sleeping things stirred. The vibration had him up and onto the porch barefoot, and even the squeak-slap of the screen door made new music.

At first things didn't look all that different. But a hint of hidden warmth had been smuggled in overnight and was now establishing itself on the light morning air. Insects seemed to appear out of nothingness, resurrected from underground tombs. Bumblebees slow-bobbed in the air like little freed birthday balloons. Birds tentatively tested their voices. Robins roused magically from the earth and hopped across the clearings, while finch and sparrow and thrush animated the high tree limbs and low brush. Silence surrendered to song. Blue seeped slowly back into the sky.

John had seen signs in the last few days, faint stirrings, the occasional glimpse. But now it seemed that while he'd slept someone had snuck into the world and spruced things up. The flat frost on the ground between cabin and woods took on the softer glistenings of dew. A few patches of wild onions appeared where only bare ground had been before, and some of the brown grass leading down into the trees had already begun shading to green.

Though still mostly bare, the woods now showed signs of vibrancy that had seemingly appeared overnight—the earliest, coral-tinted buds on the many maples woven throughout the rounded hillsides now shone bronze-burnished and blushing, the face of the forest having rouged its cheeks like a hopeful lover. Along the base of giant trunks sporadic wildfires of color threatened to erupt—the earliest sparks of bright yellow flames from wild forsythia along the tangled undergrowth, and throughout the thickets the early violet flare of redbud trees.

He stood still and was soon accepted, trusted. The birds danced shamelessly in mating rituals, and unseen creatures scurried along the forest floor. Looking up, John scanned the treetops.

The hawk sat high and silent.

Through the trees beyond the cabin John saw the sun-speckled river winding itself around wooded banks and opening wide into the opulent morning. All around him brief brushstrokes of new color were being added to a grateful canvas. He watched it all with the eyes of a boy, his own blood coursing through him like a rushing creek after the thaw.

He felt like walking.

He quickly dressed and ate, then headed down toward the water. His breath still came out in frosty puffs, but the river shook along its surface in anticipation of something wonderful. From an unseen distance came the mocking laughter of ducks. John threw stones and continued along the river's edge, rising up to the trail that would wind around a point above the reservoir toward his brother's place. It was a good distance, but he had grown stronger.

Moving with a brisk step through the thick brush on a foot-cleared trail he could reach Joey's in a little more than two hours. He felt like he could walk forever.

The woods were waking, and the man with them. Somehow, he became aware of a new wholeness, as if all that had happened—the days and nights of solitude, his new familiarity with the habitat of his memories, and now this fresh morning—had begun healing him. The cool air carried on it a kind of holiness, like the first day of creation, his world new and garden-like again, and a missing peace brushed past him on the fragrance of things coming alive. If only for a moment, everything for which his heart had been eternally homesick seemed almost within reach. He knelt and touched the coolness of his native soil with the palms of both hands.

It didn't take long to find a good, solid walking stick. He listened to the crunch of his father's boots along the leaves and rocks. In the deep shade beneath a thick-vined canopy, the forest floor had begun adorning itself with tiny hyacinth, periwinkle, violets.

Halfway around the point the land leaned steeply down, the timber darkened, and the air grew damp. The earth in places lay cut open, jagged shelves of ancient shale jutting out low and layered through exposed red clay like the folded blades of a pocketknife. He knew the creek ahead, could hear it running with the last remains of melted snow. The land tilted toward a ravine choked with heavy underbrush; he used his stick and the soles of his boots to flatten the thorns and thistle that clawed and clung to his clothes. Elusive brown thrush skittered secretively in the hedged thickets.

High banks rounded down onto cool, moss-covered earth and rock. The creek gully was old, thirty feet across and fifteen deep. Using exposed roots as hand-holds he made his way down the steep slope, until he hit the muddy shelf of creek bed beside shallow, gurgling water. Here the world felt old and immutable. Massive root systems of ancient trees emerged from the earthen banks like the petrified tentacles of giant sea monsters, exposed by countless years of water weaving and wearing away at the land. Some of the trees had over time yawned out across the water, their massive trunks deformed and bending back toward the nourishing sun. Others had not survived time; unknown years of battle had ended with entire root systems upturned, lifting with them huge mounds of earth taller than a man.

John made his way along the dryer edges of the creek bed, past and over boulders and graveled shell, occasionally pausing to listen to the wondrous quiet. High above him long, lean branches struggled for space, the grappling limbs of sweetgum and poplar rubbing and creaking together in the low-murmured moans of some secret language. Squirrels chased each other up and around tall trunks.

He closed his eyes and listened. Birdsong rang everywhere, and a boorish blue jay railed and ranted, jealous of the music. And the man knew that the woods were a living thing, entwined with and essential to his existence. Surrounded by and enclosed in them, he felt young. Listening, breathing, tasting. Clean sunlight jeweled its way through a thickening canopy of new leaves and lay dappled across the forest floor. And the languid morning passed.

Finally he found a way leading back to the sky, a fallen tree creating a ramp, and he scrambled up to the opposite bank. As he stood there the heavens exhaled, and strong, warm gusts jostled the treetops. Bright blue shone between white clouds.

He moved into the clearing, and from there watched the forest rejoicing like an ecstatic multitude all around him, waving their arms back and forth in the sky, overcome by the spirit, rejoicing in the coming salvation of spring.

A celebration had begun.

He took his time. The tentative joy he felt made him want to slow the day, and so he lingered here and there, sitting beneath trees and on rock ledges. For a while this would calm him, until the old restlessness again lifted him to his feet.

As John neared the clearing that would take him to his brother's place, an unexpected dread began settling onto him. Out of nowhere, fear.

He smelled it before he saw it. Then ahead—four huge black birds, shoulders hunched over the half-eaten carcass of a deer, ripping up red strips in blood-streaked beaks. John's footsteps startled them, and sent them heaving heavily up on wide, warning wings.

John walked faster.

He broke into the clearing and saw the trailer, its windows dark. He was still fifty yards away but broke into a full run across the yard and up the concrete steps. He threw open the door without knocking.

Joey lay in the middle of the floor, tangled and motionless. John could hear himself shouting, *Joey, Joey!* He rolled his brother over onto his back and touched his face—white cheeks, eyes sunken and dilated, lips powder-blue and cold. Putting his ear to his brother's mouth he felt only the barest breath. Again and again he called out Joey's name and pumped at his chest and breathed into his mouth, counting, praying *Sweet Jesus, sweet Jesus!* And somewhere far in himself he realized that only in times when he had feared death, his own or someone else's, had he called out that name.

Joey lay cold and still.

The phone shook in his hands so badly it took two tries to dial for help. And then John knelt at his brother's side and began all over again.

"Oh, Johnny," Maggie said. They met and embraced in the waiting area of the emergency room. "Is he..."

"They ran me out of there. They were working hard..."

"What..."

"They just don't know yet. He stopped breathing for a while."

"Oh, God, Johnny."

"The ambulance got there pretty fast, considering how far out he lives. For a while they thought about moving him to a bigger hospital. But they've stabilized him. They say he'll make it, but won't let anyone in to see him yet."

Maggie pulled away, her face now more angry than frightened. "I am so *sick* of this! What was he *thinking*?" She gripped his arms tight enough to draw blood. "What *is* it with us, anyway?" And again she turned to tears. "Doesn't he know he's killing himself?"

John said, "He's not afraid of dying, Maggie. He's afraid of living." But Maggie could only shake her head.

They sat down on dingy, worry-worn chairs.

"And where have *you* been, Johnny? It's been weeks and you haven't even dropped by. I've worried..."

"I've been...working."

"Ellen says to leave you be. Said you *art*ists need *pri*-vacy. Sounds like a bunch of bull to me, but what do *I* know?"

"I should have let you know I was okay, I guess."

"I *guess*." Her face softened. "Oh, Johnny, I'm sorry. This isn't the time. It's just all so..."

"I know. Come here, Maggie." He let her cry a while. Once she had quieted he loosened his arm and let her lean back.

"There's nothing we can do right now," he said. "We're gonna be here a while." He looked into her eyes and forced a grin. "Buy you a drink?"

They sat on a wooden bench out on the open lawn beside the little hospital, drinking bitter coffee from plastic cups. The late afternoon wind still carried enough chill to make Maggie shiver, but John put his jacket around her shoulders and she hugged it tight in front. Whenever the sun broke through between fast-passing clouds, a nice warmth soaked into them.

They talked about growing up.

"I always felt like I had to hold everything together," she said. "Like I had to be the mother for you and Joey."

"You did all you could, Maggie."

"But it was never enough."

"It wasn't supposed to be your job."

"But things had to get done, Johnny. You managed to keep out of the way, out of trouble for the most part. But little Joey, he was always in a fix. No matter how many times I tried to tell him, he'd end up on the bad side of Daddy's temper."

"I know. I always felt like I should rescue him. But I didn't know how." Sadness pulled at him. "I know things got even worse when I left…"

"Things were bad before you left, Johnny."

"Yeah."

"Poor Mama, sitting all alone, day in and day out, taking those pills. And us kids always walking through life on eggshells, trying to figure out some way to feel…"

"Safe."

"Yeah, safe. And me always washing and cleaning like some hired maid, while you hid out in your room with your books. Some days I could get everything quiet, get Joey settled into something, and we'd all relax a little."

"Yeah."

"Like the whole house was taking a big, deep breath."

"I remember."

"Some days were good."

"Yeah," John said. "There'd be no yelling or screaming, no bad sounds, things breaking…"

"And sometimes we'd all have fun together, wouldn't we?" Maggie smiled. "All of us together."

196

"Yeah, playing cards."

"Uh-huh. At the kitchen table. I'd make popcorn..."

"And Daddy would be okay, funny like he could be sometimes, and he'd get us all laughing..."

"Yeah, even Mama."

"Even Mama."

They sat for a little while without speaking, their faces offered up to the sun. Winter seemed for a moment all but beaten.

"Oh, Johnny."

"I know."

"I married two alcoholics. *Two*."

"Uh-huh."

"The first was sweet when he drank. So I figured he was nothing like Daddy. And the second one...well, you know, Leonard was mean as a snake. But sweet or mean, they turned out to be pretty much the same kind of men, really. Pitiful." Maggie looked at her brother. "And I took *care* of them. I looked after them like they were my...children." She seemed quietly astonished. "I moved out from home and thought I was finally free. I went just across the neighborhood and tried to create a new family. A well and whole family. And then I came back and forth, taking care of both, *mother*ing everybody." She looked tired. "Is that what I did?"

"I think so, Mags."

Her mouth hung slightly open. "This is not how I thought things would turn out," she said. "This is not what I thought my life would be." She paused. "But then Ellen was born. And life became about her. And I'm glad. I can dream for *her* now."

John realized at that moment that he had never considered what his sister's own hopes might have been, long ago. He hadn't thought of her as someone who might ever have dreamed of faraway places, dreams too big for their little town to hold. And seeing this now, he felt more selfish than ever. He understood, as he always had, that she was the better person.

Finally Maggie said: "Johnny, what is *wrong* with us? Mama, Daddy, you and Joey, and *me*—Lord, I wouldn't know love if it snuck up and bit me on the backside." She leaned back and held a wad of tissues under her nose. "All three of us ran away, didn't we? In different ways, into our own worlds. Is that why you drank, Johnny?"

He sat still for a moment. "It's more complicated than that, Maggie. But yeah, that's some of it, I guess. It's nobody else's fault, though. I drank because I liked the way it made me feel. Braver, somehow. The same thing's true with Joey. We drink because...because it works for us, in a weird sort of way."

"Sure doesn't seem like it's working to *me*."

"I know. It's insane. But we don't quit until it stops working for us, Mags. And as hard as it is to understand, I think Joey's drinking is still working for him."

She could only stare at him with defeated eyes that said she didn't understand. He decided to tell his sister a secret.

"My whole life, Maggie," he said, "my whole life I've felt afraid."

"*Really?*" Her head tilted. "I always thought you were the only brave one."

"I became a good actor."

"Hmm. We all did, I guess. All of us going into our separate rooms, separate roles." She touched his hand. "Maybe we still do."

They fell silent.

Finally Maggie looked right at him. "What are you going to do, Johnny? Why did you come back here?"

"I'm not sure. I thought I knew. But nothing's been what I expected, what I'd hoped."

"What were you hoping for?"

He thought about how to answer, but couldn't put it into words.

His sister touched his arm. "Was it Jessie?"

This helped him start. "Yes, in a way. I knew the time would come when I'd have to see her, speak to her. What I needed to say to her...it just wasn't something I could put nice and neat into a letter. I felt I owed her more than that." He reached down and pulled a single clover from the ground and, remembering, rolled the stem between thumb and forefinger; the little leaves spun like a propeller. "I needed to see you too, Mags, and Joey. To tell you..." His throat tightened around the words. "To tell you how sorry I was."

"Johnny."

"No, Maggie, it's okay. It's part of what I have to do, to take responsibility, finally grow up..." His voice trailed off. He put the clover stem between his lips. It tasted faintly of summer. "But it's not what I expected," he said at last.

"How?" Her voice was gentle, patient.

"That's hard to say." John barely shook his head. "It's like I fell asleep and had a long, detailed dream, Mags, a dream of a faraway place, all fantasy and lights. And when I woke up it was like no time had passed at all, in some ways, no more than a single night, maybe, and all the years I thought I'd lived in the dream vanished the moment I opened my eyes." A mockingbird scolded from a nearby branch.

Maggie took her time before saying: "Life really *has* gone on, Johnny."

"Yes. But not at the same pace, in the same way. When I look in the mirror now..."

"What?"

"I see...someone else."

Maggie heard her brother's voice darken. She remained still. "I know who you really are, Johnny," she said. "From the moment I saw you at my door I knew you hadn't come home to stay." She moved closer and curled into his shoulder. "But for now, brother, I'm awfully glad you're here."

"Joey."

The eyelids fluttered but didn't open.

"Joey, can you hear me? It's Johnny." He looked down and saw someone old and worn—needles and tubes coming out, face the color of old paper, the machines hissing and sucking air like a wounded animal. And in that face he saw much more than his brother. He saw the labored breath of a dying old man and a struggling infant, in and out, the tireless face of birth and death, heaven and earth, gods and monsters. He saw the face of his mother and his father, and he saw himself, too, wrapped in the same white burial sheets with needles in his arms. He wanted to run away. His fists clenched and he bit at the inside of his mouth until blood came.

"Johnny?" Joey's eyes squinted open. His voice was weak and muffled.

"I'm here, little bro. Take it easy. Don't try to talk."

"Shoofar."

"Yeah. Stay still. You're in the hospital in town."

"Wha'pend..."

"You took too many pills, Joey."

"Shoofar." Tears and a grin both fought their way through the tape and tubes.

"You moron," John said, touching his brother's hair.

17

Jessie stood in the open field, waist-deep in waves of broomstraw.

The wind was warm and wonderful. She held out her hands so that the soft tops of the wild, golden grass lightly tickled her palms as it swayed. With her eyes closed she rode Sky, leaning low over the broad neck, clean air in her face.

When her eyes opened, everything had grown old.

She knew that by returning here she had betrayed not only Tuck but also her own heart. But now the numbness felt almost tolerable; her own life seemed to have been forfeited, her will killed. The sun was sinking behind the barn for the third time since their meeting, and she felt both remorseful and relieved. Still, she had come again, and would stay till dark.

In some ways she did not feel surprised that he hadn't come back; she had lost faith in his returning long ago. Three days before, she had left with the halfhearted hope that their encounter would finally conclude things, closing a too-long opened book. She had emptied her heart, at least the part she wished known, turned and walked away on a prayed-for strength beyond her own, the unsteady earth beneath her feet threatening to ruin everything. Aiming her eyes toward the highway and the truck, she had clenched her jaw and refused to turn or look back, and somehow escaped alive. She had said the words, at long last, and thought—prayed—that it would be enough. In his letter Johnny had only promised to come to the barn every day until he saw her, spoke to her. And although now it barely seemed real, that had happened.

But it was not enough; thoughts of him still wore away at her. She had not spoken her full heart. She felt only half-healed, still less than whole. And though she hated herself for it, she dared allow herself to wonder if it had been enough for him, either.

When she had finally returned home that evening after seeing Johnny, the sense of incompleteness encircled and inhabited her, only perhaps more profoundly than before. While Tuck was at work, Jessie moved from room to room as if searching for something lost. The afternoon encounter now seemed a distant dream. She had seen his face—perhaps it had indeed been nothing but a dream, and he a ghost. Whatever the truth, hopeful prayers of closure had failed her. Seeing Johnny had somehow deepened her loneliness.

It did not feel like goodbye.

And so today she stood in the untended pasture, the wind blowing across her face, carrying on it the memory of belonging they had shared in this place. She let the never-quite-forgotten feelings fill her like light through long-shuttered windows.

Occasionally she felt a kind of presence, and turned only to see the brown churning sea of grass around her, and the broad bordering shore of woods. Each time, her heart raced and she took a cautious breath, both thankful and crushed that he was not there.

What's wrong with me, God?

Now the unusually warm March winds lifted. Treetops inhaled and shrugged away their long sleep. The radiant meadow hypnotized her.

Momma. I wish you were here. I wish you could tell me what to do...

Jessie watched a fleet of clouds sailing fast overhead on the full white sails of an armada, their flat, blue-bottomed hulls skimming fast across the sky as if...as if retreating from something.

Something did not feel right.

There—a dark, menacing warship gathering along the western horizon, thunderheads moving toward the swelling fields.

For three tender, torturous days, Jessie had waited.

This time, sunset would come early.

* * *

John had stayed near Joey.

Once his brother had grown strong enough, John had done all he could to convince him to enter a treatment facility only a few hours away; he'd offered to pay for it, cajoled, pleaded. But Joey would have none if it, and after only three days had insisted on leaving the hospital and going back to his trailer.

"I ain't goin' to no funny farm," he said. "Take me home."

"It's a treatment center, little bro. They're not so bad. I can tell you all about them if you really want to know."

"I really *don't*." Joey had stared hard at his brother from his seat in the car. "Take me home."

"I'll be fine, Johnny." Joey seemed relieved to be back inside the dark, dingy box, safe in his corner chair. "It was just an accident, for gosh sakes. I already told you that. Shoot fire, that woman asked me a hundred questions, over and over. She *said* I could go home. I just...messed up, that's all."

"You almost died."

"I'll be more careful."

"No you won't. You'll be less and less careful." John waved his arm at the mess around them. "Look at this, Joey. Is this how you want to live?"

Joey looked up with an expression different from any John had seen before: hurt, angry, disappointed. "How is it you, of all people, figure you can tell *me* how to *live*?"

John stopped cold, and swallowed hard. "I can't," he said.

"No," Joey said, "you can't."

It was already late afternoon when John left the trailer.

He felt more foolish than anything else; he knew there was little chance she would ever return. By the time he had walked from the road to the barn, less than an hour's light remained. But the skies were unusually dark already. The air felt alive and dangerous. He walked into the fields and listened.

Whispers.

Tilting his head, he closed his eyes and parted his lips and tried to taste something suddenly not hidden. His blood warmed and he felt the feeling fly in on ageless wings, as real as ever, this thing that had been too old and torturous for them then. Now the brutally beautiful passion that had always quivered between them shuddered through him anew, so true and real he turned and looked all around him across the empty fields.

...almost as if she's been here...

Electricity tingled against his skin; low rumbles shook the earth; the woods whispered warning. John pulled his jacket tighter against the wind, and headed for his car.

* * *

When Jessie walked into the house a dull dread penetrated her, and she knew Tuck had not been sleeping. She found him in the bedroom pulling on his boots.

"Tuck."

He stood. "Where've you been, Jessie?"

She could not speak. Their eyes met.

"I warned him," he said. Something in his voice frightened her.

"Tuck, I...this is my fault. I was alone. He wasn't there..."

Tuck looked down at her. "Don't you worry, Jessie. I'm gonna take care of things."

And she realized that in all of her husband's anger there was none directed toward her. None. She felt sick, not sure she could stand.

"No, Tuck," she said weakly, but his face was red and set. She reached for his arm.

"This won't take long," he said, ignoring her touch. He was out the door, her hand holding nothing.

* * *

A storm was coming.

John sat on the porch, watching. Far to the west, a deep purple mountain had formed, the squall line crawling up low and ominous on the western horizon.

Enough light remained for him to see the hawk perched patiently, high in its favorite oak, steadying itself against the wind. The wary woods waited; trees locked arms and readied for the blow.

John found the scene fascinating. All his childhood he had instinctively gauged the internal turning of his universe by the cyclical seasons. Growing up in this place, with its primal patterns setting the pace of his existence, the boy had observed the sure shape and certainty of time itself. Back then all of it made sense, the tireless earth moving to a rich, rhyming rhythm as old as time.

205

But in recent years he had lived too long in a place of one continuous season, a place never fully dark, never resting, a land bent on cheating time. Staring out now into the wild sky, he realized just how much he had missed watching the world writhe through the labor pains of new birth. He saw now that without all this he had been only half-living, removed from the core of who he was. He now knew these woods had been trying to speak into what was left of his heart, ever since he'd driven back across that bridge.

Far out over the water, but coming—the peculiar copper-cobalt cast of clouds harboring hailstorms, or worse. Now winter would rail against the coming spring, cold air clashing against warm, and the deep-southern storms would stomp and rage as they had for a million jealous years. He grew drunk on the air's dangerous energy, and his eyes grew heavy.

"You don't look so good, boy."

From behind closed eyes John saw the awful face, blood-drained and pale. "I'm okay," he said.

"Look real shaky to me. Need somethin' for your nerves."

"No."

"Suit yourself."

"Leave me alone."

The laugh was low and rumbling.

"Boy, I ain't even here unless you want me to be."

"I don't want you to be."

"Hmm. And yet here I sit."

"Go to hell."

The thunder-laugh broke harder, rolling from the low sky over the darkening river.

"Been there and back, boy. Been there and back."

The rockers creaked.

"We can have it either way we want it, boy, heaven or hell, right here on earth, right now..."

206

John opened his eyes at the sound of gravel growling under tires. It took him a few breaths to determine where he was. To the left of the porch he saw the truck pull up and stop. The storm was still coming; the trees had turned up the pale undersides of their young leaves. It took all of his strength to stand.

Tuck got out, took off his hat, and put it on the front seat. He closed the door, walked to about thirty feet in front of the porch, and stopped.

"This man's got somethin' that belongs to you, boy..."

The voice ran harsh-hot through him.

"Need you to come down off that porch, Johnny." Tuck spoke clear and evenly. Both hands hung free, sleeves rolled up. The wind gusted, and the big man had to raise his voice to be heard above it. "I'm fixin' to whip ya, Johnny Allen. It ain't right to whip a man on his own property."

One voice inside John only wanted to talk to Tuck, explain why he'd done what he had, shake his hand, pack the car and drive away. But then—

"What're you gonna do about it, boy?"

"Is that what you're here to do?" The voice John heard coming from his own mouth sounded low and sure and inexplicably calm. The hair tingled on his arms and neck.

"I told you I wouldn't let you hurt Jessie," Tuck said. "I told you I was only gonna warn you once."

John thought about telling him that he'd only seen Jessie the one time, but for some reason did not. "You can't run her life for her, Tuck. She has to make her own choices."

"She already has," Tuck said, his voice barely breaking. "She told me to tell you to leave her alone. She don't want you, Johnny. She said she don't want to ever see you again. She wants you to leave here forever."

John's hope folded into nothing. Dark clouds of fear and shame covered him. A lie, all of it, smoke and mirrors...

"See what I mean, boy?"

207

There was a way out.

"He owns her. But a man's always got options." The wind howled beneath the porch planks.

Then, alongside defeat came something unexpected.

"Now you see who you really are..."

John welcomed the rush of violence coming across the river, coming into him. He rolled up his sleeves, never taking his eyes off Tuck. His hands felt hard and heavy, arms strong.

Thunder rolled over them, closer now.

"Kill him."

He came off the steps and Tuck moved forward and the two men wordlessly met, fists thudding into flesh. Both threw right hands that landed; the crunch of cartilage and bone through John's knuckles intoxicated him. Both staggered back. Again and again they bore in, exchanging blows, and the skies grew black and deathly quiet.

John ducked down and hooked hard with his left at the soft place under Tuck's ribs, who grunted and bent but stayed up, swinging. Tuck's punch didn't land full, but the sheer weight of it knocked John from his feet. As he fell hard into the dirt he saw Tuck coming, and he staggered up as another arm clubbed down, throwing all he had into a punch that caught the big man's stomach. John heard the breath rush out of Tuck on a moan.

Down on one knee, Tuck looked up as John reared back, then lurched forward, chin tucked low. The blow glanced off the side of his jaw, slowing him but not enough, and then he had John's throat wrapped in both hands, rushing him backwards toward the porch rail and pinning him against the timber.

John tore down at the arms but they were hard as railroad ties. The steel hands squeezed and the dark started seeping in. He saw Tuck's face changing, closed his eyes and saw a reddening sky and heard the crackling laugh—

"You're worthless, boy!"

Rage exploded in him. He managed one last hook, short but sharp to the same spot beneath ribs, and the chokehold weakened and fell away. Tuck took two steps back and went to his knees. John collapsed in the dirt, tried to rise but couldn't. Both men sucked hard for air. But Tuck was up first and coming.

And then he stopped.

Thunderheads turned day to night. Tuck stood over John, what was left of a beaten sun reflecting off the blackness and covering both men in eerie blood-red. Tuck stood still, fists hanging at his side. For a fear-filled moment the woods went silent. Then like an angry spirit the tempest tore at the tops of the trees.

John braced for Tuck to finish him. He tried to focus, but what he saw made no sense.

Tuck was crying. He towered above, an enormous mountain with the sudden tears coming down off him in little streams.

"God forgive me," he said.

John rolled onto his side and tried to sit, pain lancing through his ribcage. He made it to one elbow. Dust swirled, blasting into his eyes. He could hardly hear the sound of sobbing make its pitiful way through the chaos.

"God forgive me," the mountain moaned again. He raised his huge head heavenward, struggling for breath, a wrathful wind whipping wildly at his clothes. "I was gonna kill him, Lord!" he shouted at the angry sky. "I was gonna murder this man..." He bent his head back down and looked at John. "And it wouldn't have mattered. It wouldn't have changed a thing." The pain in his face leached out and his features emptied of rage, became resigned, remorseful. Tuck looked like a man with all life sucked from his soul.

Rain began to fall.

"I could take your life from you, Johnny Allen," he said. "But it wouldn't matter. It wouldn't matter."

And the big man slowly turned and disappeared into the deepening storm.

John looked in the mirror and saw pain, but felt none. Half his head was covered with dirt, the collar of his shirt torn. All around his right eye the skin was already shading to purple. His lower lip showed a full gash, and half-dry blood covered his chin and part of his neck. And he felt his horrible shame rising up, his worthlessness, and he saw that all he had touched had been destroyed, everything, especially the things he loved most. He looked into the tortured face and felt already dead.

And then, as he watched, a strange thing happened.

The face smiled.

Lips pulled back from red teeth, and tears were in his eyes but he was helpless to stop the laughter that was low and deep and not his own. He reached and pressed into the wounded mouth; blood oozed and the pain surged up in him wondrously, gloriously, a searing, sensual thing. He stared at the fierce reflection for some time before splashing cold water all over his face and head and neck.

His injuries held false grace; his own blood radiated meaning. He had not realized until this moment just how much he had longed for such pain. This at last was vital, essential suffering he could see, taste, feel. The ache authenticated him in every muscle, substantiating his sense of being. The very forces of nature had granted him permission. Freedom from fear flowed over him in warm waves.

Never once did the thought feel wrong, or even unfortunate. Everything made perfect sense. All struggle fell away. The who and what of him began celebrating at the very thought of it, even before he'd walked into the kitchen and opened the cabinet. Pulling down the half-full bottle he felt a perverted peace, his purpose now solid and indisputable. He got a glass and went to the porch.

The trees shook their raised fists like an angry mob, fevered and shouting. The wind wailed against the woods and his clothes and the walls of the cabin.

He poured, then set the bottle on the crate beside the rocker. There was no real drama, none of the shame and remorse he'd rehearsed a hundred times in his head; the temporary estrangement had been farcical. He gave the glass one small, sensual swirl—legs of oily amber ran seductively down the sides. He breathed in the heady smell of escape. It was again now as it had forever been, a permanent part of him, a profane revelation of his truest self.

"Drink up."

"Don't mind if I do." A voice transformed by belonging.

And he swallowed salvation. It flowed down gracefully, burning a path through the darkness, a cleansing, courageous river of fire, the fear and loneliness and shame caught in a swift current and washed down toward their proper place in purgatory.

He drank, again and again.

The forest embraced in a blinding flash of darkness. Lightning lit the black dawn, clashing at the sky like swords. And as Heaven unleashed fury onto its cowering creation, the man walked off the porch into the gale and raised his arms in worship, daring the storm to strike him dead.

18

Jessie sat at the kitchen table, listening to the storm pound away at her home. Thunder rattled the windows. The rain fell so hard against the roof that she didn't hear the truck pulling into the drive.

Tuck came through the door, closing it quietly behind him. As he moved silently past her Jessie drew in a breath; his clothes were dirty, face bloodied. He did not look at her. She opened her mouth but no sound came out as Tuck disappeared down the hall to their bedroom. Jessie had never seen him this way, grim and oblivious, in all the years she had known him. And she had known him for nearly as long as the two of them had been alive.

She heard him hulking around in the back bedroom, opening drawers, turning on the shower. She could picture every movement, having watched him do the same things year after year. But she simply sat there, listening. The two of them inhabited the same house but, for those moments, nothing else.

Jessie could not control the contrary feelings that ebbed and flowed between her head and heart. Part of her felt guilty, but another part could not determine exactly her sins, or how or to whom she might offer penance. In a way she felt grateful for her lassitude; no matter how she tried to reach into herself for some authentic emotion, she felt little more than numb detachment. This helped mask the slow-growing fear...for Johnny, Tuck, herself.

She knew she should go to her husband, but the rain roared too heavily on the roof, and she could not rise from her chair. *Both of us just need some time to think things through*, she thought.

Jessie waited.

After interminable hours passed Tuck left the house, avoiding her, and went to work across the river, not having slept at all. He left early, around ten-thirty, as if the house with her in it made him feel too sad to stay. The two of them did not exchange a single word. And when he walked past her neither of them bothered to reach out and touch, perhaps sensing that their hands might have passed right through one another's emptiness.

Tuck headed out into the driving thunderstorm.

For several years, since Tuck had been put on graveyard shift, Jessie had lived with her environment inside-out, never quite finding any true balance with the passing of time. She had never fully adjusted to an unsettling feeling of disconnect, of something uncomfortably covert in living awake while the world sleeps. Something about it had always made her feel separate not only from her husband but from nature itself.

On this night the inverted images of day and night appeared even more pronounced. Again and again she glanced at the clock, trying to get her bearings, unsure if the sun would soon rise or set, her new day begin or end. She felt her soul would soon embark on a long, unknown journey, and she had neither map nor compass.

Once Tuck's truck had pulled out of the drive down toward the highway, she stood and walked to the bedroom mirror. She pulled the curls back from her eyes. She was not sure what the woman in the mirror would do next. And it was with some relief that she watched this stranger turn and lie down on the bed, folding her hands on her stomach, as if awaiting burial.

Finally the clock chimed once.

She stared for a long while at the ceiling, waiting, the indefinite spirit of time curling and wafting around her like colorless smoke. In the quiet she could clearly hear a steady ticking.

Twice.

The woman in the mirrored painting rose and walked to the dresser. She brushed absently at her hair, touched up the tearless eyes. There was now color in the cheeks, and new resolution in her face.

At the front door she looked out into the torrent, listening to thunder mourning off the surrounding hills.

"This won't do," she said aloud. But there was no strength in it now, not enough to hold back her longing. She took an umbrella from the entrance-way closet, and walked out into the storm.

* * *

John dreamed.

Winged demons flew at him. He raised the shotgun, leading, but each time they would vanish before he could squeeze off a shot.

"Take your time, son."

"I'm trying."

"I know." The voice was deep but kind. Johnny turned and saw his father, clean-shaven and dressed in a fine suit.

"Hi, Daddy."

"Hi, son."

"I'm so glad you're here."

"Me too."

"I guess they're gone now, huh?" The skies glowed pink and clear.

"For now. They'll come back, though."

"Will you help me?"

"I can't stay long."

"Why not?" Johnny felt like crying.

"Have to go." His father's face was young and handsome and free of pain.

"Are you happy now, Daddy?"

"Yes."

"I'm glad."

"Yes. Long time coming, son."

Johnny fearfully scanned the skies. "But what about..."

"When they come," his father said, never taking his eyes off him, *"you will have to decide."*

"Decide...what, Daddy?"

"You'll know."

"What if I can't choose?"

"We all make choices," his father said. *"Every person has to find their own way. A man always has options."* The hand reached but passed right through Johnny's face. The man's eyes saddened, just for a brief instant.

Then he was gone, the rocker still.

High above him Johnny heard a sound like chainsaws cutting through ice. He raised the gun.

"Here they come..."—guttural, chair groaning, the smell of whiskey and cigarettes covering everything like a cloud. *"You have to LEAD 'em, boy!"* The gun now too heavy to lift, barrel big as a tree trunk, buzz saws clawing their way down from a bloodied sky, screeching like bats, a relentless droning, droning, louder...

"Get ready, boy. They're fast..."

A furious roaring woke John in his chair by the cold woodstove, the bottle lying at his feet, the last of its blood dripping onto the hardwood. The room was nearly dark, but the bedroom light shafted through the door and cast hard-edged shadows around him. For a full minute he could not determine where he was; his surroundings seemed alien, like a place he might have read about in a book and up till now only imagined.

He opened his mouth and pain shot through his whole face. When he moved a cracked rib shifted inside him, and a groan escaped. He put his face in his hands, gingerly. He wondered how long he had been passed out.

The howling in his head bounced off every wall, the roof, and he realized that a brutal rain pounded away at the cabin. The little window across the room—black, then animated with lightning, then black again, a low stampede of thunder following close behind.

He struggled to stand. Bracing his left arm against his ribcage, he shuffled to the kitchen sink. Slowly the reality slipped in, and with it remorse, though less so than he had always imagined. It did not seem to mean very much, now that it had happened. He splashed water on his face and in his mouth, and spat red. Pain shot down into his legs and the room started spinning. He felt a perverse gratitude. The cabin seemed an appropriate place to die.

The rain made such a deafening din on the roof that he almost didn't hear the truck. He shook his head and ran wet hands back through his hair. Walking back into the main room, he saw the glare of headlights through the front window.

John opened the door and looked through the screen. The truck sat, motor running; nothing else moved. Then Jessie got out and opened the umbrella.

She stood still, rain crashing down onto the truck, roof, umbrella, throbbing like a million fevered drums. He watched, afraid to move, not wanting to wake.

Finally she took a few steps and stopped in front of the truck. The beams from the headlights shone like thin, twin rivers of gemstones. She stood captured between them, as if deciding on which side of fate her feet would fall, knowing that her next step would begin or end everything.

He could not see her face. He pushed open the screen door and stepped onto the porch, letting it close behind him as noiselessly as possible.

She stood there, poised between seduction and salvation. They looked at each other.

She chose.

Her steps were determined, passing through the rain-slanted shaft of light into blackness, then toward the steps, the dim glow from the windows slowly illuminating her shape. He stepped toward her, to the edge of the porch.

"No," she said. But he took another step and she stopped. "Go back," she said, faintly, the sound nearly washing away with the rain, but he couldn't move. "Go back in," she said, louder, and he backed up to the door. *"In,"* she said. And when he hesitated she slowly lowered the umbrella, first to her shoulder, then to her side, finally dropping it onto the river of earth flowing all around her, standing helplessly, wordlessly threatening that unless he obeyed she would simply allow herself to be drowned and washed forever away.

The rain drenched her. In the half-light he saw everything surrendering, an exotic flower in the storm with torrents flooding all around her. Lightning lit the trembling trees behind her—white face flashing, dark-circled eyes wide. Fear filled him and he took steps back, opening the door, backing inside, closing it between them. He stood there with his hands pressed against the screen.

Only then did she move. She came slowly up the steps, through the falling water, across another patch of black until she was there, at the door, pressing her palms against his, the screen blurring reality, softening them both

217

into smoke and shadow. He saw her face inches away...he could almost touch her, and he pushed against the shroud.

"No," she said, but a weakening whisper now, ducking her eyes away, hopelessly pushing her own hands flatter into the last, lithe barrier. They touched but could not fully feel.

"No," she tried but without strength.

"Jess," he said, and she stood back, two steps, her hands coming together in a point beneath her chin as if she were about to pray, fingers fluttering toward her mouth like moths, a mask falling away.

Jessie backed one more step but could not turn.

John pushed open the door and the veil between them swung away, his body breaking toward her. And now she did not run, the walls of water descending from the porch roof in shimmering sheets all around.

"No," but he was there and she met him, enfolding into one another, brought alive—"I love you..." "Always, always..."—her wet clothes clinging, soaking into him, and she was light and easily held.

White-silent bolts clawed at the darkness.

He tasted her. On her lips he tasted existence, a still-sweet savor of ripe fruit and the faint flavor of his own blood, the smell of fertile earth and the full falling away of loneliness, the taste of time, life, being, of existence itself.

"I've always loved you"—both their voices full of breath and fire and innocence regained—"always..." Indomitable, transcendent, the roar of the rain trembling over them, the water a translucent curtain all around off the eaves of the porch. The pain passed between their lips, and with the taste of blood came resurrection. She pushed her elbows weakly into him but then let them give way.

"I love you, Jess..."

And his arms were around her, strong. He pressed into the vital warmth of her, away from the world, from pain, from reality, burying his face into the merciful blackness of her

218

hair...and she was his, he knew it, had always known it, she belonged to him fully...

"Wait," she whispered.

And he did, as always, though he knew she couldn't stop him and knew she wouldn't even try, because there was something sacred in her word, as sacred as their love, fresh as spring morning after the rain...

"Wait."

And he did...*holding her without forcing, honoring, understanding, the thing they shared stronger than any passion, the spirit of their love more powerful than flesh, than sin, than life itself...the only thing the boy had ever known that flew above the pain, high above and out of reach of reality, of time itself...*

"Come with me," whispering, the skin of her ear soft.

"Yes, yes..." she said.

"The day after tomorrow, before sunrise," he said, and she knew she was alive.

"Yes..." a strange, short laugh escaping her mouth near his, "...the day after tomorrow, I'll wait for you until sunrise..." Waterfalls all around encasing them in silver, swirling along a surging river. "Yes..."

"Wait..."

And she took the fury from him, all of it, and drew it into herself, all his loss and loneliness, his restless heart. Again she rescued him from his fear, from himself. And her whisper was neither request nor command, only truth...that any intrusion would shatter the illusion, waking them both from a divine dream...

"Wait."

"Yes. We'll wait, Jess..."

"Until you come back," her breath-song, lightly in his ear.

"Until I come back."

They would wait.

And again he knew she had saved them both, because

there was somehow something more precious in the waiting, more holy, even...

Jessie pulled away, crying out with the pain of it, both reaching, fingers barely touching but the scorned sky flashed into the forest and burst into angry flame, splitting the world in two, her eyes, his eyes, both knowing if they disobeyed the world would drown and all would be lost. Thunder shook them. They crushed together but were not afraid.

Coalescence. Now, both knew time could be defeated. Once joined, *they could live forever.*

"Johnny..." her voice young, the thunder threatening to shake loose the feeble boards beneath their feet. She broke free, down the steps, through the falls into the violent, sobbing storm, across the water and past the umbrella tilted, half-filled, through the bridge of lights.

"If you don't come, I'll know," he shouted against the drums.

"Yes, yes," she whispered to herself, "the day after tomorrow..."

Door slamming, a deep dissatisfied moaning still connecting them both, the truck groaning, disappearing.

"Please come..." he said into cascading crystal.

"...I'll come, the day after tomorrow...before sunrise," she said, unsure if the sound coming from her was laughter or crying, if rain or tears covered her wet hands, slick and shaking on the wheel.

19

John did not sleep.

He moved through the cabin, quick, clear, more sober than he had ever known possible. Though he had been there for nearly three months, he realized that he had never fully unpacked, always ready to run. And now he understood with some sorrow that he had lived much of his life in this transient way.

The rain pounded away all night.

Dawn broke slowly, the storm draining from the sky along with the darkness. Gradually the roof grew silent, and John went to the porch. Distant thunder shuddered across the humbled earth like the purring of some great lion. What rain remained fell through the warming air with soft kindness. He leaned against one of the beams at the top of the steps and stared out at the vaporous, freshly watered world. Fantasy and reality had meshed; if not for the open umbrella still tilting in its puddle, he would have thought every moment leading to this one had been a hallucination. He walked off the porch, lifted the curved handle that had touched her hand only hours ago, and poured out the rainwater.

One more day, and one more night, he thought. *Time enough to say goodbye.*

He knew the waiting would be hard, that the day would creep torturously along. On some level he was aware of the pain in his body, and of his growing delirium from so little sleep over too many nights, but none of this mattered.

It was too early to go see Maggie and Ellen and Joey, to tell them that by the next day's sunrise he would be gone. He moved impatiently through the cabin. Finally he walked down to the water, towards the rebirth emerging on the horizon. He watched the river trembling with what was left of the rain.

By the time he returned the morning was warming, the soaked earth beginning to sigh and steam. Restless, he went out past the corner of the cabin and started chopping wood. At first, swinging the axe split a hot wedge into his side, but the pain burned away his exhaustion and he pushed through it. After a while he felt elated, each stab in his chest proving that he was awake, that everything had been real, had truly happened. Sweat formed on his forehead and the axe felt meaningful in his hands, strong strokes, woodchips flying. Finally piles of useless firewood lay scattered all around. Leaning the axe handle against the old stump, he heard a noise behind him.

Ellen stood watching.

"Johnny?"

"Hi, El."

"Getting ready for next winter?" She stood near the steps to the porch, squinting in the low-glowing sunlight.

"Getting in a little workout." He walked to her.

"Oh, *Johnny*."

"No, no, it's okay, El." He'd forgotten about his face.

"What in..."

"Tuck. He was here last night."

"Oh my... are you *okay*?" Ellen was all little girl now, about to cry. She reached tenderly toward his swollen eye.

"I'm fine. Really." He tried to smile. "Let's go in."

Ellen stopped in the middle of the main room and slowly turned, taking everything in. John was glad he'd thrown away the empty bottle.

"You're leaving," she said.

"Yes."

"Is Jessie going with you?"

"I...I hope so. She was here."

"Johnny. Oh, *my*..."

"It's okay, El. Either way, it's time for me to go. I'm leaving. Before sunrise tomorrow."

"Oh." She let him hug her.

After a moment she leaned back and focused on his face. "Looks like a truck hit you."

"More or less."

"Johnny..."

"Real life's ugly sometimes, El."

"Something told me to come check on you. I just *knew*."

"You should be in school."

"It doesn't matter." She raised her chin, eyes wet. "Have you told Mom?"

"Not yet. I'll go see her."

"She knows, Johnny. She's known all along that you wouldn't stay. She never expected you to be here for very long."

"I know."

"She'll be sad. But not surprised."

He nodded. "Thanks, El. I won't stay away forever, not anymore. There will come a time when I can come back."

"Yes." Her tears welled, then gently rolled down her cheeks. "This place will always be here, and a part of you will always belong here. But this is not your home. Your home is somewhere else. Not here, and not where you've ever been before, either. You'll find it, Johnny. You'll find it." She looked into him. "I want you to know, Uncle. I've never thought you were a coward. Never."

His throat tightened and he struggled to speak. "I've never thought of myself as anything else," he said.

"You must find your true home," she said, "and your true self."

They sat together on the top step of the porch, talking. Ellen held his hand and cried. Finally they moved toward goodbye.

"I'll pray for you," Ellen said. "For your happiness. Whatever that looks like. However you might find it."

"Soon, you'll be leaving too," John said. "Your future's out there, El, waiting for you."

"Hmm." She looked down toward the river. "It seems like all my life I've dreamed about leaving, about where I'd go, where in the big world I'd go..."

John watched her. He saw something pure and promising moving across her face, and without thinking said, "*O mistress mine, where are you roaming? O, stay and hear; your true love's coming / That can sing both high and low...*"

Ellen turned her glowing face to him, eyes young, old, filled with tremulous sadness and hopeful joy, and said in a voice true as time and new as morning—

"*Trip no further, pretty sweeting; Journeys end in lovers meeting / Every wise man's son doth know...*"

* * *

The night before, Jessie had returned so wet and wearied in mind and body that had she found her husband unexpectedly at home—a fear that occurred to her when driving back through the hard rain from the cabin—she might not have been able to even speak.

But Tuck had not been there. And knowing he was still across the river until morning relieved her, gave her enough strength to deal with the soaked clothes and take a hot shower. Soon she had collapsed onto the bed, where she lay curled in the quilts like a baby.

Her body trembled; it took her a long time to feel warm. Finally she drifted to sleep, and dreamed of an ever-widening world, far out beyond the immensity of creation.

Dawn came. As soon as much light had filtered into the bedroom she sat up, eyes open wide.

Tuck would be home soon.

But, yes, it had happened.

It was not a dream.

After a quick breakfast she dressed and went for a walk in the clean, clearing morning. The dream of the night before blended seamlessly into a changing landscape, the maple and ash now preening their branches in a kinder breeze. Sluggish wasps lofted lazily in the still-cool air, and countless unseen birds unfurled their feathers and sang for nothing less than the pure miracle of one season slain, another resurrected. And with each step Jessie could hear the ice-silent sound of winter slipping away.

She stood barefoot amid swaying switchgrass, wild lavender and dandelion and tiny blue and yellow wildflowers nestled near the ground, blossoms no bigger than the nail of her little finger splayed out in all directions. The wind shook the limbs of the plum trees, freeing thousands of cream-colored petals the size of snowflakes to float down around her, and she spread out her arms, slowly turning. She laughed out loud and then began to cry, at such a sight as a virgin sky swept so sweetly clean.

By now her long sleeves had become too much; a fine film of sweat formed on her upper lip, and she ran the tip of her tongue over the salty taste of remembering. Soon summer would arrive on the droning hum of cicada wings, the air heavy with humidity, and growing things would thrive and thick-tangle in this great, swarming, greenhouse country.

Returning from the fields, she saw ahead a sight that drew her, and her heart beat louder than the fall of her feet as she walked toward the house, a feeling buoyed by a bright vitality, lifting her, and suddenly she was in her mother's flower garden. And here, while Jessie had slept, God had dipped and brushed His handful of colors across the well-watered rows onto just-born blooms—crocus and daffodil and tulip already reaching toward the sun, purple iris poised to follow, the wooden trellises filling with water-blue wisteria that would soon hang down in heavy, grapelike clusters. Jessie cupped the emerging blossoms in her hands, and pressed her face into the slowly unfolding future.

Could it be, she wondered, *that all this beauty surged to the surface while I slept? Or was I walking through life half-alive until last night…and now my eyes are fully opened?*

She lifted a handful of black dirt and let it sift down between her fingers. And when she knelt in the healing earth, she felt a presence kneeling near.

Can a feeling like this be wrong, Momma?

The land around her had overnight grown young, and she with it.

She had one more day, and night, to wait.

Alive.

She felt *alive.*

* * *

Maggie opened her front door, then propped the glass storm door with her hip, the way she had on that first day John arrived in town.

"Well," she said. One eyebrow lifted. She let out a long sigh. "Should I even *ask?*"

"Hi Mags," he said.

"Get in any good punches of your own?"

"A few."

She just kept looking at him. Her eyes narrowed, then moistened. She lowered her chin and said slowly, "Let me guess. You've got a plane to catch."

"I came to say goodbye. For now."

Maggie took the dishtowel off her shoulder and dried her hands. "It's a nice morning, brother," she said. "Let's sit on the front steps a while."

They talked for hours.

"Have you told Ellen?"

"Yeah. She came to the cabin this morning."

Maggie blew out between pursed lips. "That girl. I guess she thinks since she's a senior she can come and go from school any time she pleases." She shook her head. "I swear, Johnny. That girl adores you. Always has."

"She's a special person, Mags. But you know that."

A small smile creased her face. "Yes. I know that." She turned and looked at him. "I know you can't stay, and I'm not going to ask any details. But any idea when we might see you again?"

"No. The truth is, Mags, I'm not sure what will happen next."

"Whatever happens, Johnny...as long as you're okay..."

"Maggie, I'm not going to lie to you. I came back here looking for...for something I've never had. Some sort of peace, maybe. And I'm not sure if I've found it or not."

They sat still for a moment more. The sun felt good on their faces. Maggie straightened her back and put her hands on her knees. "Johnny," she said, "maybe what you've been looking for is what everybody's looking for." She sighed. "And maybe we're all looking in the wrong places."

John smiled. "That's pretty much what Preacher said."

"I get the feeling, brother, that what we're really chasing after isn't something we'll find in any place...or any person. Maybe what you and I are searching for, no human being can give us."

"Maybe," he said. "That's what I need to know."

"Johnny, no matter what happens next, you know

you're always welcome here. With...us." Maggie smiled. "With your family."

This time, John let a few tears fall. His sister leaned her head on his shoulder, and cried with him. After a while, he took a deep breath. Maggie lifted her head.

"I know, Johnny," she said. "Time to go."

"Yeah." He stood, and took her hand to help her up.

"I've always been lousy with goodbyes," she said.

"Me too."

"I don't know why they're hard for *you*, Johnny. Heaven knows you've had more than enough *practice*." Maggie's laugh turned into a small sob. "I'll miss you, brother."

"I'll miss you too." He wiped a tear from her cheek with his thumb.

"I hope you find what you're looking for," she said. "Maybe you came back and discovered that Tranquility isn't the kind of place you could live in any more. But who knows, brother? Maybe you've also learned it's the kind of place you can't live without."

John smiled.

"I'll pray for you, Johnny," Maggie said. "I'll pray every day that you find happiness. That you find peace."

"Thanks, Mags," he said, hugging her. "You'll be in my heart." And he turned and walked to his car.

Maggie held the dishtowel against her nose and mouth, waving with her other hand as he drove away.

"Don't be a stranger, Johnny," she said.

* * *

John stepped up the cinderblocks and knocked on the trailer door. When no one answered he cupped his hands around the tiny window in the door and tried to see inside. Everything was dark. He put his hand on the doorknob and twisted.

"Ain't nobody home, big brother." The voice came from directly above. John stepped down one block and looked up.

"What in the world are you doing up there?"

Joey's head poked over the top edge of the trailer. He grinned from beneath the wedge of shadow made by his baseball cap. The sky above and around his face was soft and blue and forgiving.

"Watchin' the day end, bro. Just watchin' the day end."

"Joey, you moron. Come down from there."

"HAW! Naw, you come up. It's nice up here." The head disappeared. "'Round back, Johnny."

John circled around. The unfinished porch frame stuck out from the trailer's center toward the woods and the river below. Large pieces of heavy plastic that had come untacked flapped in the breeze. Joey's head reappeared above him.

"Climb up, see?"

"You idiot."

"Shoot fire, Johnny, just climb up onto that first two-by-four, then pull up from there. You ain't forgot how to climb things, have you? You big sissy." With that the head again vanished, then two feet swung over the edge. Joey sat waiting.

John managed it easily enough, hoisting up along the two-by-four framework and onto the flat surface of the narrow metal roof.

"I swear, little bro. You act like you're ten years old."

"Why, thank you, Johnny." The younger man's voice was as sincere as his smile. An open can of beer sat next to his thigh; several crushed empties lay where they'd been tossed toward the center of the roof. John started to speak, but couldn't. He felt too sad to be angry, and just scooted along the edge until he sat beside his brother.

"Shoot *fire*, bro. What happened to your *face*?"

229

"Accident. I ran into a…fist. Repeatedly."

Joey tilted his head, opened his mouth, then shut it. "All right," he finally said. "All right." He left it at that.

They stared out toward the light-excited water.

"Look there," the younger man said after while. The brief, wooded lot backed into a westward-facing cove of the reservoir; the sun glittered euphorically along the silver surface as it moved toward the horizon. "I've been watchin' this same piece of river for a long time," Joey said. "And it ain't never got old to me, bro. Still beautiful as ever. Truth is, I can't think of anywhere else in the world I'd rather be."

John looked far into the past and future. It seemed he had never gone a day in his life without seeing this place, and yet was now seeing it for both the first and last time. "I know," was all he could think to say.

They stared out without speaking. Low, sparkling light came pinched through the fine fingers of the trees. The breeze had new warmth in it, and the smell of living; the two men let it move through their hair, across their cheeks, and John forgot for a moment about everything—love, pain, loss, the cornfield and cabin and barn, the overdose, the smell of beer beside him, and they were just two young boys again, two brothers on top of the world gazing out at endless possibility. John felt exhausted with life to the point of crying for joy, and he could sense he was about to lose his voice forever, and so said— "I'm leaving."

Joey didn't move. Finally he said, "The days will be gettin' longer, now," as if he were talking to himself. Then, "I hate how short the days get in winter. I swear, I can't stand it when the sun goes down before the day's got half started." John felt his little brother turning to him. "That's how it seems in the winter, don't it, big bro?"

"Yeah." John kept his eyes pointed toward the water. The sun slipped toward the horizon.

"There's somethin' terrible sad about sunsets," Joey said. "Don't you think?"

"I guess so."

"Yeah. Real pretty and all, but sad, too. Like the end of somethin' beautiful, somethin' that ain't ever comin' back. Another day'll come, Johnny, but not this one. This one's gone for good, and there ain't no gettin' it back. Ever." Joey sighed, and John felt his own lungs empty.

Then, because the younger man knew what was coming, he said—"Let's not talk about anything for a little bit, big bro."

"Okay," John said. They sat with their legs dangling over the edge, high above the need for words, for reasons or responsibilities, the last of the sun's warmth radiating up around them from the aluminium roof.

Joey leaned slightly back, gripped the edge of the roof, then lunged forward; his spit flew out and landed a good thirty feet away in the dirt. He looked at his brother.

"Pitiful," John said. He gathered his own and let it fly, but at the last minute tilted his head down slightly, causing his to fall just short of where Joey's had landed.

"HAW!"

"Dang," John said.

"I beat ya!" The younger man beamed. "I finally beat ya!"

"Guess I'm losing my touch."

"Too much city livin', big bro," Joey said, and then both again grew silent.

After a while, Joey said, "Old Spice."

"What?"

"Daddy wore Old Spice. Remember?"

"Hmm. I do."

"Yeah." Joey took a breath. "You remember the closet?"

John felt suddenly cold. "Yes."

"Me too," Joey said quietly. "I don't know why it was so scary when he'd throw us in there, but Lord knows it was."

231

"It was the dark," John said.

"Yeah. That was it. Blackest place ever. I don't mind the dark so much, you know, the regular kinda dark, with some moonlight at least, or some stars. But God, that closet was black. Black as death." Joey paused. "I hated that closet, more than when he'd take his belt to us, even, more than anything."

John cleared his throat. "I hated hearing him turn that lock," he said. "I knew where we were, just an ordinary closet. But when he put us in, and threw that lock..."

"Yeah. And stuff hangin' around our heads, touchin' our heads, like..."

"Like fingers."

"Yeah, like ghost arms comin' outta those sleeves. And bats, big bro, like bats, I always thought."

"Uh-huh. Hands. And bats."

"Yeah. Shoot fire."

Quiet again. Then—

"His clothes were in there, though, Johnny. His shirts."

"Yes."

"And they *smelled* like him."

"Like Old Spice."

"Yeah. And that's what I remember most, bro. Not the bats or the ghost sleeves reachin' down on us, but the smell of Old Spice. That's what I remember." Joey sniffed, and a little moan escaped. "And I've got one of 'em."

"What?"

"I've got one of his shirts. I asked Maggie to get me one, after Daddy died." Joey's words choked. "She asked me what I wanted, and I said nothin', I didn't want a dang thing. And then later I told her I'd changed my mind. I told her to get me one of his shirts. And I've got it, and I ain't ever washed it. I just keep it, pull it out of the drawer sometimes."

"Old Spice," John said.

"Yep. Smells really good."

They watched the orange ball sinking, at first slowly, until the fire was finally touching the lip of the water; then the end came swiftly, as if some great fish beneath the river's surface had taken hold of unsuspecting prey and dragged it under. Dusk fell around them like blue smoke. And together they silently mourned the death of another day.

When their silent, shared sorrow became too much, and the chill woke them from a dream of winter ending, Joey said:

"Johnny, you believe in God?"

For some reason, the older man decided to tell the truth. "Well, Joey, there have been times when I wasn't so sure if he was there or not. And then there've been other times, really bad times when I needed him most, he showed up. Or at least, *something* showed up."

"Like somethin' or somebody showed up and saved your ass, you mean?"

"Yeah. That's exactly what I mean." John could feel the air getting colder. "The truth is, little bro, a lot of the time I'm just not sure."

"Yeah," Joey said. Again the quiet settled. Then, "How 'bout Heaven? You believe there's a Heaven?"

John forced a little laugh. "Hell if I know," he said. "I guess so."

"Yeah. I think so, too." Joey slumped. "You think...whadaya think happens to somebody...you know..."

"I don't know." John spoke it hurriedly.

"Aw, come on, Johnny." Joey sounded like a little boy. "Ain't you ever wondered? 'Bout what happens to somebody who dies...like the way Mama did."

John felt afraid. He wanted to yell at Joey and tell him to shut up. He wanted to climb down and start running and not stop, ever. He gripped the edge of the roof.

"Johnny?"

Something in the voice sounded so young and sad. And John drew out of his own fear and into his brother's. "Joey," he said.

"Well, shoot fire, Johnny. Ain't you ever wondered?"

"Yeah. Yeah, I've wondered."

"Me too. I mean, when somebody dies like that. It's a sad thing."

"Yes, it is."

"I swear, Johnny, I wasn't tryin' to do that. I just forgot how many I'd taken, I reckon. I ain't the happiest guy in the world, maybe, but that ain't no way to go."

"No."

"But if somebody...does that...you think they go to Heaven anyway? You think God forgives people when they do that, Johnny?"

John had to breathe in and out very slowly so that the woods would stop spinning, so that he could answer, so that Joey wouldn't be afraid. He forced himself to say, as calmly as possible—"I'll tell you this, little brother. If there's a Heaven, Mama's there. If there's a God, Mama, of all people, is with him."

The two men looked at each other in the dying light.

"You really believe that, Johnny?"

In that moment John realized he did not know exactly what he believed any more. But he also knew that his little brother needed him. And so he added without thinking— "And she's young again, too, Joey, young and pretty. All the bad times gone for good, as if they never happened. No more hurt in her eyes. She's young and smiling and full of life. And she isn't feeling any pain or fear. It's just like she's been reborn, and everything made brand new." John reached out and put his hand on his brother's shoulder. Suddenly Preacher's face came into his mind, young and strong now, and the words strangely didn't feel like a lie. "God loves us, Joey," he said. "And there's not a blessed thing we can do about it." He took a breath. "That's what I believe, little bro."

Joey turned. Surprisingly, there were no tears on his face. "Then that's good enough for me," he said.

The wind picked up, gentle but cold.

Joey kept looking into his brother's eyes. "Sometimes he'd leave us in there all night," he said. "That closet was dark as death. Why would somebody do that, Johnny?"

"I don't know."

"Me neither. But I know I couldn't have made it without you. What would I have ever done if you hadn't been there with me, Johnny? I swear, I think I might've died from fear. That was the darkest place I ever saw, blacker than anybody will ever know."

"Yes it was."

"But you always got me through it, big bro. You took care of me, told me not to be afraid. I knew I could make it, as long as you were there with me. You always said mornin' would come, and I believed you. I figured even though I wasn't brave, together we'd make it. I figured you was brave enough for the both of us."

John bit down hard on the inside of his cheek, and his vision blurred until he could no longer see. He tried to say his brother's name, but couldn't.

"Mornin' always comes, though, don't it, Johnny? No matter what."

John felt his brother's eyes on him, but was afraid to look anywhere except straight down toward the dark water.

"Morning always comes, Joey," he said at last. "No matter what."

As soon as they had climbed down and gone inside, Joey slid straight into his worn recliner in the corner without turning on a lamp. John stood awkwardly in the middle of the tiny room, the muted light coming through the little window barely illuminating their faces.

235

"I'm leaving Tranquility," he said.

The visor of his cap hid all but Joey's chin in shadow. "When?"

"Tomorrow. At sunrise."

"Shoot fire, Johnny," the shadow said quietly.

"Yeah."

"Seems like you just got here."

"I know."

"Where're you figurin' on goin'?"

"I don't know, exactly," John said. "Some place new."

"I reckon I knew you would." Joey killed the rest of a beer and crushed the can in his claw. "I reckon I always knew."

"Joey, I sure wish you'd rethink things."

"Don't start, Johnny. It ain't gonna do you no good."

"Joey…"

"Listen, bro," he said, suddenly standing and meeting John in the middle of the little room. "My life belongs to *me*. It's mine to live, Johnny, one way or the other. My life ain't your life and it never has been, never will be."

"I know."

"Well, I need you to know somethin' else." He put his hand on his big brother's shoulder. "And you need to hear me good: I love you, Johnny. I always have. *All* of us have, the whole time. I never blamed you when you left, and I ain't blamin' you this time, either." His eyes filled and so did John's. "Every man has got to go his own way. Your way was always different, even when you was little. But none of us blamed you when you got outta here. Shoot fire, I'd have got away from Daddy too, I reckon, if I'd known how to do it."

John felt like someone shouting into a storm, throwing a rope to someone drowning, but the person couldn't see it.

"But then again, maybe I *wouldn't* have, either. 'Cause my life is my own," Joey said, determined now. "Shoot, you ought to understand that. Nobody else knows what I'm talkin' about. Everybody figures I can just quit drinkin' and smokin' and takin' pills any time I please. Like I'm supposed to snap my fingers"—he raised his right hand to do so, then looked surprised not to have enough fingers—"and say hocus pocus and be just dandy." His face hardened. "But it ain't always that simple, is it?"

"No, it isn't."

"I reckon we gotta get tired enough of dyin' before we start livin', huh, bro? See, me and you, we're way more alike than we are different, ain't we?"

"Yes."

"Like Daddy, sort of."

"In some ways, yes. Yes, we are."

"'Cause you tell me the truth—didn't nobody ever talk you into gettin' sober, did they?"

"No."

"And I'll bet jail didn't get you sober, or losin' that fancy place you lived in, or nothin' else either, did it?"

John took a deep breath. "No, Joey. As a matter of fact, you're absolutely right."

Joey leaned his head back and did a slow, sure nod. "And each of us has to make our own choices, don't we?" His eyes for the first time showed the frailest hint of hope.

"Yes," John said. "We do." And though the truth of it frightened and frustrated him, in that moment he let go of his end of the rope.

"Now listen, bro," Joey said, his face breaking into a grin. "I know you'll be comin' back. 'Cause you ain't runnin' no more, are you? And you've come home now, and no matter where else you go, a part of you will *still* be here. Shoot fire, Johnny, a part of you was here the whole time."

"I'm not sure, Joey..."

"Well, I *am*." His face broke into a full, toothy smile, tears now all over his stubbly cheeks. "I know Daddy said I ain't never had a lick of sense. But a man's got to find his own way. You gotta go find yours. And I reckon I'm gonna have to find mine, all by myself."

"You're not Daddy, little bro."

Joey stood very still. "Well, I am, and I ain't," he said. "And the same goes for you." His eyes looked old, and painfully young. "Nobody else but you and me is ever gonna understand that, are they?"

"No," John said. "Nobody but me and you." He reached and touched his brother's arm. "Don't cry, Joey."

Joey shook his head.

"Just this one, last time, big bro. One last time."

From the door John said, "Take it easy, Joey. Watch those pills, you moron." He watched his brother slide back into his chair in the shadowy corner. The little room was growing cold. John felt like a man looking into the permanent face of winter.

But Joey only grinned.

"Hey, Johnny. Which one?"

Johnny kept his hand on the doorknob, and turned.

"Tennessee girls, little bro. Tennessee girls by a mile."

Joey smiled wide, and lifted his beer in a toast.

"Haw-HAW! I thought so, big bro. I *thought* so."

20

Jessie listened to her husband's steady breathing.

She had waited until late afternoon to return from her long walk through the woods, knowing that by then Tuck would have given in to his exhaustion. After peeking in to make sure he was asleep, she had slipped quietly across the room to sit in the cane-bottom chair by the window. Although she remained very still, she thought that perhaps Tuck might wake, sensing her presence; a part of her prayed he would open his eyes, while another part desperately hoped he would not.

Outside, night settled over the land. Jessie watched the light drain gradually from the room, the colors and dimensions of things slowly fading into a flat, monochrome gray. She saw herself and everything around her growing fainter until all the familiar shapes dissolved to nothingness. As her eyes adjusted to darkness, she could still see the outline of her husband's shoulders, rising and falling beneath the covers.

She waited.

Tuck would wake around eight as always, shower, put on his work clothes, and have something to eat. Then he would leave around eleven, just as he had for the last several years.

Now she watched him sleeping, and imagined how once the house was empty she would pull out the old suitcases and begin packing her things, putting the essentials for her new life into a few bags. The thought made her feel faint. She did love Tuck; leaving would not be possible, surely, but now neither would staying, and thinking of it actually happening created a kind of passion in her that she had for a long time believed would never come again. She felt exhilarated, ashamed, emptied, filled.

Thoughts came to her, fast and out of sequence. She thought of how strong Tuck's arms felt around her, and how his skin smelled of leaves and wood and fresh air. She thought of how they had shared countless prayers together, asking God for a child of their own, and how during the long seasons of God's silence Tuck had proven strong enough to both hold her and cry with her. And she thought of the day they were married, the pastel sunlight coming all rose and green-golden through the stained-glass windows. She thought of these things, and knew the remaining hours until sunrise would be the longest of her life.

She sat very still with her hands folded in her lap, her husband's breathing and the ticking of her father's clock from the next room the only sounds in her whole world.

* * *

From the porch John watched the moonlight cast dancing diamonds onto the river. Pale light touched the tops of the trees and terraced down through the branches. A powdery luminescence covered everything.

He looked at his watch. The night turned so slowly, John felt he'd been sitting there all his life, waiting for dawn.

He wondered. About how he could have ended up here, on this porch, staring out onto this place where he was born. He wondered how life could have led him in so many directions, into other worlds and relationships and experiences, yet all along drawing him unknowingly back toward this still place, for some sure purpose.

He had not slept in a long time. He wanted to keep his eyes open, to see as much as he could, *feel* as much as possible. After a lifetime of searching for truth, he had finally discovered that feelings mattered more than knowledge. As he sat watching the fixed fireworks sparkling in the sky and on the water, John decided that he knew nothing at all. And there was a peace in this surrendering, in seeing that any human understanding of creation would always be at best distorted. All his life he had vainly sought answers, meaning and purpose through the idolatry of people, places and possessions, only to learn that the things he considered treasures had in the end been less than dust.

In all the places he had traveled, none had felt like home. Even here, now, his incessant sense of homelessness remained. Of all the beings he had touched, none had made him whole. Each of them had taught him something, perhaps, and some of them he had even loved, in a way, with what little true love lived within him. But through all the years none of the people had been *her*. He had gone to the edges of the earth and stood on the shores of many seas, and wondered where else in the world he could possibly go to either escape or find her. And yet every time he turned his back on her, Jessie stood facing him.

But not only her. Over the last months he had become aware of another truth. He knew now that he had been running away from another haunting face, the face of his father. Ultimately he had discovered that his father's face was in many ways his own.

And so he sat with the stiff canvas collar pulled up around his ears, eyes growing more and more heavy, the dew settling on him as if he were a part of the sleeping earth. Waiting. What he imagined to be the last and greatest of his dreams still remained, only a few miles away.

* * *

Jessie moved about the house like an anxious child.

She was afraid to talk to him. Each time she pictured saying goodbye in her mind, no matter how she framed it, she could foresee nothing but pain and sorrow. She would not be able to do it. Her only hope was to steal away.

She knew the sounds in the old house; water flowing through the pipes told her Tuck was up, showering. He would have to leave soon. She moved mechanically about in the kitchen, getting something ready for him to eat.

When he sat down at the table, she knew there could be no easy way. He laid his heavy arms on either side of the place mat. His eyes were puffy and his knuckles split. He would not meet her gaze.

Every remaining ounce of her self-sufficiency drained away. She put the plate in front of him and moved quickly to the window at the sink.

Finally the awful silence drove her back to her chair. "Tuck..."

He looked down, chewing, jaws flexing.

"Tuck." She repeated, her hands gripping the edge of the table. "I'm sorry."

He looked up at her.

"Sorry for what, Jessie?"

"For...breaking my word." She knew her words were pathetic, ridiculous. "For everything."

"What do you want me to do, Jessie?" he asked. The voice was so plaintive that it broke her heart. She could not think of a single word to say. Their eyes briefly met, and she had never seen anything so sad as his, or, in their emptiness, so frightening. He looked like a man who had lost his soul. He waited, his face full of hurt and hope, and when she didn't say anything more he put his fork on the still-full plate and stood.

"I'm goin' on to work," he said. There was no anger or any other emotion clinging to his voice, only a brutal fatigue. "Might as well...go on in." He turned to walk out. But something stopped him. He turned back to her and reached out his hand, lightly pressing his palm against her cheek. Instinctively, she reached, touched, felt the ragged scabs on his knuckles.

In that moment Jessie, looking into his face, almost asked him not to go. The sadness she saw in her husband nearly woke her from the dream. Something rare and delicate and valuable urged her, ever so briefly, to hold on to Tuck and never let go.

Jessie rose and fell against his chest. His arms went around her, unquestioningly. She opened her mouth against the warmth of his flannel shirt, breathing him in, and she tried to speak but only misery came out. Her mind shouted the thoughts—*I've lost myself, Tuck. I don't know who I am anymore, and I'm dying.* She heard him say her name but all she could do was press her head against his chest, the sobs shaking them both, *Save me, save me,* but all her breath was gone and he had to hold her up. "Jessie," her husband said, the voice part question, part prayer, everything going blank in her mind, and she wanted to stay there in the warm darkness and sleep forever.

Through the years, Tuck's arms had always been strong enough to hold her to earth, even in the darkest storms. But she felt unworthy of his strength now. Leaning back her head, she looked into his sad, gray eyes.

And they both knew. There was nothing she could say, no words that meant anything. She could not ask Tuck to save her, or ask him to let her go. She felt that she had already ruined them. That she had killed them both.

Tuck closed his eyes, gently released her, then turned and left the room. For the first time in her life, Jessie wondered why she had been born.

She managed to remain out of his way, sitting in the unlit living room, until she heard the truck pull away.

For a long while she remained very still, staring across the room at the moonlit mantel. She watched the hands of time somehow repositioning themselves without seeming to move—once, twice, then three times, chimes broke the deathly quiet. But she was not fooled; like the hands of the clock, she only appeared to be motionless. In reality Jessie saw her life imperceptibly orbiting closer and then farther away, with or without her.

None of it seemed real—the suitcase opened on the bed, the sounds of drawers and closets opening, closing, the growing hollowness of the old house. Her thoughts held no real shape, only a humming urgency.

She dared not look behind, or too far ahead.

Now there was only the slow ache within her, the ticking clock, the coming sunrise.

* * *

"Sometimes we look for something or someone to fill us up, make us whole. But that's a tough job for any human, son. Tough job."

The voice was calm, calming. The rockers creaked against the wood, synchronized with the cricket's chanting. It seemed to John that the two of them had been sitting there together for a lifetime.

"She's all I've ever wanted."

"A man's okay until he starts wanting something, Johnny. She's part of what you want. But not all."

A chill found its way into his dream, and the boy felt afraid.

"That other man has been here."

"I know."

"I've never asked him to come." He felt a rising resentment. "He's been here more than you."

"I know."

"Why is that, Daddy? Why is it you let him hurt me? How come you never..." Sorrow welled up into his eyes and his father began to blur and wash away. "How come you never..."

"Saved you?"

Tears fell onto the weathered planks like rain.

"Yes."

"I'm no savior, son. Just a man, plain and simple. We can't go back in time and change things, Johnny. No matter how much we'd like to."

"At least take me with you."

"I can't. I wish I could."

And Johnny feared his father would not come to the porch any more.

"Will I see you again?"

"I hope so, Johnny. With all my heart."

The man smiled, then stood. And Johnny would have given his whole life just to be able to hold his father close. But they didn't touch. The dream weighed heavy on him, pressing him into his chair.

"Sun will be up before long, son."

"Do you know if she'll come?"

His father looked at him, those star-eyes dazzling, and tilted his head.

"You think she'll save you."

"I don't know."

The man turned back to the water.

"Maybe she already has."

* * *

245

Jessie closed and latched the two suitcases, then took them into the unlit living room and set them down near the entrance to the front hall. She went back for a last check.

In the bedroom she paused at the bureau. She touched the silver-handled brush, and looked up into the mirror. The strange woman staring back at her froze, as if just caught stealing; behind her, the room started spinning, and she grabbed at the dresser but couldn't hold on, turned to escape, falling, floating helplessly down at the side of the old spindle bed.

With the world collapsing all around her, she buried herself in the sanctuary of her prayers.

Time stopped.

Silence startled her awake.

Opening her eyes, for a moment she struggled to remember where she was. Then the familiar room, the time-wearied furniture, the rug where she had knelt—*how long ago?*—and now sat with her legs curled into her chest, head leaned against the side of the mattress. Her heart flared briefly with a fear that nothing had been real—not the letter or the barn, the storm, or the kiss that had resurrected her. And then with both relief and remorse she realized all of it had happened, and that now everything was about to forever change.

But something in the house felt all wrong, too still. She lifted her head, focusing deeply into the quiet, listening.

The mantel.

The old clock.

The house had lost its heartbeat.

Panic filled her—How many hours had passed?

The windows remained black.

There was still time.

She stood and walked through the door into the darkened living room. The barest light from the picture window shone on the white wood of the fireplace, the mantel shining like a shrine. She felt drawn to it, gliding...her fingertips now lightly tracing through the carved wood, the round, delicate glass door on tiny brass hinges. The two thin hands sat still, life drained out before they could declare the dawn.

The clock had for so long been the pulse of her home that its silence now roared through every room of her being. In this void she finally heard through the clatter of her own thoughts, and breathed in as deeply as possible.

Love is never selfish...

A whisper escaped her lips—

"Momma?"

Truth paled its way into her on soft, white wings.

Love runs deeper than the pain, always...

She realized she was not alone, and turned.

Tuck loomed like a boulder on the loveseat at the window. The outside world lay covered with bruised darkness; a high tide of white light poured through the panes, illuminating the top half of the room. In this glow he was only visible from the waist up, moonbeams baking his broad back, shoulders bent and head bowed in supplication. Off to one side, rounded shadows of the tops of her two suitcases could be seen rising up from the gloom. From where she stood, her husband looked like a man kneeling in a graveyard, praying at the foot of headstones.

She walked slowly toward him.

Jessie.

What, Momma? I can't hear...

Your heart...

Riding beside her father in the musty old truck... throwing a blanket across Sky's steaming back...clear mornings, chilled twilights, silver moons glowing down on long, fenced fields...bright, sanguine sunlight and the smell of hay and honeysuckle wafting through ragged cracks in a barn...

Your heart will know.

And now, the sweet weeping of the white garden swing, her mother and father sitting together, holding hands... Tuck standing at her front door, hat held gently in his fingers...the creaking of old pews, and walking beside her father, toward the altar where she'd been christened and baptized with cool water... Tuck in a fine black suit, waiting there with the preacher, sure and strong and unafraid...the smooth satin of her mother's own wedding dress against her skin, and velvet light filtering through stained-glass windows, turning everything the color of roses...

And all the past and future fell away with each soft step.

At the end of this, the longest of journeys, she realized she was no longer breathing. She could not see his hands. Kneeling, she reached down into the blind shadows between them, and covered his hands with her own. He lifted his up, into the light, opening.

In his palm he held the brass key.

"I came back," he said softly. "I forgot to wind the clock."

Time had waited.

And her heart knew.

"I have something to tell you..." she said, but Tuck gently reached and stilled her lips with the tips of his fingers.

"I've loved you my whole life, Jessie," he said. "And I'll love you forever, if you'll have me."

It took all her power to get the words out, before she fell into his arms.

"We'll have each other..." she said.

Forever.

* * *

248

Johnny dreamed he was flying.

Riding the wind like a hawk, watching, listening. Everything below paused, for one last, motionless moment—the world awaiting rebirth, all of it silent and breathless with expectation. He could see himself, too, down there on the porch, head fallen forward onto his chest, drifting in a place somewhere between sleep and waking. With the slightest tilt of his wings he rose up, above the currents, higher, until now he hovered in space, watching the slow rotation of the earth, and the broad line of light being slowly drawn across the river, woods, cabin—the satellite of his separate selves turning inexorably toward dawn, in the holy realm of earthly and heavenly fathers...

"She ain't comin'."

The voice shot into him. He began to fall.

"Can you hear me, boy? She ain't comin'."

Back inside his body now—John panicked, but couldn't open his eyes, couldn't move. "There's still time," he tried to say, his chin still tucked into his chest, his voice pitiful and small against the vacuous silence.

"Time's run out."

"Please. I've always loved her..."

"Give it up, boy. You didn't really expect it, did you?"

Grief welled up. "No."

"Life ain't a book, Johnny Allen."

The black cackling of vultures.

"It's time, boy. You know what to do."

Deafening laughter echoed off nothingness and was gone.

The silence that followed was at first awful in its emptiness. But then, slowly, he realized the quiet was one of design, poised, suspended between the not-dark, not-light time, the holy, silent space between when the crickets pause their music and the birds begin their own, as if God were taking a deep breath...

...a strong but gentle hand, reaching down, gently shaking him by the shoulder. And Johnny opened his dream-filled eyes to see, beautiful but brief, his father's face above him, eyes filled with stars.

"Happy birthday, Johnny. You'd better wake up now. It's almost dawn. We're goin' huntin', remember?"

John opened his eyes.

A bare glow, at the tops of the trees. Vermillion veins ran just beneath the pale skin of the sky.

The chair, the porch, all real. The world still cold but pulsing, palpable. Fingers flexing in jacket pockets, the jagged air rich with the smell of earth and leaves, time, and gunpowder. The all-too-human sense of longing, clinging to the remnants of a dream now lost.

Darkness winged away.

It took several minutes before he could summon enough strength to move. Stiffly, he leaned forward and covered his face with his hands. He pressed his palms hard against his eyes, trying to eclipse the coming truth. But the deep-soul sadness rose up, intangible as twilight, inevitable as life and death. Cracks of pink began to form in his false night, and finally he lowered his useless hands. He could not hold back the morning.

He waited. For sounds of life. Tires on gravel. The warm breath of eternity in his ear. He waited until the woods around him began to stir, the dense, smoky blueness redefining itself with the outlines of trees and the soft shapes of haze-covered hills. He watched reality gradually reincarnated, changing like the imperceptible hands of a clock, until the gathering light glowed golden and the air woke with the scent of dew-kissed evergreens.

He waited, watching, until the sun burned away the last of his hope.

Morning had come without her.

"Go on. Get it over with." The voice, cruel again, but this time from within himself, no longer a dream.

John Allen stood.

He looked out through the brightening woods and down to the river, out beyond the wide waters into the hanging mists, wondering where else on earth he could possibly go. Every indulgent fantasy had failed him. Now he succumbed to the full futility of his life, to the exhaustion of his vain struggle against time, against time's very Creator. He felt so profoundly weary that the thought of endless sleep brought with it a sort of resigned peace. It seemed to him that the only true rest a man would ever find might be in dying.

"Do it."

John went inside to the kitchen, opened the cabinet, and pulled down the full bottle. Then to the bedroom closet, and the shotgun.

He stood on the porch. The weapon hung firm and heavy in his left hand, the bottle in his right. The sun was slowly setting the woods on fire. He went down the wooden steps and out to the clearing beside the cabin.

"You ain't nothin' but a coward, boy."

John stood and looked up into the treetops. The stone-still shape of the red-tail hawk could be seen now, staring down like a gargoyle.

"You're just takin' up air..."

His father's boots made sounds along the earth, toward the woodpile. With each step the blood flowed into his hollow helplessness, and they were his steps now, his very own, closer, toward the big stump.

"You ain't got no choice, boy."

The ground seemed to roll beneath him, and he had to kneel to keep from falling, broken now, like a man before a sacrificial altar. He set the bottle on the stump, bracing himself, and bent down until his forehead was pressed against the cold, rough wood.

And for one long, still moment all the earth and sky hung under and over the man, the day uncertain whether to begin or end, to be born or buried.

Finally, he stood. He walked back toward the river, counting in his head, fifteen, twenty steps.

Then he turned and raised his father's gun.

"A man's always got options," he said.

Thunder petrified the forest.

He unleashed one, two, three rounds—firing, pumping, firing, the strong, solid shocks to his shoulder brutal but real and good, the deafening ring in his ears clean, clear, cutting—four, five. The wounded woods howled like a dying animal, then became silent.

The stump was half gone. He lowered the gun to his waist; tiny fragments of wood and glass floated through the air like confetti all around him. The smell of whiskey wafted by, then vanished.

John scanned the trees. The hawk was gone.

He stood there a long time, waiting until the forest dared breathe again.

Then he walked into the cabin and laid the gun on his father's bed.

His bags were already in the trunk.

Epilogue

The man drove across the bridge.

The sun had mostly made its way above the east rim of the waking world. Below him the river ran wide between rolling hills covered in the soft, iridescent moss-green foam of spring.

In his rearview mirror the north bank of the river grew smaller and smaller until it was gone. Ahead, the woods swept down into emerald meadows along both sides of the highway. He did not know where he would go, only that it would be to a place he had not yet traveled.

Still, a faint glow of hope had risen with the sun. He knew that through a power beyond his broken heart he had been given the rare chance to regain something lost. He had encountered ghosts both real and unreal, and at long last said goodbye.

Now he understood that the sacred place for which he had always longed would not be found in his irretrievable past; home did not lie on either side of this or any other river, but in the deeper waters of his truest self. He would seek a strong and steady current, one that might bear him to a place of belonging, where faith could finally overcome fear.

From this point on, he alone would choose whether to be haunted by his dreams, or healed by them.

And in another faraway world, the woman looked out over the bronzed, wind-bent broomstraw, wave after wave lapping at the surrounding greening shores like some great ocean in a dream. But unlike the landscape of dreams, the earth beneath her feet felt solid and real. Across the swaying fields she saw spring coming, and knew other seasons would follow—budding, blooming, folding, falling, the immortal soil tilled by time's tireless hands.

At the crested treetops, the bluing horizon now manifested as embrace rather than enclosure, her home welcoming her back with open arms. Though the hushing sounds of rain would forever fall on a roofed porch in the deep-wounded woods of her heart, the storm within her soul had passed with the night. Courage rose like new morning.

Jessie knew.

Love, though elusive, had not abandoned her after all; love had pursued, fought for, and won her; love, lifted on the wings of faith, would remain forever, long after the years had stolen the blush from every earthly garden. Now her world shone radiant in the dawn, the air bittersweet with faint but familiar hints of hay and honeysuckle.

And from where she stood, fresh color could be seen here and there flirting out from the forest, the dogwood just beginning to bloom, April only days away.

Acknowledgements

First and foremost, I thank God, who continues to bring wonders into my life. A lot of people have been involved for many years in the writing of this book, whether they knew it or not, by sharing their lives with me, and thus teaching me what real life looks and feels like. I have many to thank: all the enviable inhabitants of the Magic Valley, both past and present; my father, James W. Robinson, who encouraged my writing very early on, and my step-mother Betty, who has always enthusiastically supported my work; my sisters Joette and Jennifer; Bryan Haislip, who not only provided the opening poem that inspired this story, but also the verse "written" and recited by Ellen to John during the fishing scene; my extended family and friends, including my "test readers", who suffered through primitive drafts and managed with a straight face to tell me to keep plugging along until I got it right; Anne Trudel for early proofing and praying; the entire ProdigalSong ministry team—Frances and Larry Vaughn, Kim Garrison, Sherry G. Thomas, Michael Euliss and Mary Jean Bentley, who so generously give of their talents and love; Tim Jones—friend, encourager, writer, prayer warrior; my fabulously funky friends and literary agents, Ang and Dan DePriest, who from the very start have been more family members than business associates – Sistah, Brutha, this prayer could never have been answered without you; Tony Collins, who championed this book from the beginning and made it all happen, project editor Simon Cox and all the gifted professionals at Lion Hudson in England and Kregel Publications in the US; my trans-Atlantic editor, Jan Greenough, whose firm but sensitive hand made for not only a better novel, but indeed a better novelist; Kregel's publicist Amy Stephansen; and, of course, my loving wife, Teresa (who proved quite the editor herself!) and my two kids, MR and JB, who put up with my intolerably long hours at the computer...a humble and heartfelt thanks to you all.